Triple Crown Publications presents

STT

LOVE

DISCARD

A Triple Crown Anthology by

Δ

Keisha Ervin

Δ

Danielle Santiago

Δ

Quentin Carter

Δ

T. Styles

Δ

Leo Sullivan

Compilation and Introduction copyright © 2007 by
Triple Crown Publications
PO Box 6888
Columbus, Ohio 43205
www.TripleCrownPublications.com

Library of Congress Control Number: 2007928281
ISBN: 0-9778804-6-X
ISBN 13: 978-0-9778804-6-1
Authors: Keisha Ervin, Danielle Santiago, Quentin Carter, T. Styles, Leo Sullivan
Photography: www.TreagenPhotography.com
Cover Design/Graphics: Aaron Blackman Davis – www.elevado.us.com
Typesetting: Holscher Type and Design
Associate Editor: Brett Gill
Editorial Assistants: Elizabeth Zaleski, Nazlihan Kavak
Editor-in-Chief: Mia McPherson
Consulting: Vickie M. Stringer

First Trade Paperback Edition Printing June 2007

10 9 8 7 6 5 4 3 2 1

Printed in the United States of America

This book is dedicated to you: Our Triple Crown Readers.

Words could never truly express my appreciation for you and your devotion to my company. Triple Crown Publications has been a labor of love and certainly not without its ups and down, bumps, bruises and back-stabbing muses. We've experienced the joys of launching careers and the betrayals of those we considered close and have helped make dreams come true. They say being a CEO is a very thankless, yet rewarding job.

Imitation is the most sincere form of flattery; we are flattered daily. More personally, you won't find people who use their own money to help you or believe in your dream. I put my money where my heart was, and that was in the careers of my authors.

Authors come to us for a career, and we deliver this to them. What can I say?
5 years, 1 million books sold, 2 languages and over 20 best-selling authors.

Street Love is our dedication to you, giving you stories by some of the most talented writers of this genre.

Enjoy!
                    Vickie M. Stringer
Queen of Hip-Hop, Street Lit, CEO, Righteous Hustla

AFTER THE STORM

An excerpt from Keisha Ervin's fifth novel, Torn

Triple Crown Publications presents . . .

After the Storm

PART ONE

Sitting on the edge of her bed, Mo gazed around her lavish bedroom and wondered if it was all worth it. It was 3:00 in the morning and she was at home alone for the second day in a row. Quan, her boyfriend of nine years, was out in the streets doing god knew what. She'd called him over a million times and he hadn't bothered to pick up the phone once.

She knew he was wit' another chick, but without any proof, all she could do was go on her woman's intuition. Rolling up a vanilla Dutch, she shook her head in disgust, because she knew no matter how much shit he put her through she wasn't going anywhere. Mo and Quan had been together since she was fifteen and he was eighteen. He was her man and she was his ride-or-die chick.

The two had weathered the storm more than once, but with nine years invested into their relationship and no ring in sight, Mo was getting fed up with the bullshit. She was tired of pretending that she didn't give a fuck if he cheated or lied. She was tired of acting like she didn't give fuck if he left or if he stayed. She was tired of pretending that clothes, money and jewelry would erase the pain of him not being there. Plain and simple, she was sick and tired of being sick and tired.

Nobody knew the ache she felt in her heart every day. They didn't know that she secretly hated herself for loving

Keisha Ervin

Quan so much. They didn't know that the thought of him being with another woman tore her up inside. Mo wasn't an angel, either. She'd cheated a couple of times, too, but it was only after years of turning her cheek to Quan's indiscretions.

After lighting up the cigar filled with weed, she placed it to her lips and inhaled deeply. Mo had hoped that smoking a blunt would help calm her nerves, but so far it seemed to only make matters worse. Instantly she began to feel even angrier. All night her phone had been ringing off the hook with prank calls. Nine times out of ten, it was Sherry, the girl that Quan had been cheating on her with.

A year ago, Mo and Sherry had a heated argument over Quan at Mo's best friend's beauty salon. Sherry called herself putting Mo on blast in front of everybody, but her plan backfired. Mo cussed the skank out. But she couldn't front, some of the stuff Sherry said did cut deep, especially the part about her not being able to have children. Mo and Quan tried for years to have a baby, but each time she reached two months she would miscarry. So naturally, once she learned Sherry was three months pregnant with her man's baby, Mo's entire world came crashing down.

Everybody, including her best friend Mina, urged her to leave him alone but Mo just couldn't gather up enough strength to do so. Quan was her heart and soul and the two of them had been together far too long for her to give up now. Plus the fact that he swore up and down that the baby wasn't his did help some. But deep down inside Mo knew the truth.

Glancing at the clock, she noticed that it was now 3:55, so she picked up the phone again and tried calling Quan's cell but was only met with the sound of his voicemail. "*Yo, this Q, leave a message.*"

After the Storm

Even more heated that he hadn't picked up the phone, Mo waited for the beep and said, "I hope you enjoying fuckin' that crusty-toe bitch 'cause please believe when you walk yo' retarded lookin' ass in this house it's gon' be World War III up in this muthafucka!" Pressing the pound sign, she ended the call and hung up.

I can't believe this nigga tryin' to play me, she thought. *And after all we've been through.* Mo had met Quan when he was a petty hustla. He was broke for the most part, but she saw potential. Back then he treated her like the queen she was. At first their relationship was cool. It was everything that love was supposed to be.

They never went a day without seeing or talking to each other. It was nothing for him to lavish her with affection and to show her how much he cared. Remembering the good ole days, Mo walked over to her jewelry box and pulled out the first piece of jewelry Quan had ever given her. It was a 14-karat gold necklace with a gold name plate in the middle. Quan had stayed on the block day and night just to get it.

In return she surprised him with a tattoo of his name written on her wrist. From that moment on, Quan knew that she was his and did whatever he could to take care of her. Mo never wanted for anything. They lived in a million dollar crib in the Central West End section of St. Louis and drove only the finest whips.

Their house was breathtaking. It had seven bedrooms, three bathrooms, a game room, an outdoor pool and a home theater. Mo decorated the entire house herself. She had impeccable taste. For her love and loyalty Quan blessed Mo with designer clothes, diamonds and furs. She didn't have to work, but for fun did a little modeling on the side. Quan made sure his boo was straight and Mo loved him dearly for

Keisha Ervin

that, but she wished in her heart that things could go back to the way they used to be.

Hearing the phone ring, she placed her necklace back into the box and reached for the phone.

"Hello?" she answered with an attitude, expecting it to be Quan or the prank caller.

"Whaaat, you in the house tonight? You ain't out in the streets?"

"Nah, West," Mo replied dryly, realizing it wasn't either.

"Oh, well, where yo' man at?"

"I don't know. You tell me."

"Damn, that nigga ain't there? I been tryin' to reach him all night."

"Is he ever here?"

"Ahh, don't be like that, Babygirl, you know he out there in the streets on the grind," West spoke deeply into the phone.

"That's what's wrong wit' niggas now, they always out in the streets," she snapped, rolling her neck.

"Yeah, I agree. Ain't nothing out in them streets. But that's what's wrong wit' niggas though. They start fuckin' up, givin' space for a nigga like me to take over."

"West, what you know about takin' care of a woman?" Mo asked, intrigued by the sound of his voice.

"Yo, that ain't even for you."

"C'mon, tell me. I'm a big girl, I can handle it."

"Yeah, that's what yo' mouth say, but we'll see. Tell my boy I'ma holla at him."

With that, he hung up. Shaking her head, Mo placed the phone back onto the receiver. She couldn't get West's words out her head. They had been flirting back and forth with each other for years, but Mo knew where to draw the line.

After the Storm

West was her man's best friend. There was no way she could take it there.

Just as she was about to pick up the phone to call Quan again, she heard the sound of the front door open and Quan's heavy footsteps approaching the bedroom door.

"What you still doing up?" he asked as he placed his keys on the dresser.

"No, the question is where have you been?!" she shot back with her arms folded underneath her breasts giving him the "and you bet not lie" look.

"I was wit' West and them."

"Nigga, quit lying 'cause West just called here lookin' for you! I know you was wit' that bitch!"

"What bitch you talkin' about now, Mo?!"

"Sherry, nigga, that bitch!"

"Man, I wasn't wit' that girl. Go 'head wit' that. It's late, a nigga tired, c'mon, ma, don't start," he said, slipping off his pants and Prada tennis shoes.

"Don't start? Nigga, I've been callin' you all night! And why the fuck didn't you answer yo' phone?!" she spat, mushing him in the head.

"'Cause it didn't ring and you bet not put yo' hands on me no more!" he warned, getting into her face.

"It didn't ring? What kind of bullshit-ass lie is that?!" she shot back, not the one to be easily intimidated.

"On the real, I think I broke it."

"Yeah right, whatever, Quan. You full of shit!"

"Mo, baby, calm down. Let's just go to sleep," he reasoned, trying to take her hand.

"Don't touch me! I don't know where yo' dirty-ass hands have been!" she snapped, getting up and preparing to leave.

"Where you think you going?" he asked, pushing her

back down onto the bed.

"Leave me alone, Quan! I'm going into the other room!"

"What for?"

"'Cause I don't wanna be no where near yo' trifling butt," she said, trying to get back up.

"Man, sit yo' ass down! You ain't going nowhere!" He pushed her down again.

"Will you stop?!"

"Man, just shut up and come wit' it," he whispered as he pulled up her pink negligee, revealing her 34 C breasts.

"Quan, I said leave me alone. Just let me go in the other room, a'ight?" she whined, trying her best not to moan.

"Shh, c'mon, ma, just let a nigga get some in peace. I know you feel how hard my dick is," he pleaded while pushing her legs apart.

At that moment Mo knew that putting up a fight was useless. Quan's head game was lethal to say the least and every time he went down on her she was guaranteed to cum at least twice.

Ready to handle his biz, Quan placed her onto her back. Wanting him to taste her, she parted her lips for him. Quan got the hint and dove in head first. With both of her thighs in his hands he sucked on Mo's pearl-shaped clit until she screamed out in ecstasy. With expert precision he licked the right side of her clit, causing her to shake and moan. Just as he expected, Mo started to cum in his mouth. Quan loved it. She tasted just like candy.

"Oooooh just like that," she panted, holding onto the sheets.

"You like that, baby?"

"Yes!" she squealed as he flicked his tongue across her clit even faster.

After the Storm

"Ooh, baby, please make me cum again!" she begged.

Doing as he was told, Quan parted her pussy lips even wider. Wanting to please his boo, he sucked on her clit some more, until Mo came in his mouth again.

"Aaaaaah!"

"Damn, boo, yo' pussy taste good."

"Oooooh … that shit feel so goddamn good! Baby, pleeeease make me cum!"

The faster he licked the more Mo begged. He placed two fingers inside her pussy while still sucking on her clit. The combination caused Mo to cum again for the third time. Quan was just about to replace his tongue with his dick when his cell phone began to ring.

"I thought you said it didn't work?!" Mo panted, coming down from her orgasmic high.

Ignoring her, he roughly slid his thick seven-inch dick inside her slit. Quan wasn't the biggest nigga in the world, but he knew how to work it well. The only thing Mo could do after he put it in was gasp for air and hold on for the ride. Holding her legs in the air, Quan pumped in and out of her at a feverish pace.

He loved Mo's feet, so while fucking her brains out he licked and sucked each and every toe. Mo was in agony and in heaven all at the same time. As soon as he put his dick in her, she felt torn between whether she should love him or leave him.

Should she stay or should she go? A part of her wanted to leave him alone and move on. But then the other part of her wanted to love him until it hurt. Flipping her over, Quan began to beat it up doggy style.

"Ooooh … baby … that's my spooooot!" Mo began to scream as she clawed the cotton sheets.

Keisha Ervin

"You like it when yo' man beat it up, don't you?!" he questioned, smacking her right ass check and then the left.

"Yeeeeees!"

"You want me to hit it fast or slow?"

"Ooooh, baby, hit it slow! Hit it slow!" she squealed.

"'Cause you know ... when I hit it slow ... yo' pussy get real wet." Quan slowed down his pace, hitting her with rough, slow pumps.

And Quan was absolutely right 'cause as soon as he began hitting her with the death stroke, Mo's pussy became wet as hell. It was hard for him to keep his dick from sliding out, her pussy was so moist. Mo loved it when he fucked her hard but slow. Turning her head so that she could get a good view of him, she reached in between her thighs and placed two fingers on her clit and started to play with it. Mo knew that Quan loved it when she did that.

Spreading her ass cheeks apart, he watched as he fucked her soaking wet pussy while she played with her throbbing clit. Mo's pussy was the best. It was fat and creaming with juices, just how he liked it. Mo had to bite down on her bottom lip just so she wouldn't scream out his name as she gazed over his honey-colored physique.

Quan was that nigga. There was no denying that. He was a cocky son of a bitch but he was hers. His entire presence was commanding and intriguing. He had a low cut with waves, sleepy brown eyes, a strong regal nose, sexy suckable lips and a smooth beard. Mo's real name, Monsieur, was tattooed on the left side of his neck. He reached almost six foot three in height and had a body any woman would want to caress. Just the sight of him made Mo want to bust a nut.

"Ooooh ... baby ... fuck me!" she continued to beg while rotating her fingers across her swollen clit.

After the Storm

"You gotta learn how to trust me, ma," Quan groaned, thrusting his hips from side to side making sure he hit every last one of her walls before he busted a nut. "You gon' trust me?!"

"Yes, baby, yes, I'ma trust you!"

"You love me?!" he questioned, feeling the nut build up in the tip of his dick.

"Nigga, I'ma love you forever." With that said, they both came long and hard all over each other.

PART TWO

The next morning, Mo awoke to a sun-filled room with only her in it. Immediately, she began to feel stupid, but when she looked over and saw a small blue Tiffany box with a card attached lying on top of Quan's pillow, she lightened up. Completely naked, she sat up with a smile a mile wide plastered on her face, hoping and praying that what was in the box was a ring.

Pulling the ribbon, she lifted the top only to find a set of keys. Confused, she placed the keys back into the box and opened the card. It simply said: *Go outside*. Jumping out of bed, she slipped on a pink Agent Provocateur robe and headed down the steps to the door. She was so excited she thought her heart would jump out of her chest it was beating so fast. Mo almost shit herself. She couldn't believe her eyes when she walked outside.

There, sitting in the driveway, was a brand new silver

Keisha Ervin

2007 G55 Mercedes-Benz truck. The damn thing was kitted out with eighteen-inch chrome Giovanna rims plus tinted windows. Mo barely wanted to touch it, it was so pretty. The chick was cheesing hella hard as she walked over to her brand new truck. Once she got up closer, she noticed another envelope with a card inside.

This nigga must really feel guilty, she kidded herself while opening the card. *Meet me where we first met at 1:00.* Wondering what time it was, Mo ran back in the house to check the clock. It was 11:15. She knew that it was gonna take her at least an hour to get dressed, so she hurried and took a quick bath. An hour and a half later she was on the highway heading for the Jennings Station Road exit. Mo bumped Beyoncé's *"Upgrade U"* as she took Jennings Station Road all the way up to Natural Bridge. Spotting the barber shop, she stopped, put the truck in park, hopped out and went inside.

It didn't take much for Mo to spot her man amongst the sea of dudes standing around. Quan always stood out in a crowd. There he was, posted up in his favorite b-boy stance, rocking an all-white LA cap, white tee, Red Monkey jeans, and low top Air Force 1's. He and his boys were in deep conversation, but Quan still peeped Mo walking up. As soon as she entered the shop his dick became hard.

Mo had to be about the flyest bitch in St. Louis. She was five feet ten with the body of a goddess and a booty so fat that she turned heads wherever she went. Her face was pure and angelic and her skin was a tantalizing Middle Eastern shade. She possessed long black hair, doe-shaped eyes, high cheek bones and succulent, heart-shaped lips. Her 34 C breasts were full but firm and her tiny waist, thick hips and perfect set of dancer legs could fill out any pair of jeans.

After the Storm

Quan had to admit, his boo stayed fly. She was a dime piece for real. Every nigga in the shop had to adjust his dick as she approached. Mo looked good as hell. She rocked a white fitted tee, tied in the front, a pair of extra tight, skinny leg jeans and red Christian Louboutin platform heels. Soft curls framed her face. Silver hoop earrings were in her ears, three necklaces were draped around her neck and silver bracelets filled her wrist. Chanel lip gloss adorned her lips.

"What you doing up in here?" West asked as he eyed Mo up and down with a lustful hint in his eye.

"Mind ya business, homeboy. I came to see my man. Why, you got a problem wit' that?" she asked, giving him the same look.

West was sexy as hell. Every time Mo was in his presence her nipples would get hard, but he was Quan's man and fuckin' him would be going against the code, so she kept her flirtation and lustful glances to a minimum, hoping and praying that Quan would never notice.

"Nah, I ain't got no problem wit' that. Do you?"

"Why would I? But anyway, thanks for my truck, baby." Mo wrapped her arms around her man's neck and hugged him tight.

"It's all about you, ma. You know that." He pulled her away from the crowd, hugging her back just as tight. "But why you got these tight-ass jeans on?"

"Come on Quan, don't start."

"I'm just sayin' though, ma, look at the way you got these thirsty-ass niggas staring at you. They can barely keep they tongue in they mouth. I don't like that shit. You gon' fuck around and make me have to put one in a muthafucka."

"I can't help that I have a bad-ass shape. There ain't nothing I can do about that."

Keisha Ervin

"Whatever, conceited, just watch what you put on when you around my boys from now on, alright?"

"A'ight, a'ight, whateva ... but how did you get down here? All of your cars were still in the garage when I left home."

"I had West come get me. We had to take care of some business, but I'm done now, so I'm tryin' to spend the day wit' you."

"Word, that's what's up?"

"Yep, so c'mon." Quan took her by the waist and led her out the shop and over to her truck. "This muthafucka fly, ain't it?"

"Hell, yeah! These bitches really gon' be hatin' now," Mo boasted as she passed him the keys and slid into the passenger seat. "So, baby, where we going?"

"It's a surprise. Just sit back and chill. I got this."

Twenty-five minutes later, they pulled up to Spanish Lake.

"Quan I can't believe you remembered!" Mo exclaimed as she jumped out of the truck. She loved being near lakes, oceans and waterfalls. The sound of water trickling or splashing just soothed her.

"We haven't been here in years!"

"I know. I figured you'd be happy," Quan said, meeting her in the front of the car.

"Yes. Thank you, baby. I love you so much." She hugged him tight.

"I love you, too, ma."

Gently holding her hand, he led Mo over to the lake. It couldn't have been a more beautiful day. The sun was beaming brightly from the sky and not a cloud was in sight. There was a slight breeze in the air, causing the tree branches to

After the Storm

sway from side to side, but other than that it was perfect. For the first time in a long time, Mo felt whole. Moments like this made her remember why she loved Quan so much. He felt the same way. Putting a smile on her face and making her happy was all he cared about.

She was his everything. There was nobody in the world he trusted or needed more. Quan loved Mo more than she knew. She was the apple of his eye—just looking at her brightened up his day. Mo was his best friend, his lover and his reason for living and breathing. Her smile made him smile. When she hurt, he hurt. She completed him and stayed on his mind at all times.

Mo thought that he didn't give a fuck about her or her feelings. He knew it was his fault her feelings weren't the same. There was a time when all he had to do was walk in the room to make Mo smile. But now it seemed like the only things that made her happy were trinkets and gifts.

"This is so nice," she sighed, leaning her head up against Quan's chest as they gazed at the lake.

"Yeah, it is."

"I wish we could spend more days like this together."

"Me too, but you know a nigga gotta make moves, ma."

"I know. It's just that I hate all the arguing and fighting we've been doing lately. I just want things to go back to the way they used to be. Like … remember when we used to catch the bus together?"

"That was so fuckin' long ago. A nigga was straight bus passin' it back then." Quan laughed, shaking his head at the thought. "Yo, remember when before I got my Cutlass I used to pick you up in crack head Willie's car?"

"Yeah, I could've killed you! Had me ridin' around in that basehead's car thinkin' it was yours."

"And remember when yo' ole dude caught me in yo' room that day when you was supposed to be at school?"

"How could I forget? My daddy beat my ass when you left." Mo cracked up laughing.

"You was scared as hell."

"Don't front, you know you was, too. Up there trying to hide in my closet."

"Shit, yo' daddy wasn't gon' kick my ass."

"Punk!" she teased, playfully hitting him in the chest. "Yo, you hear that? Oh my god, Quan, somebody playin' our song!" Mo shrilled in delight as he led her over to a park bench to sit.

"What song?" he asked as he sat her down onto his lap.

"Don't play, you know *'They Don't Know'* is our song."

"Oh, I hear it. *Don't listen to…what people say…they don't know about…'bout you and me.*"

"Baby, stop, that right there ain't even for you." Mo giggled as he sang into her ear.

"See what happen when a nigga try to be nice?"

"You know I was just playin'. I love it when you sing to me," she said, giving him a light kiss on the lips. "But on the real I couldn't have asked for a better day."

"Me either. I needed this. I don't never get a chance to just chill."

"Ahh, look at that little cutie over there." Mo pointed to a little three-year-old boy with chocolate brown skin and curly hair. "He is too cute."

"Yeah, he is."

"Quan, I'm sorry I haven't been able to give you a baby." Her bottom lip began to quiver as tears slid down her cheek.

"I told you it's cool, ma. I love you with or without kids. You're all I need."

After the Storm

Turning around to face him, Mo gazed into his eyes and whispered, "It's killin' me inside though, baby. Every time I'm around Mina and her son I wanna break down and cry 'cause I know I'll never be able to experience something like that. And I know it's a possibility that Sherry's baby is yours—"

"I don't even know why you keep bringing that shit up. I told you that baby ain't mine," Quan said, cutting her off.

"Okay, Quan, but it still hurts."

"I know, baby, but having a baby with you isn't going to add to my love for you. You not being able to have one is not going to make me love you any less." He wiped her eyes, stopping her tears. "You my boo and soon a nigga gon' make you his wife so stop trippin' off that shit."

"You're right." Mo nodded her head.

"A'ight?" he said, lifting her head up to face him.

"Alright."

"No, I said a'ight." Quan tickled her stomach, causing her to double over in laughter.

"Alright, alright!" Mo laughed, pushing his hand away.

Hearing his phone ring, Quan lifted Mo up so that he could go in his pocket and retrieve it.

"Hello? Yeah … a'ight … I'll be there in a minute. What the fuck I just say? I said I'll be there! One." Quan turned to Mo. "Look, ma, I'm sorry but I gotta jet. That was West, me and him gotta go take care of something."

"It's cool. I understand." She sighed, really not wanting the day to end yet.

Back in the car, Quan started up the engine and said, "Open up the glove compartment for me, I think I left something in there."

Doing as she was told, Mo opened it up only to find yet

Keisha Ervin

another small blue Tiffany box.

"What is this?" Mo flashed a broad grin.

"Just open it."

Once again Mo's stomach was in knots hoping and praying that maybe, just maybe, this time it was the ring she'd always wanted. This time her prayers were answered. Opening the box she was presented with a flawless, 7-carat diamond and platinum engagement ring with diamonds encrusted into the band.

"Is this for real?"

"What you think? I told you I was gon' make you my wife."

"Oh my god, Quan, we getting married for real?" she exclaimed as he placed the ring onto her finger.

"Yep, just set a date and I'll be there."

"Baby, I love you so much! I can't wait to show Mina and them!"

PART THREE

After taking Quan home to retrieve one of his five cars, Mo hopped back on the highway headed toward Mina's Joint salon and spa. It was a Friday, so the place was packed. Mo was greeted with a warm welcome as soon as she walked through the door.

"What up, Mo?" all the stylists asked.

"Hey, everybody!"

"Well, look what the cat dragged in. We ain't seen yo' ass

all week," Delicious, Mo's friend and stylist, said.

"Delicious, hush 'cause a bitch got good news."

"What? Jay-Z left Beyoncé for Rihanna? Oh, no, better yet Remy Ma finally took that tired-ass blond weave from out the front of her head?"

"Neither." Mo rolled her eyes. "Me and Quan are engaged!" she gushed, showing off her ring.

"The world must be gettin' ready to end. Gurl, let me see that ring!" Delicious brought her hand closer so that he could get a better look. "Oh, shit! This muthafucka hot! Ain't got no flaws or nothing! Quan really outdid hisself! Congratulations, Miss Thang, you finally locked that nigga down!"

"Congratulations, Mo!" everybody in the shop roared.

"Thank you."

"What is going on out here?" asked Mina, Mo's best friend of sixteen years, as she appeared from the back of the shop.

"*Gurl*, you ain't gon' believe it! Quan tired ass finally asked Mo to marry him!" Delicious joked.

"Watch it, nigga, that's my fiancé you talkin' about now."

"You go, girl!" Mina hugged her friend. "So when y'all gon' set a date?"

"I don't know. I'm just happy he finally asked," Mo answered, taking a seat in Delicious' empty styling chair.

"All I can say is it's about time you locked that nigga down. Hell, as much shit he put you through he should've been gave you a ring," Delicious continued.

"Right. I just hope now he'll act right."

"Let me tell you something, getting a ring or having good pussy ain't gon' change no man ... but a fire-ass blow job will make a nigga reconsider his position."

Keisha Ervin

"You ignorant as hell!" Mina hollered out, laughing.

"Shit, he ain't lyin', he tellin' the truth," Mo agreed. "It took me nine years of dealing wit' his bullshit just to get the ring. It's probably gon' take nine more years to get his ass down the aisle."

"I hope not. Don't think like that."

"You're right, girl, I have to stay positive. Maybe Quan is tryin' to change."

The words weren't even good out of Mo's mouth when her cell phone began to ring. It was Quan.

"Hold up y'all, this my boo. Hello?" she gushed.

"Where you at?"

"At the shop, why?"

"Nothing, I was just callin' to check on you. I might be home a little late tonight. Me and West still taking caring of business."

"Ok, just call me when you're on your way home."

"Will do."

"One," Mo replied, hanging up, but she quickly remembered that she forgot to tell Quan that she loved him. Flicking her phone open, she dialed his number and placed her phone up to her ear. Prepared to hear ringing like she normally did, Mo was instead met with the sound of voices in her ear.

"Hello?" she spoke, confused and not getting a reply. *Quan must still be on my line*, she thought.

"Quan! Quan!" Once again she got no answer, but Mo could still hear voices and from what it sounded like it seemed as if they were moaning, so she listened in closely.

"Let me eat your pussy."

"You don't want no head first?"

Hearing Quan and a familiar female's voice, Mo's heart

instantly stopped beating and she became enraged.

"*C'mon, Sherry, nah I ain't eat your pussy all day. A nigga been feenin' for this shit, ma. Let me do what I do and don't be screamin' while you nutting, you gon' wake up the baby.*"

"Mo, what's going on? Who is that?" Delicious questioned as he saw tears begin to build in her eyes.

"Shh!" she shushed him so he would be quiet.

"*Damn you got a fat-ass clit. You gon' cum in my mouth?*"

"*Yes, baby! Ooooh I wanna cum all over you!*"

"Mo, who is that?" Delicious continued.

Paralyzed, Mo sat still. She wanted to answer him but her lips couldn't find the strength to move.

"Girl, give me that phone! 'Cause you know I will cuss a muthafucka out!" he yelled as he yanked the phone from out of her hand.

"Hello … hellooo … " he listened in a little closer. "Ah uh … oh no he didn't … gurl, you don't need to be hearing that shit," Delicious snapped, hanging up.

"Mo, what's wrong?" Mina urged, trying to shake her friend from the trance she was in.

"That was Quan," Mo whispered as her entire world seemed to come to an end. All of the air in her lungs had left. The room was spinning and tears of sadness streamed down her face.

"What happened? Did something bad happen?"

"He was wit' another girl," Delicious answered, knowing Mo couldn't get out the words.

"How you know?"

"'Cause I heard them in the background fuckin'."

"Oh my god."

"Look, I gotta go. I gotta get outta here. I can't breathe." Mo jumped up, frantically searching for her keys which were

Keisha Ervin

already in her hands.

"Uh ah, Mo, I don't think you should be driving like this."

"I gotta go, Mina! Just let me go!"

Mo rushed out of the salon and ran to her car. Inside, she slammed the door shut and placed her head on the steering wheel. The tears that pelted her skin felt like heavy rain drops as they fell from her eyes. At that moment Mo felt as if she had died. There was nothing in the world that could make her feel better or ease her pain. She was tired of playing the fool for Quan over and over again. She was tired of fighting with herself over whether she should leave or stay.

Staring out the window, Mo watched as rain poured from the sky. She had never been so hurt and confused in her life. *How could he do this to me? He said he loved me*, played over and over again in her mind. For years, Mo noticed the phone calls Quan would get where he had to leave the room. She knew he fucked other women, and hated it.

She tried to be blind to his cheating ways but now that it was smack-dab in her face, Mo knew she had to do something. Trembling, she adjusted the rearview mirror and wiped her eyes. The only thing on her mind at that moment was revenge. She had to make Quan hurt just as much as he'd made her hurt over the years, so she scrolled through her phone and called West.

"Hello?"

"Hey West, how you doing?"

"Good. What's up, Babygirl? You don't sound too good."

"Oh, I'm fine. Is Quan with you?" she asked. Mo just had to reaffirm what she had heard.

"Nah, I ain't seen that nigga since he left the barber shop wit' you."

After the Storm

"Oh, okay, so what's up wit' you? What you doing?"

"Nothing … chillin'. Gettin' ready to head over to Tropicana to play some pool. Why, what's up?"

"Is it okay if I meet you over there?" she asked, already knowing his answer would be yes.

"Yeah, you can slide through."

"Okay, I'll be there in like ten minutes."

"A'ight."

"One."

It really took Mo fifteen minutes to get there due to the severe thunderstorm that plagued the afternoon sky. Mo didn't have an umbrella with her, so she ran as fast as she could to the entrance. But running didn't help any. Her clothes were drenched.

Searching the place for West, she tried to spot him, but couldn't because the pool hall was so dimly lit. Then suddenly she felt a hand grab her shoulder. Turning around, she found West. The nigga looked even sexier than before. He was tall with broad shoulders, an adorable face, a low cut and a goatee. West was rocking the hell out of a white, sky blue and tan striped Polo shirt, baggy khaki shorts and Air Force 1s. The man looked good, damn good. Suddenly Mo didn't feel as guilty about what she was about to do.

"Damn, shorty, the rain really got you," he said, eyeing her wet top, which did nothing to hide how hard her nipples were.

"Yeah, it did." Mo blushed, running her hands through her wet hair.

"I'm surprised you called. What's the deal? What my man do now?" West asked as he grabbed a cue stick from off the wall.

"Look … I didn't come here to talk about Quan. I came

Keisha Ervin

21

to see you."

"Oh, really? What you wanna see me for?" he asked, barely above a whisper.

"Don't make me say it," she whispered back, turning her head, slightly embarrassed.

"Nah, say it." West got into her face. "I wanna hear you say it."

"I want you to fuck me."

Seconds later, Mo and West were in the back of her truck getting it on. His lips enveloped hers as she unbuckled his pants. Mo knew that what she was doing was wrong, but at that point she really didn't care. Quan's thoughts or feelings no longer mattered to her.

The fact that it was raining only seemed to intensify her pleasure. She could hear raindrops hitting the windows and thunder striking the sky. Mo couldn't wait to feel West inside her, and he couldn't wait to get her clothes off. West had imagined for years what it would be like to sex Mo. She didn't know it, but he'd planned on putting her in every position imaginable. Pulling up her shirt, he unsnapped her bra and took one of her swollen nipples into his mouth.

"Damn," Mo moaned as he licked, sucked and pulled her nipple in and out his mouth like he was a newborn baby.

Caressing and sucking her breasts, he used his free hand to unbutton her jeans and pull them down. West used his fingers and plunged them deep into her vagina.

"Ahhhh!"

"You like that, ma?" he whispered as he finger fucked her and played with her clit all at the same time.

"Yes!"

Not wanting to waste any time, he told her to scoot up.

"I wanna taste you," West groaned as he pushed her legs

After the Storm

all the way up to her chest. Mo's pussy was directly in his face.

"Damn, ma, you got a fat-ass pussy." He smiled devilishly as he planted his face in between her thighs and went to work.

"How it taste? Tell me how good it taste!" she moaned, arching her back.

"Yo' pussy taste good as hell, ma. It taste like strawberries and cream."

"Well taste me, baby! Lick my pussy until I cum!"

Doing as he was told, West held both of Mo's thighs in his hands and feasted on her kitty. His tongue tantalized and assaulted her pussy with every lick. Mo was in absolute bliss. West could almost eat pussy as well as Quan. *I guess the saying is true, birds of a feather do flock together,* she thought.

The nigga was working her pussy over with his tongue. Every lick felt sinful and soft to the touch. Rubbing and squeezing her nipples, Mo called out his name. She could feel an orgasm nearing, but before she came she had something she needed to do. Mo reached for her cell phone on the floor of the car and dialed Quan's number. West was so into what he was doing that he didn't even notice. For the first time in a long time, Quan picked up on the first ring.

"What's good? Where you at, baby?"

But Mo didn't answer, instead she placed the phone away from her ear and screamed, "That's it baby ... lick this pussy!"

"Mo?!" she heard Quan yell.

"Oooooh ... West ... I think I'm gonna cum!"

"Cum for me, ma! I wanna taste every last drop!" West moaned, flicking his tongue even faster across her clit.

"Mo?! I swear to god if you doing what I think you're

Keisha Ervin

doing I'ma kill you!" Quan barked into the phone as he tried to concentrate on the road.

"Yes ... ooh ... yes ... right there ... ooh I'm cumming ... I'm cumming ... Fuck, I'm cumming!" With that said, Mo turned off her phone, hanging up in Quan's ear. Unbeknownst to her, as soon as she hung up, Quan's car ran into the dividing wall on Highway 70.

PART FOUR

Mo arrived home a little over an hour later. After West ate her out and made her cum three times, she decided that was punishment enough for Quan. She'd wanted to seal the deal and take it all the way, but couldn't. West eating her pussy was one thing, but him fuckin' her was another. Niggas had died for less than that, and after Quan heard them, Mo knew that the both of them were in deep shit.

But she wasn't about to stick around and wait for her ass-whooping. Mo had already made a reservation at the Marriott. Placing her purse down on the dresser, she walked over to the closet and pulled out one of her suitcases. Before she began to pack, something told her to check her voice-mail. She had five new messages.

"Mo, this is Nicky! Pick up the phone! Quan's been in a terrible accident!"

Mo couldn't believe her ears. Quan being in an accident was most likely her fault. Saving the message, she listened closely to the rest.

After the Storm

"Girl, where are you at?! I've been tryin' callin' your cell phone and everything! Look, the ambulance took Quan to Barnes Hospital! They said that he got a concussion! Call me as soon as you get this message!"

Mo didn't even bother calling Mrs. Mitchell back. She snatched her purse off the dresser and headed out the door.

The emergency room at Barnes wasn't as crowed as usual. Only a few people sat awaiting service. Mo hated hospitals. The last time she'd been in one, Mina had been badly beaten. Hesitantly, she rang the bell on the nurses' station, fearing the worst.

"Hi, how can I help you?" a short, pudgy nurse by the name of Wanita asked.

"I'm looking for my fiancé, Jayquan Mitchell."

"Doctor Calvert is in the room with him now, ma'am. You're his fiancée?"

"Yes."

"You just missed his mother. She'd been trying to reach you."

"Is he okay?" Mo questioned nervously.

"Yes, he's gonna be fine. He only suffered a mild concussion and wound to the head. We're trying to get him to stay the night for observation, but he doesn't want to. The doctor is in there with him now."

"I hear what you saying, man, but I can't stay here!" Quan yelled as he stormed out the room.

Instantly, his eyes locked with Mo's. Pure hatred was written across his face as he looked at her. Quan's chest heaved up and down as he balled up his fist, he was so angry. Mo had never seen him look like that before. She felt like shit as she eyed the thick bandage across his forehead. Blood was all over his shirt, jeans and shoes. She even noticed a couple of scratches on his face and arms.

"What the fuck you doing here?!" he barked, scaring the hell outta her.

"I came to check on you," she said softly.

"Listen, Mr. Mitchell, you need to rest. I strongly advise that you stay the night," Doctor Calvert urged.

"Man, fuck what you talkin' about! I'm outta here!" Quan turned to leave.

"Quan, where you going?! You need to listen to the doctor!" Mo said, trying to grab his arm.

"Get the fuck off me! It's yo' fault I got in the accident in the first place!"

Unable to defend herself or her actions, Mo stood there quiet.

"Yeah, that's what I thought! Now get the fuck out my face!"

"I know what I did was fucked up, but please just let me take you home!" Mo begged.

"Mr. Mitchell, I don't know what's going on with you and this young lady, but I would really feel better knowing that you got home safely since you refuse to stay," Dr. Calvert added.

"Whatever, just don't say shit to me!" Quan warned, putting his finger in Mo's face.

The ride home from the hospital was filled with unspoken words and the heavy air of broken promises. It was still raining hard outside. Mo could barely see out the window as she drove. The DJ on the radio said that there was a tornado warning in the St. Louis area. But a tornado warning didn't mean anything to Quan or Mo at that time.

Neither of them knew what to say or do. There was so much confusion and hatred in the air. Quan didn't even let

After the Storm

the car pull all the way up to the house before he hopped out. He didn't want to be anywhere near Mo. Words couldn't describe how mad he was at her. If he didn't love her so much, he would've killed her by now.

Following him into the house, Mo headed for the steps only to hear him say, "I want you out of my house by tonight!"

"Excuse me?!"

"Don't make this hard. Just get yo' shit and step."

"You know what, Quan, fuck you! And just to let yo' ignorant ass know, I was already leaving anyway! As a matter of fact, here!" she yelled, taking off her ring and throwing at him. "Give this piece-of-shit-ass ring to that bitch, Sherry! I'm sure she'll love it!"

"You know what, maybe I will! At least she didn't fuck my friend!"

"She should have 'cause I know I sure enjoyed it!" Mo spat as she walked up the steps.

"Oh, you enjoyed it?!" Quan questioned as he followed her.

"Did I stutter, nigga?!"

"I swear to god I should knock you in yo' muthafuckin' mouth!" Quan balled up his fist as he noticed her suitcase on the bed. *Damn this bitch really was leaving*, he thought.

"I wish you would!"

"Why you fuck my boy?!" he snapped, yoking her up by the neck, pushing her up against the wall.

"How could I fuck yo' boy?! How could you fuck that bitch?!"

"What are you talkin' about?!"

"Don't play stupid!" Mo snapped back, pushing him off of her. "I heard you and that bitch fuckin' on my phone!"

Keisha Ervin

"I wasn't fuckin' her! I was over there visiting my son!"

The mention of the words *my son* seemed like a knife stabbing Mo in the heart. Without thinking of the consequences, she hauled off and slapped the shit out of Quan. Concussion or no concussion, she was gon' fuck him up.

"You lied to me! You said the baby wasn't yours!" she yelled, hitting him repeatedly in the face.

"So you gon' go and fuck my boy, Mo!" he said, trying his best to restrain her.

"How long you been fuckin' that bitch?!" Mo tried her best to slap him again.

"Yo, chill!" he barked, grabbing her by the neck and slamming her down. Mo's head hit the floor hard. With her pinned he yelled, "And you say you love me! Bitch, you just like all these other hoes!"

"Get off me!" she yelled, trying to get up.

"Not until you calm yo' ass down!"

"I said get off me! Let me go!"

"Mo, when I get off of you, yo' best bet is to leave this muthafucka straight up," he warned, letting her go.

"I gotta go, and you been fuckin' that bitch! This shoulda been a wrap! Nigga, you should've been told me to leave! I would've left!" Mo began to cry uncontrollably.

"Oh so you gon' cry now, Mo? Like straight up? You cryin' for real?"

"Why you have to go and fuck that girl?! What, I wasn't good enough?!"

"You good enough for the hood now! How many times have you forgiven me?! Huh?! Yo ... I know I fucked up! I know the way I was livin' was wack! But it is what it is! I wasn't gon' tell you I had a baby wit' that chick 'cause I knew it was gon' hurt you! I loved you too much to do that to you!

After the Storm

But now … after you done fucked my boy … I ain't got nothing but hate for you!"

"First of all … I didn't fuck him! Yeah, I could've but I didn't! And second, how the fuck you gone say you hate me after all the shit you've put me through?! All those nights you sacrificed our relationship just for some pussy … I was the one home alone wondering where the fuck you was at and who you were with! I was the one who stood by yo' side through it all! So don't blame me for all of this … it's your fault, not mine!"

"Yo, save it, ma, 'cause I ain't even tryin' to hear you right now. You fucked my boy, ain't no turning back from that!"

"Whateva, Quan! I'm wrong, you're right, whateva!"

"Just shut up and get out! As a matter of fact, let me help you!" he declared, pulling her clothes off their hangers and onto the floor.

Mo just stood there in complete silence. She was tired of arguing with him.

"What, you ain't gon' help?!" He turned and looked at her.

"Fuck you! I'm out! You can keep all that shit!"

Quan knew no matter how much shit he talked that he didn't want Mo to leave. He couldn't be without her if he tried. He couldn't even imagine her not being in his life. She was his rib.

"Where you think you going?!"

"I'm leaving! That is what you want, isn't it?!" Mo quipped with an attitude as she placed her hand on the door knob.

"It's up to you, ma. I don't give a fuck whether you stay or go."

Keisha Ervin

"Sometimes I wish I never met yo' sorry ass!" she screamed as she opened the door.

But as soon as she stepped foot outside, all the lights on the block went out. Turning around, she saw that the lights inside the house went out as well. The wind was blowing with so much force it almost knocked her over. And on top of that, rain and hail were falling from the sky. Mo wasn't going anywhere in that kind of weather.

"I thought you said you was leaving?"

"You know I can't go nowhere in that storm!" Mo slammed the door shut.

"After I find this damn flashlight I want you gone!" Quan barked as he searched for a flashlight. It was pitch black inside, so he really couldn't see where he was going.

"Fuck!" he yelled as he bumped into the corner of the coffee table. Rubbing his knee Quan continued his way into the kitchen. Ten minutes passed by, and he still hadn't found the flashlight. "Where the fuck is the flashlight?!"

"Maybe if you were home sometime you would know where it was at!" Mo yelled back as she lit a few candles that were placed around the living room.

"Well since you here all the time come help me find this muthafucka so you can step!"

"So you gon' send me out in that storm, Quan?!"

"Whateva, Mo, just don't say shit to me. Just help me find the flashlight!" he yelled, coming back into the living room to find it lit by candles.

"Kiss my ass, Quan! Why don't you go upstairs or something?!"

"Don't tell me where to go! This my goddamn house!"

"Whateva, stand yo' stupid ass there then," Mo replied while taking off her clothes.

After the Storm

It was hot as hell since the air conditioner was no longer on. Mo took everything off but her bra and panties. Quan tried his damndest not to stare, but her body looked good enough to eat. Flickers of light danced across his face and sweat beads filled her succulent breasts and thick thighs. Mo was a bad bitch and even at that moment Quan couldn't deny that.

She noticed his eyes on her but ignored him. Instead she plopped down on their suede couch. Following suit, Quan stripped down to his wifebeater and boxers. Not wanting to be anywhere near her, he sat on the floor and leaned up against the wall. Both of them sat in deep thought. Quan knew Mo was hurting and wanted desperately to go over and console his boo.

Though they weren't married, she was his wife, his life, his hopes and dreams. Quan never loved anybody the way he loved Mo. But to hear his woman making love to another man, especially his boy, tore him up inside. Mo might as well have shot him dead. Now things were all fucked up. She'd fucked his man and he'd had a baby on her. There was no way their relationship could survive after all of that.

Mo was thinking the same thing as she stared at the ceiling in agony. Quan didn't know it, but she was crying. All she could think about was the way he used to love her. He used to treat her with the utmost respect. But in Mo's eyes, having a baby on her with another girl was the ultimate sign of disrespect. *Maybe if I hadn't nagged him so much he wouldn't have strayed*, she thought as she wiped her eyes for the umpteenth time.

Getting up from the floor, Quan walked over to the closet and pulled out his old portable radio. It was the same radio he and Mo used to listen to back in the day. Mo

Keisha Ervin

watched him as he fumbled through an old box of cassette tapes. As much as she tried not to be, Mo couldn't help but be attracted to him.

Quan was beautiful in a thugged out way. After putting the tape in, he turned and faced Mo. Marvin Gaye's *"Just to Keep You Satisfied"* was playing softly, filling up the room. Everything Quan wanted to say was in that song. So much built-up pain and frustration was in him that he couldn't even stop the tears that fell from his eyes. In the nine years they'd been together, Mo had never seen Quan cry.

"So that's what it takes?" Mo asked.

"What are you talkin' about?"

"It takes for me to get grimy for you to see how much you hurt me?"

"I can't believe you got me up here cryin' like a lil' bitch," he laughed.

"You made me cry, too," she replied, getting up and going over to him.

"Man ... you don't know how much this shit hurt."

"Yeees, I do. You do remember Sherry don't you?"

"Not now, ma."

"Well, when Quan? We gon' have to talk about this sometime."

"You wanna talk? A'ight, let's talk. Why you fuck my boy?"

"You want the truth?"

"Nah, I want you to lie," he said in a sarcastic tone.

"'Cause I wanted to hurt you, that's why. When I heard you on the phone with that bitch I spazzed out, and the first thing on my mind after that was to hurt you as much as you hurt me."

"But my boy, Mo?"

After the Storm

"I mean, what you want me to say, Quan? That I'm sorry, 'cause I'm not. You wasn't sorry when you fucked that bitch," she answered truthfully.

"Oh so we playin' tit for tat now?"

"Why it gotta be tit for tat when I do something, but when you do something it's all good?"

"I can't even front, I noticed for years how that nigga would look at you, but I ignored it," Quan responded, ignoring her comment.

"So what's up wit' you and Sherry?" Mo questioned, changing the subject.

"What you mean what's up wit' her? Ain't shit up wit' her. Today was the first time in a long time I took it there with her. I swear," Quan lied, still unable to tell the whole truth.

Knowing full well he was lying, Mo shook her head in disbelief.

"So what now?" he questioned, looking down at her.

"I don't know ... you tell me."

Unsure, Quan sat in silence, staring out into space, knowing it was going to take more than love to pull them through this time.

PART FIVE

The next morning, Mo and Quan lay on the floor in the front of the fireplace, knocked out. The two had fallen asleep there. They didn't know it, but the lights were back

Keisha Ervin

on. Waking up, Quan rubbed his eyes and focused his attention on his surroundings. It took him a minute to realize where he was at first, but once he did, all the prior day's events came flooding back.

All the yelling, cussing and fighting filled his mind. No matter how hard he tried, Quan just couldn't seem to get Mo's moans out his head. Over and over her voice echoed in his ear like a song stuck on repeat. *'Oooooh ... West ... I think I'm gonna cum ... Fuck, I'm cumming! Oooooh ... West ... I think I'm gonna cum ... Fuck, I'm cumming!'* "Damn, I can't believe she really fucked my boy," he whispered out loud.

Tired of thinking, he shook his head and tried to get up, but couldn't because Mo's head was on his chest. Looking down at her face, Quan instantly became heated all over again. Nothing could erase the pain she'd caused. At that moment all he wanted was for Mo to be as far away from him as possible. He couldn't stand the sight of her face, let alone her skin touching his, so he pushed her off of him and onto on the floor.

"What you push me for?" she asked, waking up.

"I couldn't get up wit' you on me," he answered nonchalantly.

"Oh, what time is it?"

"I don't know. The lights are back on," Quan answered, opening up the window shades.

"I see. So what you got going on today?"

"Shit. I might stop in the hood. Probably go get a shape up."

"Uhmm, Quan ... I know I shouldn't be askin' you this, but ... what's gonna happen to West?"

"What?" Quan spun around with an angry look on his

After the Storm

face.

"What ... are you ... going to do ... to West?" she spoke a little slower.

"Why?"

"'Cause I wanna know."

"But why? I mean, you mighty concerned about a muthafucka you claim you ain't got no feelings for!"

"Here you go," Mo snapped as she shot up from the floor.

"Nah, nah, nah, don't run! Don't walk away! Why you worried about that man?!" Quan said, blocking Mo's path.

"I'm not worried about him. I just asked you a question."

"You got feelings for that cat, don't you?"

"You really buggin'."

"Nah, I don't think so."

"Whateva. I ain't got time for this. You tryin' to start an argument!"

"I must be right 'cause you ain't tryin' to deny it!"

"Whateva, Quan! Think what you wanna think!" she yelled, bypassing him and heading into the kitchen.

"You know what? You really something, ma," Quan chuckled, following her.

"What the fuck are you talkin' about?!" Mo snapped, irritated and confused.

"I can't believe you had the audacity to sit up there and ask me what's gon' happen to that man. You need to be happy ain't shit happened to you!"

"Boy, please." She waved him off while opening up the refrigerator.

"You been wanting to fuck that nigga, haven't you?!"

"I'm not gon' argue wit' you! It's too early in the morning for this shit."

"Damn, I can't believe it's true," Quan said more to himself than to her.

"I can't believe you even coming to me with this dumb shit!"

"It's cool, ma. You ain't gotta admit it." Quan smirked. "But check it, I got something I wanna tell you."

"What?!" Mo yelled, slamming the refrigerator door shut.

"This right here," he said, pointing his finger back and forth between them, "ain't gon' work."

"Say that again?" Mo questioned, stunned.

"Look, I'm tryin' not to hurt you, but I ain't feelin' this."

"What the fuck you mean you ain't feelin' this?!" She rolled her neck.

"How many more ways do you want me to say it?! I don't want you no more? This shit ain't workin'? I can't keep fuckin' wit' you? Which one works for you?!" Quan shot sarcastically.

"You's a selfish son of a bitch, you know that?! It was okay when I stayed wit' you after the numerous times I caught you cheatin' on me! But the one time I mess up you wanna say it's over! Negro, please!" Mo spat, mushing him in the head.

"What the fuck I tell you about putting yo' hands on me!" he snapped, grabbing her by the neck then pushing her away.

"What you gon' do Quan, beat my ass?! I wish you would touch me! I'll have every last one of my brothas come over here and whoop yo' ass!"

"Mo, please. Get somewhere and sit yo' ass down!" Quan mean mugged her as he went back into the living

After the Storm

room and snatched up his clothes. As he dressed he told Mo, "Now what you need to do is start packin' up yo' shit so you can be the fuck up outta here by the time I get back!"

"Nigga, I ain't going nowhere! We ain't breakin' up until I say so!"

"Yeah, a'ight, ma, if that's what it's gon take to make you feel better, then go ahead and tell yo'self that. But don't be surprised if you come home one day and all yo' shit gone."

"Is that a threat?"

"Keep fuckin' wit' me and find out," Quan promised as he grabbed his keys and left.

"You know what? Do what you gotta do, boo!" Mo yelled as she watched him leave.

Exactly an hour later, Mo was on the road heading toward Quan's mother's house. As she drove along the highway, Mo wondered if she made the right decision by leaving. Quan had threatened plenty of times to put her out, but never before had she actually taken him up on his threat by leaving. But this time Mo figured she'd show his ass.

Not only did she call his bluff by leaving, but she also fucked up some of his shit in the process. Mo wished she could see the reaction on his face when he came home to find all of his clothes and his precious shoe collection destroyed. *See how you like them apples, muthafucka.* She chuckled as she pulled up into his mother's driveway.

As Mo walked into the house, a sense of calm came over her. She always felt at peace around Quan's mother. The house that he set her up in was exquisite. It was made of white stone with three different levels. The floors were made of Virginia Vintage wood and chandeliers hung from the ceiling of each room.

"Ma!" she called out.

Keisha Ervin

"Yeah!"

"How many times do I have to tell you to lock this door?" Mo placed her bags down.

"Oh, girl, please, don't nobody want me." Mrs. Mitchell smiled, greeting her with a hug.

As usual, she was stylishly dressed. That day she wore a short-sleeved linen top, jeans and wedge heels. Her brown sugar skin complexion showed no sign of wrinkles or stress even though all of her life she had to struggle. Her eyes were shaped like almonds, and her nose and lips were full and round. Thick, jet black hair filled her head and rested delicately on her shoulders. Nicky Mitchell was beautiful. Mo hoped she looked half as good when she was her age.

"Is Quan alright? I know that he didn't want to stay at the hospital," she continued.

"He's fine, I guess." Mo looked away and shrugged.

"You guess? What happened last night? I kept on askin' him but he wouldn't tell me."

"Nothing, we just got into it, that's all."

Giving her a quizzical look, Mrs. Mitchell knew that Mo wasn't giving her the full story.

"It must have been a big argument. You brought your luggage over here."

"Okay ... me and Quan sorta had a little disagreement and ... I need to stay here for a while."

"Come on in the kitchen, girl."

Doing as she was told, Mo followed Mrs. Mitchell into the kitchen and sat at the island on a barstool.

"What was the little disagreement about this time?" Mrs. Mitchell questioned as she took a seat. "'Cause y'all gon' be back together in five minutes anyway."

"Ma, it's worse than the time he hit me. Quan had a

After the Storm

baby on me wit' another girl," Mo explained as her eyes welled up with tears. Already knowing about her son's infidelity, Nicky simply inhaled deeply and shook her head.

"Did you know?"

"It's not about whether I knew or not." Mrs. Mitchell confirmed her suspicions. "It's about how you feel."

"I just don't know what to do. I mean ... I can almost deal with the fact that he cheated ... but a baby? How he could do that to me? How could he make me feel like I was the only one and then go sleep with her? I have stuck by his side and dealt with his shit for nine fuckin' years and this how he gon' do me! And I'm sorry mama for cursing, but I just can't believe it. Like how could he lay down with her? How could he have a baby with her?" Mo's bottom lip trembled. Tears were rolling down her face at lightning speed.

"Quan is all that I have ever wanted! I don't want nobody else, ma! I ain't never loved nobody the way I love him! Like it hurt so bad I can't even breathe! If he ain't want me no more he could've just said that! He could've let me go?! He ain't have to go screw that girl behind my back!"

"Mo, let me tell you something. Quan ain't gon' never leave you alone. It's up to you, baby. What you need to realize is that you're the prize, and until you realize that, ain't nothing ever gon' be right. Quan gon' continue to do what he want to do and when he want to do it, but you have to be the one to say enough is enough. What I wanna know is ... why do you keep going back? What is it about my son that you love so much that you just can't let go?"

"I don't know. I just love him," Mo sniffed as she tried her best to stop the tears that were falling.

"Let me tell you something, if the only thing you can say is 'I don't know ... I just love him' then, baby, you got a

Keisha Ervin

lot to think about, 'cause love ain't no 'I don't know, maybe' kind of thing. Real love makes you feel free and optimistic like you can conquer the world. When you truly love someone, you will do any and everything to keep that person from harm. You will never lie, because to do such a thing would never even cross your mind, and from what I've seen over the years, neither you nor Quan have done any of that."

"I know, ma, but you don't understand." Mo continued to sob, frustrated.

"Understand what? Tell me what I don't understand."

"I have loved him since I was fifteen. I don't know what it's like to be without him. And sometimes I feel like if I let go of Quan I'ma have to let go of you, too."

"Baby, listen, my love for you ain't going nowhere. Whether you're with my son or not, I'ma love you. You are still going to be my daughter. That will never change, you hear me?"

Mo was crying too hard to answer, so she just kept her head down and nodded.

"Listen, girl." Mrs. Mitchell held Mo's face up with her hand. "Wipe ya face and stop all that cryin' 'cause cryin' ain't gon' change the situation. I'm tellin' you for your own good, leave … Quan … alone. This is his mother tellin' you this. Not some chick out on the street or one of yo' lil' girlfriends, but me … his mother. Now what I won't do is tell you that you can't go back to him 'cause I know how you young folks are, but don't say I didn't warn you," Mrs. Mitchell said. She got up as she heard someone entering through the front door.

"Who is that?"

"Me, mama!" Quan replied.

After the Storm

"Umm speak of the damn devil."

"Where you at? I need to talk to you!"

"In the kitchen!"

Choking back the rest of the tears that filled her throat, Mo wiped her face with the back of her hand. She would be damned if she let Quan see her cry again. Once he reached the entranceway of the kitchen, Quan spotted Mo and became enraged.

"What the fuck she doing here?"

"First of all you better watch yo' goddamn mouth, and second, this is my house! Mo is more than welcome to be here! Now if you have a problem with that then you can skip yo' happy ass on up outta here!"

"You always taking her side! You don't even know what she did to me! While she coming over here running her mouth, did she tell you she fucked West? Did you tell her that, Mo?!" Quan barked, charging toward her.

"And what you think you about to do?" Mrs. Mitchell questioned, blocking his path. "You ain't getting ready to touch her up in here! 'Cause if you do you we all gon' be thumping! Now try me if you want to!"

"Why you taking her side?!"

"I ain't taking nobody side! If you was wrong, you was wrong! The same thing goes for Mo! But my door will always be open to her. You understand?" Mrs. Mitchell warned. "If you gon' be fuckin' this person and if she gon' be fuckin' that person then what is the point of y'all being together? The shit is just ridiculous! Both of y'all need to stop! Just let it go! Now, Mo, if you did sleep with that boy, then you was dead wrong! If it done got to the point where you feel as though you have to do some low down dirty mess like that, then you really need to let it go! Now if ya'll

Keisha Ervin

gon' go back to each other then that's all on you! But this foolishness needs stop!" Inhaling deeply, Mrs. Mitchell tried to catch her breath. "Done made my blood pressure go up! Let me get up outta here before I end up cussing both y'all the fuck out."

Pissed, Quan leaned up against the wall. He could tell that Mo had been crying and though he didn't want to feel a thing over her tears, his heart just wouldn't allow him to be so selfish. Despite the pain they'd caused one another, he still loved her. But his mind kept on reminding him of her betrayal and he just couldn't get over that. Mo, on the other hand, was so sick of crying she didn't know what to do, but the words Mrs. Mitchell had spoken still rang in her ears, causing her to cry even more. Everything she'd said was true, but loving and leaving Quan alone was something she didn't want to do. 'Cause the thought of them being over for good felt like what she imagined dying helpless and alone would be like, and Mo didn't want that.

She wanted to feel whole again. She wanted to try to make things work. They could do it. They'd done it before. As she gazed into his chocolate brown eyes, Mo felt defeated and became weak.

Flashbacks of their lovemaking entered her mind. She could feel him biting her neck and her screaming his name. She could hear him groaning in her ear the words, "I love you." *Damn, why can't I just leave this nigga alone?* she thought, trying her best to shake the memories.

Quan was nothing like the ebony prince in her daydreams. Looking at him, Mo wondered, *Why do I even love him so much?* Maybe it was the way he made her feel special and showered her with attention, or the fact that his family welcomed her with open arms. The only thing she knew for

After the Storm

sure was that nine years, three miscarriages, numerous flings, innumerable heated arguments and a few knock-down, drag-out fights later, she was deeper in love and more confused than ever.

PART SIX

It was a warm September day. Mo had been at Quan's mother's house for almost a month. She thought that he would give her some space to think and heal, but it seemed like every other day he was stopping by for stupid shit. Either he was hungry and wanted his mother to fix him something to eat or he'd drop off his clothes to be washed. Sometimes he would just come over for no reason but to sit and watch television.

He never acknowledged or said a word to Mo. He wouldn't even look in her direction. Since he wanted to be ignorant, Mo decided two could play that game. She would intentionally dress up and leave the house for hours on end. Quan pretended like he didn't care, but he would sit there and wait for her return each time.

He didn't want to admit it, but Quan was dying without his boo. One night he even went as far as to play on her phone, he missed the sound of her voice so much. Mo was knocked out in bed asleep, with her face sunk into the pillow, when the ringtone of LeToya Luckett's *"Torn"* awakened her. Startled by the music, she jumped up, clutching her chest. Disoriented, she wondered where the sound was coming from before she realized it was her cell phone ringing.

Looking over at the clock on the nightstand, she noticed that it was 2:00 in the morning. Perplexed, Mo wondered who could be calling her at that time. She found out when she gazed at the screen. It was Quan. Rolling her eyes to the ceiling, she picked up her phone and groggily whispered, "Hello," only for him to hold the phone for a minute and hang up.

What the fuck? Mo pressed end and called him right back, but Quan didn't answer. He simply looked at the phone and let it go to voicemail. Sucking her teeth, Mo snapped her phone shut, turned over and went back to sleep. Forty-five minutes later her phone rang again. It was Quan calling back, and just like before, when she picked up he held the phone and then hung up. Irritated beyond belief, Mo called him back once more but Quan still wouldn't answer. Unlike the first time, this time Mo decided to leave a message. "You's a stupid ass," she spat. Twenty minutes passed by before Quan decided to call again.

"What?!" she answered with an attitude.

"Damn, what's up? Why you got an attitude?"

"What you mean what's up, why I got an attitude? You keep callin' my phone playin'."

"Girl, gon' wit' all that, ain't nobody call you."

"Quan ... yes, you did."

"Look, I ain't call you. My phone must have dialed your number on accident."

"Twice?"

"Man, please, whateva. What was you doing?"

"I was 'sleep," she responded as if he were dumb.

"So what? You can't call nobody? We ain't friends no

After the Storm

more?"

"We'll always be friends."

"Well, why you ain't call and tell me you love me today?"

"Why you ain't call and tell me?"

"Why you think I'm callin' now?" he shot sarcastically.

"But at 2:00 in the morning, Quan? I was 'sleep."

"Well go back to sleep then. I ain't mean to wake you up."

"Alright."

"I'll call you tomorrow."

"Okay."

After that, Quan was good. He'd heard her voice and held a conversation. But he knew that sooner or later another urge would arise that only Mo could cure. Quan wasn't used to being without her. He wanted her back home where she belonged. He was tired of being without her. She was his best friend. He never related her love to pain. No one understood him like she did. Being without her was driving him crazy. He wanted things to go back to the way they used to be.

Quan hated spending his nights alone. He tried replacing her with Sherry but Sherry just didn't do it for him. He loved her, but he wasn't in love with her. Sherry was fun to kick it wit', talk to and fuck, but that was about it. His son was the only tie that bound them. On one particular day, Mo, Mrs. Mitchell, Quan's brother's girlfriend Tara and one of her friends were in the kitchen gossiping when Quan decided to make another unexpected visit. The first person he spotted was Mo.

"Oh, it's a whole bunch of y'all in here today," he joked. "What's up, Ma?" Quan kissed his mother's cheek.

"How you doing, baby?"

Keisha Ervin

"Good. What's up, Tara? Where my nephew?"

"Wit' yo' brother."

"Oh. What's up, Chloe?"

"Hey, Quan."

"What y'all chickens in here yappin' about?"

"Who you callin' a chicken?" Tara challenged, rolling her neck.

"You right y'all ain't no chickens, more like a bunch of rats."

"Ahh!" Tara gasped.

"I'm just playin'," Quan laughed. "Nah, for real what y'all talkin' about?"

"We're discussing relationship issues, and I know you gon' speak to Mo?" his mother questioned, displeased by her son's behavior.

"My bad. What's up, Mo? I ain't even see you right there." These were the first words he'd spoken to her in weeks.

Giving him a nasty look, Mo rolled her eyes.

"Mama, you want me to check on the cornbread?" she asked, ignoring Quan.

"Will you please?"

"What you cooking?" Quan quizzed.

"Some collard greens and cornbread. You want some?"

"Nah, I'm good. In a minute I'ma head over to Sweetie Pie's, but first I'ma get me something to drink." He opened the refrigerator.

"So, Mrs. Mitchell, like I was saying, the guy I'm messing wit', Earl, be trippin'. Half the time when I call him he don't answer the phone. Then when we do talk it's like for maybe five or ten minutes. And the only time he call me is when he on his way to work or when he on his break," Chloe

After the Storm

stated, needing advice.

"Do y'all spend any time together?"

"I see him maybe once a week, if that. He claim he be tired all the time."

"I don't mean to butt into y'all conversation, but why you fuckin' wit' a nigga name Earl anyway? You must be hard up for a man. Ain't that somebody daddy?" Quan interrupted as he fixed himself a glass of Kool-Aid.

"First of all, watch your goddamn mouth, and second, say you're sorry! That was so rude!" Mrs. Mitchell scolded.

"What? I'm keepin' it real! All y'all gon' do is sugar coat the shit. Yo, Mo, you want some?" he asked, placing his cup up to her lips.

"No!" She moved her head away.

"Here, take a sip, it's cold."

"What is wrong wit' you? I don't want any," she said, looking at him like he was crazy.

"Nothing. You just looked thirsty."

"Well, I'm not."

"Go 'head, Chloe, finish tellin' yo' story," Mrs. Mitchell instructed, giving her son a weird look.

"Like I was saying before I was *rudely* interrupted, I don't know what to do. I mean I really like this guy and he acts like he like me but I hardly ever get to see him."

While the women chatted, Quan took a seat on a barstool and admired the way Mo was dressed. She was casually cute in a wifebeater, skin-tight pencil leg capris and five-inch gold heels. A pair of gold hoop earrings and two long, gold necklaces decorated her outfit. Mo's long, thick black hair was flat ironed bone straight with a part in the middle. Quan loved when she wore her hair like that. It was one of his favorite styles. *Damn, I miss her*, he thought.

Keisha Ervin

"So what you think I'm doing wrong, Mrs. Mitchell?" Chloe continued.

"Have you ever read *He's Just Not That Into You*?" Quan chimed in, adding his two cents again.

"Excuse me?"

"I take it you haven't. Look, yo' boy is doing his thing."

"And what does that mean?"

"Man, I ain't got time to be explaining this to you. I got my own problems to deal with. Ain't that right, Mo?"

"Hmm, you tell me," she shot back sarcastically.

"Nah, tell me what you think, Quan. I wanna know what y'all men be thinking."

"Check it. The dude ain't feelin' you like that and he got a girl, so my advice to you is to do like me and Mo did and split."

"Oh, you have lost yo' mind," Mo stated, ready to slap the taste out of his mouth.

"Hey, I'm just tellin' it like it is. When a nigga feelin' you he gon' let it be known. And evidently whoever this cat is she messing wit' ain't, 'cause if he was, we wouldn't be having this conversation right now, ya dig?"

"But why couldn't he just come out and say that? Why he gotta lie and play games?"

"Has he hit it?"

"Quan?!" Mrs. Mitchell exclaimed with her mouth wide open.

"Mama, calm down. We all grown up in here. Now, has he?"

Gazing around the room Chloe reluctantly answered, "Yeah."

"Then that's why. It must have been good and he liked it so he keepin' you around as his li'l side piece. If you don't

After the Storm

like being a jump-off then quit messing wit' him."

"Oh my god ... I can't believe he was using me. I really liked him." Chloe's face turned sad.

"Hey, that's the way life goes."

"How you gon' give somebody relationship advice?" Mo scoffed. "You don't know if that man got a woman or not. He could be tellin' the truth. He could be tired."

"Chloe, straight up don't listen to them. They gon' have you sittin' up here lookin' stupid wit' a broken heart. I'm tellin' you."

"You would know about broken hearts, wouldn't you?" Mo remarked.

"Yeah 'cause since the moment you left mine has been," he said sincerely. For once, Quan was telling the truth. Suffocated by his response, Mo was frozen stiff.

"Okay ... is this conversation about me and my boo or you two?" Chloe asked, perplexed.

"Don't worry about all that. Mo, I'm getting ready to head over to Sweetie Pie's, you want something?"

"No."

"You sure?"

"I said I'm fine," she stressed.

"What about us?" Tara shot with an attitude.

"What about you?"

"I know you gon' ask us if we want something to eat."

"You want something to eat, Tara?"

"No."

"Then what you ask for?" he asked playfully, mushing her in the head.

"Don't be mushing me in the head, punk!" she laughed, hitting him back.

"This your last chance, Mo, I'm getting ready to go."

Keisha Ervin

"Okay, go."

"Come on, girl, quit frontin'. You know you want some of they mac and cheese," he joked.

"Girl, you betta go with this boy before I smack him," Mrs. Mitchell insisted.

"But I don't want to," Mo lied, knowing damn well she did.

"Please, just go for me. 'Cause he is driving me nuts."

As they made their way outside, Mo watched the way Quan swaggered to the car in his familiar thugged out way. She loved to see him walk. There was just something so sexy about his stride. If there was one thing she couldn't deny, it was her attraction to him. He looked good as hell in an army fatigue baseball cap, white tee, jeans and Tims. As usual, he wore his diamond stud earring, but this time he switched up and rocked a diamond pinky ring on his right hand. But no matter how fine he was, Quan was the type of nigga that brought out her violent streak. Any and all sense she had went out the window when she was in presence.

"Do you mind if I stop by the house before we go?" he asked as she buckled her seat belt.

"I don't care, Quan," she responded dryly.

"You know you owe me for fuckin' up my shit."

"I don't owe you nothing," Mo smirked, gazing out the passenger side window.

"Yeah, a'ight, we'll see."

Fifteen minutes later they pulled up to their house. Mo hadn't seen it in so long that it felt like she was in foreign territory.

"You coming in?"

"What you want me to do?"

"You can stay yo' ass out here if you want to. I don't

After the Storm

care."

"Whateva, I think I left my flat irons in there anyway," Mo snapped, getting out. After pretending to look for her irons, she stood by the door with her arms folded across her chest.

"What you standing there lookin' all crazy for? Have a seat," Quan said, turning on the stereo.

"I thought we were going to get something to eat?"

"We are, just chill for a minute."

Mo hesitantly took off her purse and placed it on the couch. Quan had turned on the fireplace, so she took a seat in front of it Indian style. Tank's heartwrenching ballad *"Please Don't Go"* was playing softly, soothing her ears. Tears immediately welled up in her eyes. She knew Quan was playing the song for her. Holding back her emotions, Mo kept her composure.

"You know that shit you did was fucked up," he announced out of nowhere.

"Did you ask me to come in here so we can argue 'cause that's what's gon' happen if you keep on talkin'."

"I just can't get over the shit," he chuckled, taking a seat on the floor next to her. Without asking, Quan grabbed each of Mo's legs, placed them on his lap, and took off her heels.

"What I wanna know is, besides your mother, who else knew?"

"Who else knew what?" Quan pretended to play dumb while massaging her feet.

"Who else knew about the baby?"

"Nobody," he lied. He would never sell out his boys, especially not Cam. If Mo found out her brother knew, she would kill him.

"I can't keep doing this shit wit' you, Mo," he continued.

Keisha Ervin

"I can't keep doing this wit' you, either. It's like one minute I love you and in the next breath I hate you. Sometimes it feels like being wit' you is like dying a slow fuckin' death. It shouldn't be like this. Loving you shouldn't be this hard."

"I feel you. I be thinking the same thing."

"I mean, don't get me wrong, I love you, but this shit is crazy. I shouldn't have to fight with you on a daily basis."

"You right, you shouldn't, but you gotta learn how to trust me, ma. Without trust things between us gon' always be fucked up."

"But how am I ever gonna be able to put my trust in you after this? Huh? You had a baby on me. I can't forgive you for that," Mo explained in agony.

"Why not? I can forgive you."

"Quan, please. No you can't."

"How you gon' tell me what I'm gon' be able to do?"

"'Cause I know you. I don't even see why we're even having this conversation. Things will never be the same between us."

"Don't say that, ma. We can work this shit out."

"I want to, Quan, I do, but—"

Frustrated, Quan cut her off and yelled, "But nothing! Quit saying we can't make it work 'cause we can! Don't you know I can't see myself being wit' nobody else but you? Even when I sleep at night all I see is you! Maybe if it was somebody else and the history was different I could cut all my ties and move on, but you're a part of my life, Mo! I've tried to move on! Believe me, ma, I've tried! But all I do is think of you! It's like I can't get you outta my head or something! A nigga been sick, ma, for real. And yo, I know what I did was fucked up, but I love you and I'm sorry! Just come home,

After the Storm

a'ight?"

"But Quan—"

Tired of going back and forth, Quan palmed Mo's face with his hands and silenced her with a kiss. As he enveloped her lips Mo could feel her spirit rise and leave her chest. Here they were, doing it again. Filling each other up with promises they knew neither would keep. She knew this feeling of ecstasy wouldn't last, but the sweet taste of sin erupted each time they kissed. Her legs were wrapped around his back as she became lost in his eyes once again.

Quan was lost as well. He knew that what they were attempting to do was wrong, but the feeling of fleeting joy consumed him. He knew that if he asked her back he'd promise that things would be different. He wouldn't let her down or make her suffer. But Quan could never be what Mo wanted him to be. *Why can't we just trust each other?* he wondered as a tear fell from his eye onto her face. This needed to end, but here they were trying to defeat failure again.

With tear-filled eyes Mo told herself that at the first sign of disappointment she was gone. But loving Quan felt so fulfilling. When things were good he filled her insides with butterflies. Then when things were bad he instantly morphed from her lover into her opponent in a matter of seconds. *When is this gonna end?* she thought as they gazed into each other's eyes, exchanging breaths.

Lovingly, Quan placed his lips upon hers and kissed her with so much intensity that she felt as if she were drowning. Drowning in a pool of uncertainty, that is. The touch of his hands caressing and massaging her face felt like heaven. Suddenly his hand was in between her thighs. One finger, two fingers, three fingers, four.

Mo knew that once she came and the pleasure of forbid-

Keisha Ervin

den passion faded, pain would take its place and the cycle of abuse would began all over again. But she couldn't think about that right now. His lips were exploring hers, tantalizing and teasing. Quan's tongue tasted so sweet. She could never let this feeling go. She would be an absolute fool if she did.

No one could love her like him. Quan felt the same. Mo was the forbidden fruit he'd been chasing for years. He knew from the beginning that they weren't meant to be. Their relationship wasn't supposed to last this long. The band had stopped playing and packed their bags a long time ago, but here they were trying to defy the odds once again.

Deep within her heart Mo could feel his love for her fading. Things would never be the same. How could they be? But then he quickened his pace, causing her stomach to contract. Each and every thrust sent sparks of fire throughout her body. Arching her back, Mo begged for more. Hurt and abandonment were just around the corner. One more stroke and they would be there.

Drawn to the sincerity of pain, Mo's torso began to convulse. Quan was cumming, too. They felt so good in each other's arms. Coming down from their orgasmic high, Mo and Quan lay side by side, breathing heavily. What would happen now? She wasn't his and he wasn't sure if he necessarily wanted her to be. Holding her chest, Mo tried to cease the heartache she felt inside from exploding onto her cheeks. *This has to stop. I can't keep doing this*, she told herself. Sensing her agony, Quan pulled her close. She lay on top of him.

He couldn't pretend that he didn't want to try again. Being with her sometimes felt so dramatic, but he loved how when he talked, she smiled. He loved how when he looked in her eyes he saw himself. She was his favorite and he was

After the Storm

hers. He wasn't the best, but he was all she knew. As Mo's face rested on his chest, she felt at peace. That was, until she heard the sound of Quan's phone ring. Out of habit, she reached over to grab it but Quan quickly took it out of her hand.

"Just lay down, ma, I got it." He kissed her forehead and slid from underneath her to go in the other room. Mo shook her head and thought, *Here we go again.*

Allure of
the Game

By Danielle Santiago

Allure of the Game

"How in the hell did this hood rat, low-level-hustlin' bitch get connected with Butta?" Suef demanded as he paced the barbershop floor, veins bulging on the sides of his shaved head. Trenton and Abdul sat in barber chairs opposite one another, eyes transfixed on his movement. Without warning, he pushed open the door of the barbershop and stepped onto the decaying concrete. His polished leather shoes clicked as he spun and looked at the old East Side building that stood as the front of his operations. The brick of the façade was decaying as fast as his own supply.

He walked back inside, locked the front door and flipped the sign.

"We closin'?" Abdul asked. Suef shot him an annoyed look and proceeded to throw anything and everything within his reach. Although he seemed out of control, Suef had a feeling he would be having this tantrum, at around this time, ever since he woke up to the news about Arnessa, the hood rat, low-level-hustlin' bitch.

"First I have the cops in my pocket bust her muscle, Eugie!" he screamed, tipping over a tray of scissors and razors. "Then I step up to her main supply and promise to buy triple her weight," he added, skipping a set of clippers across the linoleum, "but thanks to Butta's help, this girl just keeps steppin' up! I was trying to be polite, seeing that this is a bitch and all, but this ho is really starting to annoy me."

Danielle Santiago

He stopped to take in the scene he had created. Trenton and Abdul sat on the edge of their chairs while sunlight slanted in on the scattered scissors, making the floor sparkle like freshly fallen snow. It was so still, the only thing moving were the motes of dust kicked up in his rant. To Suef, it was a perfect moment. He was a professional. This, moving weight, or being pissed about not moving weight, was his profession. Beads of sweat ran down his temples and he stared at himself in one of the dirty mirrors hard enough to break the glass, but inside he was ecstatic with his performance as the number one man in the operation, the role he felt he was born to play.

"How you wanna handle this?" Trenton asked, pitching his chubby body forward, seemingly always ready for whatever. In reality, he was the type who liked to beat on women but couldn't go one round with a man. He was all bark—the only time he had any bite was when he had a gun or his boys backing him.

"I'm ready to catch that bitch and put the pistol on her. Shit, that's the problem, shoulda went at her hard from the door," Suef stressed.

"You can't solve everything with violence," a soft voice said from the corner of the room. A young, handsome guy in jeans and a white T stood at the bottom of the spiraling metal stairs that lead to the loft above the shop.

"Who the fuck is that?" Abdul asked, looking at Trenton, who only shook his head and shrugged in reply.

"Dis my cousin," Suef answered, "up here to help us out. He looks young, but he's got half of Atlantic City on lock."

"Atlantic City?" Trenton asked. "Man, what's some fuckin' Jersey boy know 'bout shit?"

"Watch it, T," Suef warned. "He knows enough to put your soft ass in the ground."

"Listen, Suef," Trenton said, "just hear me out ... you

Allure of the Game

don't got to do shit to Arnessa. Just put the pistol on that pretty little sister of hers. Send that bitch a message live and direct."

An evil grin appeared on Suef's face. "Bitches get all emotional when you bring family into it. Gettin' at her sister will make her back all the way down. Why didn't I think of that shit? Trent, you's a smart nigga."

Trenton looked at his watch and said, "It's almost three and I know where to find her right now."

* * * * *

Going to Loly's Dominican salon on 8th Avenue for a fresh doobie had become a weekly ritual for Arnessa and her little sister Cenise. Before her abrupt disappearance from their lives, Maria, their mother, had always stressed the importance of hair and skin care to her daughters. Although Arnessa had strong tomboy ways, she took great care of her hair, even bringing her own expensive products to the salon. Both she and Cenise had thick, jet black hair that hung below the middle of their backs. In public, Arnessa never wore her hair a loose. She usually kept it wrapped up with hair pins or in a bun pinned at the nape of her neck.

Where is Cenise? Arnessa wondered, sitting under the dryer with a head full of large gray rollers. Cenise, being very prissy, almost always beat her sister to the salon. Pulling out her Nextel she tried to reach Cenise on her walkie-talkie. After several unsuccessful attempts, she dialed her number, only to get her voicemail. *She probably went to the nail salon, that's the only time that girl don't answer that phone.* Arnessa picked up the latest issue of *"Don Diva"* from the chair next to her. Unable to focus, she flipped through it aimlessly and put it right back down. Cenise's whereabouts were not the only

Danielle Santiago

thing on her mind.

A little over two months had passed since Arnessa had linked up with Butta, who she soon found out had kingpin status. Now she was making money hand over fist. With the good grade of cocaine Butta was giving her at a low price, she was selling it faster than she could re-up. Instead of twice a week, she was now sending dope to Baltimore Monday through Friday. Thanks to Butta's better-priced, top quality heroin, she even had to hire a second transporter. With spring ushering warmer temperatures into the city, business was only getting better.

Making such large sums of money made Arnessa nervous. She knew that this was the type of money that attracted professional stickup kids. Arnessa was pulling in so much money that she no longer stashed it inside Timberland boxes in her closet. All of her funds were now hidden inside furniture in storage units throughout the city – one in Brooklyn, one in Queens and two in the Bronx. Most days Arnessa felt that there was no one she could trust. She no longer felt comfortable in her own skin.

Once her hair was blown bone-straight, wrapped and pinned, Arnessa left the shop. She hopped in her brand new black Dodge Magnum, her first car, her biggest purchase ever. She only bought it after Butta advised her to. "You gotta get a car," he told her, unable to fathom why she didn't already own one, and how she'd made it thus far without one. In the short time that she'd known him, Arnessa had learned a lot from Butta. Whenever he was around, she watched and listened intently, absorbing any knowledge or skill he put out.

Arnessa entered her apartment and immediately observed Cenise's book bag and purse lying in the middle of the hall. Cenise's bedroom door was cracked. Arnessa pushed it open and saw her little sister balled up in the middle the bed, still wearing her Catholic School uniform. "Neesie, why didn't you meet me at the shop?"

Cenise didn't answer.

Arnessa walked over to the bed and she touched Cenise to wake her. Cenise's body was trembling. She turned to face Arnessa. Her hair was disheveled, her eyes were bloodshot and her bottom lip was split. Her appearance floored Arnessa. "Cenise, what happened to you?"

Cenise stared at her blankly.

"Cenise, tell me what happened to you!" Arnessa said, nearly screaming.

Feeling ashamed, Cenise lowered her eyes, and in a tone slightly above a whisper, began speaking. "I was walking from school on my way to the shop. I was on 144th when this guy came out of nowhere and pointed a gun at my stomach. He slapped me so hard I couldn't feel-feel my-my mouth."

Arnessa's heart dropped.

Tears rolled down Cenise's face. "Then he stuck his hand up my skirt. Nessa, he put his fingers inside of me!" Cenise sobbed.

Vomit tickled the bottom of Arnessa's throat. She swallowed hard to keep it down. She tried hard not to cry, but the tears flowed uncontrollably. Arnessa grabbed Cenise. Hugging her tightly, they cried together. "That's all he did, right?" Arnessa asked, holding out hope that he hadn't raped her.

Arnessa felt her sister's head nod against her shoulder. "But …"

"But, what?" Arnessa pulled back and looked at her.

"He told me to tell you …"

"Tell me what?"

"Suef said give up the blocks or he would be back to see me again."

Burning anger replaced the hurt that Arnessa initially felt.

Danielle Santiago

This wasn't a random act, this was a message. The worst part was they used the only person she loved to deliver it. On the inside, Arnessa was raging. She had to take deep breaths to keep from exploding in front of Cenise. Calmly, she told her, "Baby girl, it's going to be okay. I want you to take a shower. I'm going to care take of this." She hugged Cenise one more time and left the room.

I can't believe this muthafuckin' coward dragged my baby sister into this. Arnessa's hands shook nervously as she dialed Butta's number.

It rang a few times before he answered, "What up?"

"Can you come by the crib?"

Arnessa's voice didn't sound right to him. "Is everything aight?"

Unable to mask it, she answered, "Nah."

Not wanting to walk into any type of trap, he questioned her a little further. "What's going on?"

"Ole boy from the East Side sent some nigga at my little sister."

"Say no more. I'm on my way."

* * * * *

Fifteen minutes later, Butta arrived with his boys, Shawn and Mannie. They all stood in the kitchen listening to Arnessa as she repeated what Cenise had told her.

"You think your sister would recognize him if she saw him?" Shawn asked.

"I'll ask her." Arnessa walked out the room.

Shawn, an average-looking dark skin dude, stood about 5'9". For the most part he was pleasant looking, proving the old adage that looks can be deceiving, because he was a straight murderer. "Suef and them niggas still be at that fake

Allure of the Game

barbershop every day. Let's ride by, see if she see the dude. I know it's one of them faggots, if not Suef himself, who stepped to her."

"Yeah." Mannie nodded in agreement. Like Butta, he too was Dominican, although he was often mistaken for a Puerto Rican, with his fair skin and black, wavy hair that he kept in two long braids that hung below his shoulders. "Them dickhead niggas still be down at that barbershop, the one on the East Side."

Arnessa came back into the kitchen. "She said she'd know 'em if she saw him.

Butta pulled Arnessa out into the hallway. "Pack whatever you need for you and your sister. Give your bags and car keys to Mannie."

"Where're we going?"

"I got somewhere for you to go. Shit is about to go down. Y'all can't stay here. I'm quite sure Suef knows where you live."

"Butta, I don't think they'd run up in here, and if they do, I got burners."

She is so damn hardheaded, he thought. "Yo, we about to handle this shit on your behalf. The next time Suef or his boys come at you, it's going to be more than gun pointing and fondling lil Cenise. The next time it's going to be kidnapping, rape and murder." For some reason he wanted to protect her. Maybe because she had innocence about her, a naiveté regarding how serious the game really was. On the low, he liked her, but thought she acted too much like a dude.

Reluctantly, Arnessa agreed. Quickly gathering clothing and toiletries for herself and Cenise, she gave everything to Mannie, who left in her car.

She and Cenise left in Shawn's silver Navigator with him and Butta. The dark tints on his truck concealed their identi-

Danielle Santiago

ties as Shawn drove slowly by the barbershop where Suef and his crew hung. When Cenise saw Trenton standing out front chatting on his cell, she lowered her eyes, too afraid to look up.

"Is that the dude?" Arnessa asked. "Don't be scared, he can't do nothing else to you."

Still afraid to look at his face again, she nodded, "Yeah, that's him."

Butta looked over at Shawn. "Go to my crib, scoop Mannie, then we'll come and deal with him."

* * * * *

Butta's house was amazing, to say the least. Arnessa didn't even know such houses existed in New York. Hidden behind tall trees, the three story brick home sat atop a hill on a winding road in the posh Riverdale section. Arnessa's Magnum was already parked in the driveway when they arrived. Mannie came out of the house and got in the front passenger seat of Shawn's truck.

"Y'all stuff is in the guest rooms upstairs," Butta told Arnessa and Cenise as he ushered them through the garage into the house. "The kitchen is fully stocked. Make yourself at home." He walked out, shutting the door behind him, leaving the two girls standing in the kitchen entry. The huge gourmet kitchen had marble countertops, a massive stainless steel refrigerator and a stainless steel double oven embedded in the wall. A center island with a gas burner stove top separated the kitchen from the den area.

"You want something to eat?" Arnessa asked Cenise.

"No," she replied, staring at the floor, "I wanna go lay down. Just feel like when I wake up tomorrow it will all be over." The poor girl's spirit was broken. She'd been violated in

Allure of the Game

the worst way.

Arnessa hugged her little sister tightly. "I'm sorry this happened to you." She began crying.

"There's no reason for you to be sorry. You didn't do anything."

"I didn't protect you."

* * * * *

After a long, hot shower, Arnessa put on her favorite Victoria's Secret pajamas, a fitted pink cotton T-shirt and a pair of pink-and-white-striped boy shorts. She removed her hairpins and brushed her hair down, as she did every night. Instead of wrapping it right back, she let it hang. The hairpins were giving her a slight headache.

Arnessa stuck her head into the room Cenise was staying to make sure she was okay. Her little sister was sound asleep. The attack on Cenise had Arnessa really rethinking her position in the game. Maybe it *was* time for her to give it up. Although they were often at odds with one another, Arnessa would die if anything happened to her sister. Besides that, she couldn't bear the thought of anything happening to herself and leaving Cenise in the world alone. At the end of the day, they were all each other had.

Hungry, Arnessa went downstairs for a snack. She nearly jumped out of her skin when she saw Butta sitting on the couch. "I thought you were gone."

"Nah, they went ahead without me," he said, looking up from the book that he was reading. He could not take his eyes off of her. Butta had never seen her in anything other than the baggy sweats that she wore every day. Now she was standing in front of him in a tight T-shirt that barely contained her 34 Ds, which sat up fine with no bra. Arnessa's body was tight, no

Danielle Santiago

stomach, and she had a nice-sized butt, too. Not too big, but not small, either. It had a nice round shape which the shorts were amplifying. He was even more amazed by her luxurious, jet black hair. He had a thing for long hair.

I knew I should've put on some sweats. Arnessa wanted to break and run back upstairs, embarrassed to have him looking at her body. Butta sensed her uneasiness and diverted his eyes back to the book. Attempting to play it cool, Arnessa headed into the kitchen to get what she came for.

For the first time, Butta really looked at Arnessa. He saw a female who was doing what she had to do in order to provide for herself and her younger sister. Arnessa was so cool and laid back, he often forgot she wasn't a dude when they were around each other. Butta knew that she was tough, but not as tough as she would have people think. He could tell that what happened to Cenise was taking a toll on her already. Arnessa was intelligent and extremely street smart for a twenty-one-year-old chic. She was built for the game, but she was no Kisa Kane.

At any moment, the game could destroy Arnessa, and Butta knew it. The sad part about it was that besides Cenise, the game was all she had, ever since her brother Deon was murdered. Unable to cope with his death, her mother had abandoned her and Cenise years ago.

Although Arnessa was trying to hide her emotions, Butta knew that what happened to Cenise had her shook up. Arnessa's vulnerability was like a walking aphrodisiac to Butta. He got up and went into the kitchen, where she stood in front of the open refrigerator. The hem of her boy shorts barely covered the bottom of her protruding ass. *Should I cross this line or keep it business?* Butta asked himself, feeling his dick swell. *Nah, let me fall back.* Turning to walk away, he caught another glimpse of her ass. *Fuck that.* He walked right up on her, and as he reached over her to get a chilled bottle of Evian, he intentionally rubbed his dick against her so she could feel how hard it was. She attempted to move, but there was nowhere to go but in the refrigerator.

Slipping his hand into the waist of her shorts, he massaged her hips.

"What are you doing?" she questioned, feeling her nipples harden.

"Are you hungry?" he asked, totally dismissing her question.

"Nah, I'm straight."

He pulled her closer to him, shut the door then backed her against the refrigerator. Eyeing her luscious body, he noticed her hard nipples. She attempted to walk away. Pushing her back into position, in a low tone he said, "Don't do that, ma. You know what I went through walking over here?"

Doing her best to be strong, she asked again, "Butta, what *are* you doing?"

"I can't even front. Your ass is beautiful. I mean … I knew you was cute. I thought about gettin' at you, but I put that shit on hold, trying not mix business." He took her arm and placed it around his waist.

"Butta I don't know—"

"You don't know about what? You don't know if you feeling me?"

She diverted her eyes from his.

"No, look at me. Tell me to leave you alone." He ran his tongue up and down her neck. "Tell me to get off of you." Butta slipped his hand in the front of her shorts, running his fingers over her swollen clit. "Tell me you don't want me, and I'll stop, that's my word. I won't come at you again."

Without Arnessa saying a word, they both knew she was giving in.

Danielle Santiago

Taking the lead, he pulled her shirt off. "No more talking," he said, pulling her shorts down. Kissing her body gradually, he eased onto his knees. "Open your legs, let me show you something."

Doing as she was told, she watched as he licked her clit with the tip of his tongue. Ecstasy shot through her body, a feeling she'd never felt before. Her knees buckled, and she had to grab the back of his head to keep from falling. Licking her clit once more, he said, "You're not ready for that." He stood up and took Arnessa by the hand, leading her into the den and over to the couch.

Butta took off his wifebeater as Arnessa unbuckled his pants, her hands shaking nervously. He grabbed her hands. "Relax, I got you."

Lying back on the oversized vanilla couch, she asked, "You sure this isn't just a fuck?"

"I wouldn't dare fuck you." He lay between her legs. "I'ma take care of you." He sucked on her lip and kissed her passionately. He attempted to penetrate her, but found it difficult. "Are you a virgin?"

"Un-uh," she answered, opening her legs wider, helping him in.

"Damn." He closed his eyes, enjoying the sensation. Arnessa's pussy felt like a hot, wet vice grip on his dick; he nearly nutted. "You sure somebody done been up in here before?"

"Yes, one person ... three years ago," she replied, a little embarrassed.

Trying to be gentle, he started out stroking her slowly, rolling his hips up and down. He could tell that she was inexperienced, which turned him on even more. While running his fingers through her hair, he looked into her slanted eyes. "Stay here ... let me take care of you."

Allure of the Game

"Why you wanna take care of me?" she moaned.

"It's something about you, plus this shit out here ain't for you."

"I take good care of myself. I'm not a charity case."

"I didn't say you were." He ran all the way up in her and paused. "You don't need to be in the streets beefing with Suef, or no other niggas."

"So what you want, for me to give up my blocks to you?"

He gave her a hard thrust and said, "Let's be real, Arnessa, if I wanted your blocks," he gave another hard thrust, "I would've had 'em."

At the moment, with the way he was sliding his rock hard dick up and down in her, she felt like he could have whatever he wanted. "I like making my own money," she moaned.

"You can keep your money on the street, but you … you need to fall back," he said, sliding his hands beneath her ass. Lifting her slightly, he spread her cheeks apart and drove deeper inside of her.

"Ahhhh," Arnessa screamed out, her eyes fluttering from the pleasure that he was pounding into her.

He licked her ear, then whispered, "I'ma handle that B-More package for you, too. You keep sending them chicks down there alone, them niggas gonna take that work and kill them one day." He lifted her legs up over his forearms, going right up the middle.

"Ooh-ooh, oh, *Butta*, wait, stop." Arnessa's body tensed up, her legs began to tremble, her pussy contracted in and out and creamy liquid flowed down, saturating his dick. She was experiencing her first orgasm, and Butta had given it to her. At that point, he had her mentally wrapped.

He pulled out and saw her cream covering his brown dick. "Turn over," he told her. Holding her by the waist, he entered her from behind. She grabbed a throw pillow and bit down on

Danielle Santiago

it to keep from screaming aloud. Butta moved her hair out the way and sucked her neck while sliding in and out of her. "You belong to me now. This is *my* pussy."

Enjoying the long strokes he was giving her from the back, she simply nodded in agreement. Butta ran the tip of his tongue up her spine. Arnessa responded by arching her back and poking her ass out, exactly what he wanted her to do. Beginning to climax, he squeezed her waist tighter, pumping harder and faster, all the while telling her, "Don't no nigga touch what's mine. Understand?"

"Mm, oh, mm," she moaned.

He yanked her hair, thrusting into her even harder. "Did you hear what the fuck I said?"

"Yes," she panted.

Groaning in pleasure, he exploded inside of her. With his dick still in her, he asked, "Whose pussy is this?"

The way he was coming at her was controlling, arrogant and confident. Arnessa loved it! Hesitantly, she answered, "It's yours, Butta."

* * * * *

Inside a warehouse in Manhattan's Meatpacking District, Trenton sat naked, his hands tied behind the chair, his legs spread open, each bound to a chair leg. His mouth was covered with gray duct tape. When Shawn had snatched him out of his car, he didn't even put up a fight. Instead, he began copping pleas. "You can have my money, just let me go."

"I don't I want your money! I'm here for you, young boy," Shawn told him through gritted teeth, then knocked him out with the butt of his gun.

"So you like delivering messages?" Mannie questioned Trenton, standing in front of him. "Deliver this then." He lift-

Allure of the Game

ed his foot and stomped on Trenton's dick. The pain was so excruciating, he nearly blacked out. His brown skin was covered in blood and bruises. "We run those blocks, nigga. Next time you got a message, come see me!" Mannie punched him with the back of a gloved fist, knocking him and the chair over.

Shawn picked up a brick and slammed it into Trenton's face. His jaw split in two and he instantly lost consciousness. Mannie looked at Shawn. "What the fuck, man? We not supposed to kill him." They had been beating the living shit out of him for more than two hours.

"That nigga is *not* dead," Shawn laughed. "Throw some of that pig piss on him, he'll come around."

"Man, you tripping, I'm not touching that shit! We done beat his ass enough anyway. He fucked up bad," Mannie said, looking at the blood running from the side of Trenton's face.

Shawn agreed. "Untie his bitch ass and let's go. I'm starving."

* * * * *

"Girl, where have you been?" Tasha questioned, opening her apartment door to let Arnessa in.

"Laying low," Arnessa replied.

"Nessa, I haven't seen you in over three weeks! Wait a minute. Are you actually wearing something that shows your figure, and are you carrying a purse?" Tasha asked, examining Arnessa's pale yellow Juicy sweat suit and the brown leather Gucci bag in her hand. "And your hair is hanging. You look so pretty. What the fuck is going on?"

"Cut it out, Tash." Arnessa followed Tasha down the hall into the kitchen, where Tasha was cooking. "What's that? It smells good," Arnessa said, taking a seat at the glass dining

Danielle Santiago

table.

"I got turkey wings, cabbage and macaroni and cheese. I know you want a plate."

"Sure do." Arnessa smiled. She loved Tasha's cooking. The girl could throw down.

"Nessa, how come you don't bring me the B-More package no more? And why them dudes take the trips wit' me an' Janine now?"

Arnessa sighed. "You still getting money, right?"

"Yeah," Tasha answered, turning to face her.

"Aight then, that's all that matters."

Tasha twisted her lips and said, "I see laying low ain't changed that slick-ass mouth."

Arnessa knew Tasha had a right to ask those questions, seeing that *she* was the one stuffing heroin into *her* vagina three times a week and transporting it down to Baltimore. "My bad, Tash, I'm stepping back from handling the packages personally right now. And those dudes going wit' y'all in case one of them niggas try some fly shit."

Tasha prepared Arnessa's plate and set it in front of her along with a glass of her homemade sweet tea, which Arnessa loved. After grabbing a plate for herself, Tasha sat across from Arnessa. "So, bitch, what's going on? You done just up and disappeared."

"I told you I'm laying low. You know a lot of shit been going down in the streets with Suef."

"You got to come better than that, you done showed up at my door looking all feminine and shit, which I been trying to get you to do for the last two years. Something else is going on wit' you, *home girl.*"

Arnessa contemplated her answer. *I should tell her, she is my only friend.* It had been three weeks since she'd gone to stay with Butta. No one else knew about their relationship outside of Cenise, Shawn and Mannie, or so she thought. Once Shawn's baby's mother caught wind of the relationship, she and all her chicken head friends were buzzing.

"I'm staying with Butta now," Arnessa replied.

Looking up from her plate, Tasha asked, "You staying with him, or are you *staying* with him?"

Unsure of what their relationship really was, she answered, "I think we're together."

Tasha's mouth fell wide open. "Are you jayin' Butta with his fine Do-mini-can ass?"

Arnessa simply blushed.

Tasha laughed. "You finally got you some dick ... it's about damn time."

The two girls chatted for a little while longer. Then Arnessa had to leave to get Cenise from school. After Cenise's run-in with Trenton, Arnessa drove her to and from school every day to ensure her safety.

Following Butta's automotive advice for the second time, Arnessa sold her Magnum and purchased a fully-loaded black Infiniti FX45. He'd initially told her to get rid of the Magnum in case Suef had any ideas for repercussions against her. A different car would throw him off for a while. Before she got the FX, she'd tried to buy a Grand Cherokee, but Butta, who'd accompanied her to the car lot, changed her mind. "Get you something nice yo, enjoy your money," he encouraged, knowing the only thing that she cared to splurge on was Cenise, which was something that he admired about Arnessa.

When Arnessa saw the FX, she fell in love with it, but she didn't feel comfortable with the nearly $50,000 price tag. "Butta, I like it, but it cost too much."

"Ma, if you want that, I'll give you half the money. I think you should have this car though. You hustle hard for your paper, treat yourself sometime, baby. 'Cause you can't it take

Danielle Santiago

with you."

What she wouldn't treat herself to, Butta did, lacing her with quite a few trinkets and treats. Not because he was trying to spoil her or buy her, but because he wanted her to be more lady-like. Around the middle of her second week at his house, he noticed that she kept all of her small belongings like her money, license and ATM card in her pockets. When he'd thought about it, he'd never seen her carrying a purse. The following evening, when she returned to the house, the couch in the den was filled with shopping bags from Louis Vuitton, Gucci, Prada, Saks and Bergdorf. Each bag contained two or three purses, along with the matching wallet or billfold. A couple of the bags were for Cenise, who now thought Butta was just the coolest.

Later that same night, when Butta came in and got into the bed where Arnessa was lying awake, she told him, "Thanks for the handbags. They're all really pretty, but you didn't have to—"

Cutting her off, he placed a finger across her lips. "You're a lady now ... my lady."

* * * * *

Lil Wayne's *"Receipt"* filled the car as Arnessa sat outside of Cenise's school, waiting for her to come out. Without alerting her phone, Butta's voice came over her Nextel speaker. "Ma, where you at?"

Pressing the PTT button on the side of her phone, she chirped him back. "Picking Cenise up from school."

"What else you got to do?"

"Um, I'm running Cenise and her friend a few places."

"Meet me at my people's spa that I showed you on 7th. Let them take your whip and go."

"Aight," she responded.

Butta closed his phone. "She's on her way," he announced to Kisa, Sincere and Eisani.

"Now, what is it that you want us to do?" Eisani asked Butta.

"E, she the same girl you picked the handbags out for. I want y'all to take her shopping with y'all." Butta pulled two bundles of money that totaled a little over fifteen thousand from the pockets of his jeans and set it on Kisa's desk. "Pick her out some hot shit, yo. I want her to get some fly shit. I'm talking about skirts, dresses, blouses, jeans, shades, shoes—"

Kisa interrupted him, "Butta, you upgrading bitches now?"

Everyone laughed, including Butta. "Come on, Kane, you know it ain't like that."

"I'm fucking with you, B, I can tell you like her though. I've never heard you talk about a girl the way you talk about this *Arnessa*."

"I know," Sincere interjected, "all he been talking about is Arnessa since he picked me up this morning."

"That's enough, that's enough," Butta said, grinning. "I'm feeling her for real, plus she so cool. I can't wait for y'all to meet her."

* * * * *

Once inside the bustling luxury spa, the receptionist led Arnessa upstairs to Kisa's office. As Arnessa entered the room, Butta stood up and pulled her to him, hugging her tightly. He kissed her. "Hey, baby."

"Hi," she said in a low voice, not at all used to being affectionate in front of others.

Beaming, he introduced her everyone. "This is Arnessa.

Danielle Santiago

Arnessa, this is my brother, Sincere, this is his wife Kisa, but we call her Kane, and this is Eisani ... she not nobody special."

"Shut up," Eisani said, then told Arnessa, "It's nice to meet you."

"Same here." Arnessa smiled nervously, feeling insecure in the presence of Kisa and Eisani. The two of them were beautiful and exquisitely dressed, as if they just stepped off the pages of Vogue. They both exuded power and confidence without saying a word. Feeling inferior to another female was not something that Arnessa was used to.

"We outside when y'all ready," Butta said, leaving with his arm around Arnessa.

As they walked down the stairs, Arnessa asked Butta, "Where are we going?"

"I gotta make some runs with Sin. You're going shopping with Kane and Eisani."

Arnessa stopped walking. "Butta, no, I don't know them. You and I can go shopping this weekend. I'll get whatever you pick out," she pleaded.

Standing on the stairs, he rubbed her face and assured her, "That's my family. They going to take good care of you, get you right for our trip."

"What trip?"

"We're going down South in a couple of weeks for a wedding."

Apprehensive, she sighed and said, "If this is what you want."

"It's not just about what I want, Arnessa. It's about preparing you—"

"Preparing me for what?" she snapped. "To be a lady?"

"Yes, but no, that's not the only thing. I mean, I'm into you—you know that—and I only want to see you shine at anything you do. If for whatever reason we don't work out, I want you to leave me a better woman."

* * * * *

Over the course of the shopping day, Arnessa got more than clothes. She gained two new friends. At first appearance, she thought Kisa and Eisani were stuck up, but she soon learned that they were the exact opposite. She found them surprisingly down to earth and easy to talk to, like the older sisters she never had. An added plus was that they both knew what it was like to be in the game. Arnessa reminded Kisa of herself when she was younger, a wild child, sort of a loose screw. She liked her instantly.

Shopping should have been Kisa's middle name; she was addicted to it. She lived for it, no matter if it was for herself or someone else. Arnessa became Kisa's muse, they swept through every high-end designer and department store in midtown. The trunk of Eisani's S550 was filled with so many shopping bags they could barely shut it. By the time they reached the last store, L'impasse, Arnessa and Eisani were exhausted, but not Kisa.

"I hope this is it," Eisani said.

"You don't have to come in," Kisa replied, "I came to get something to wear tonight. Arnessa, you wanna come in and get something for the party?"

"What party?" Arnessa asked, confused.

"My cousin Kennedy is having a book release party tonight at Strata. Butta is coming, aren't you coming with him?"

"I don't know. He didn't say anything to me about it."

"You don't have to go with him, 'cause you're going with us."

* * * * *

Danielle Santiago

A few hours later, the girls were at Eisani's loft, having drinks and getting dressed. Eisani and Kisa's younger cousin Tyeis came over to touch up Kisa's hair. She ended up doing Arnessa's hair, too. Tyeis' hands were anointed. Every time she picked up her scissors or curling irons, she created magic. She cut the front of Arnessa's hair into long flowing layers with a straight razor and gave her feather curls around her face.

"Tyeis got your shit looking good," Kisa told Arnessa as she entered the vanity area of the spacious bathroom and handed her a caramel martini.

Getting up from the vanity stool, Arnessa took the glass. "I don't know if I can drink this one, too. That last one got me feeling a lil tipsy."

"You don't drink much, do you?"

"Rarely," Arnessa responded with a giggle.

"Sit back down," Kisa instructed. "Let me put some make-up on that cute face." Kisa opened a brand new box of Bobbi Brown foundation and began applying it to Arnessa's face. "You know, I've never heard Butta talk about a girl the way he talks about you. Hell," she laughed, "I've never really heard him talk about any girl."

"Yeah, *right.*"

"I'm serious. Trust me, you're special," Kisa said, applying eye shadow to Arnessa's lids. She took another sip of her drink. "Real talk, Butta is a good dude. Most of all, he's loyal. Take good care of him and he'll always take care of you." Kisa gulped the remainder of her martini.

The liquor and the level of comfortableness led Arnessa to disclose something personal to Kisa. Up until now she had no one else to discuss the subject with. "I don't know if I'm doing it for him, sexually."

Kisa coughed, spitting out her drink. "Huh?"

"I think he wants me to go down on him," Arnessa said, embarrassed.

"If you don't want anybody else to do it, you better."

"It's not that I won't do it … I don't know how."

"Hmm?"

"I've only been with one other person."

"No wonder you're so special," Kisa joked. "I take it you would like a few pointers."

"Exactly," Arnessa replied, blushing.

"Wait one second. I'll be right back." Kisa returned with two bananas. She handed one to Arnessa. "Peel this." Kisa proceeded to teach Arnessa how to give a blow job by demonstrating on the banana. She also gave her a few other sexual tips that she guaranteed would drive Butta crazy.

* * * * *

"What you know about that, I know all about that," Arnessa rapped along with T.I. as she walked through Strata with Kisa and Eisani, her newfound friends. It was packed wall to wall. All eyes were on Arnessa as she entered the VIP area clad in a sleeveless, beige, empire waist mini-dress that looked spectacular against her brown skin. Very low cut in the front, the dress showed off her nice chest, and the golden-brown Dolce & Gabbana peep-toe pumps accented her shapely legs. The four martinis that she'd consumed at Eisani's gave her a burst of confidence and helped her walk smoothly.

Arnessa looked absolutely stunning. Butta had to do a double take when she approached him. Twirling around and giggling, she asked him, "You like?"

Butta scanned her body from top to bottom, then glanced over at Kisa and Eisani, who had big grins plastered on their faces, proud of Arnessa's new look. Turning his attention back

Danielle Santiago

to Arnessa, he pulled her into a big bear hug. "You look beautiful, baby."

She wiggled from his embrace. "I want to dance," she said, moving her hips to the beat.

"Have you been drinking?"

Smiling all silly, Arnessa nodded her head while dancing seductively.

Shawn walked over and stood next to Butta. "My dude, she cleans up very well."

"Yes, she does," Butta said. Unable to take his eyes from Arnessa, he wrapped his arm around her. "I'm ready to be out."

"We just got here," she complained.

"*Y'all* just got here, *we* been here. I gotta get you home, you got me wanting to do some things to you," he said, rubbing her ass.

That one touch had her thinking, *Fuck this club shit.* "Aight, but let me go say bye to Kane and Eisani."

Arnessa made her way over to where Kisa and Eisani were standing with Sincere. She paid no attention to the man walking toward her until he shoved her to the ground. He then bent over and asked her, "How's your little sister?"

When she looked up she saw that it was Suef. Before Arnessa could give any type of response, Sincere came over and laid Suef out with a hard right, and began viciously stomping him. Butta, Shawn and Mannie quickly followed suit. Eisani and Kisa rushed over, helping Arnessa to her feet. From the corner of her eye, Kisa saw Suef's right-hand man, Abdul, charging toward Sincere. Reacting quickly, she stuck her foot out, tripping him. Abdul crashed to the floor only inches from Sincere's feet. He grabbed Sincere's leg, trying to pull him down. Eisani got a champagne bottle from a bucket and smashed Abdul in the face. Sincere turned his attention

Allure of the Game

to Abdul and began stomping on his chest.

Club bouncers pushed their way through the crowd toward the altercation. When they saw it was Butta and his crew, they stood back for a moment before stopping it. If it had been anyone else they would've picked them up and threw them into the street. Instead, the head bouncer, who they all knew from Uptown, walked over to them. "Come on, fellas, that's enough, that's enough."

* * * * *

Suef's reference to her little sister pissed Arnessa off more than being shoved to the ground. It bothered her so much that as soon as she arrived home, she ran straight upstairs to Cenise's room. Arnessa was relieved to find her sound asleep. In a few weeks, Cenise would be graduating from high school. Arnessa was sending Cenise, along with her best friend Nomie, to Oakland. They were going spend the entire summer at the home of Nomie's aunt before leaving for college. Both girls would be attending Spellman, in Atlanta. Cenise, who had been on the A honor roll since kindergarten, received a full scholarship covering her four years of tuition.

Arnessa was relieved that Cenise was going away, not because she was tired of her or anything. Inside, she already knew that once her sister was gone, she was going to miss her tremendously. Her relief came from the fact that Cenise would be far away from the drama that was unfolding daily. Arnessa walked over to the bed and stared down at Cenise. For a brief moment, it was like looking at her mother. A tear snuck out of the corner of her right eye, sliding down her cheek as she thought about how different their lives would've been if their mother Maria hadn't abandoned them.

Some days Arnessa longed for her mother, but most days

Danielle Santiago

she hated her. A lot of days she wished her mother had died, rather than disappeared. That way she could've just grieved and moved on instead of being emotionally confused. Every time Arnessa made an attempt to let it go and move on, she thought of her high school graduation, and her hatred for her mother only magnified.

Arnessa would never be able to forgive her mother for missing the biggest day of her young life. She vividly remembered walking across the stage, knowing that Maria wasn't there. The hurt she felt was so painful that after the ceremony she became physically ill.

Wiping her eyes, Arnessa bent over and kissed her little sister's cheek. Deep down, Arnessa held out a small hope that Maria would show up for Cenise's graduation. Pulling the covers up over Cenise's shoulder she thought, *It doesn't matter if she ever shows up ... I'll always be here for you.*

On the way to her bedroom, Arnessa overheard Sincere giving Butta advice. She stopped to listen.

"You got to get rid of that nigga immediately," Sincere expressed. "From the door, when he sent his people at Arnessa sister, you shoulda bodied him and the nigga he sent. Fuck all that back and forth shit. You forgetting how to do this?"

"Fuck no!" Butta exclaimed.

"Aight, then you need to put a lid on this nigga, like yesterday. He young, he disrespectful and he smelling himself. I'm telling you, handle him before he handle you."

* * * * *

"Now if this ain't just some wrong-ass shit," Suef said, shaking his head. "Hiding out in my own hood like some little bitch." He wanted to pull back the curtain and peer outside, but he knew some of Butta's team could be watching the

Allure of the Game

barber shop downstairs. "If it weren't for you, cuz, I'da starved to death up in here."

"You gonna starve anyway, Suef," his cousin replied, setting a bag of groceries on the table. "In three months you 'bout lost all your blocks, or at least the dudes you had working them. Half your crew been taken out. The only reason I'm walking is that nobody's ever seen us together. I don't even know enough dudes with burners in all of Atlantic City to deal with Butta's army."

"Cuz," Suef said, "I'm not getting these blocks back. I know that." He got up from the couch and paced in small circles around the crowded loft. "Not yet, anyway. But, I gotta ask you ... you remember that favor you owe me?"

"I ain't killin' no bitch, Suef," his cousin replied.

"And I ain't askin' you to kill anyone," Suef said.

"Then what you want?"

"You're a smart guy," Suef said, pausing to adjust from his bent posture. He straightened up and puffed out his chest. "I want revenge."

What Suef didn't realize was that he was the only one fighting for those blocks, because he needed them. Butta's money was long. The cash those blocks brought in was nothing compared to what he made distributing cocaine and heroin up and down the East Coast.

For Butta, it was all about respect. With every passing day he was becoming increasingly annoyed that no one could find Suef. The majority of Suef's team had been murdered or severely injured at Butta's orders, which pretty much ended Suef's short reign at the top. That wasn't good enough though. Butta would not be able to relax until Suef was dealt with. As long as Suef was alive, Butta would continue to be tense, expecting him to strike at any moment.

All Butta really wanted to do was kick back and spend

Danielle Santiago

some quality time with Arnessa. They'd fallen hard for one another, in spite of everything that was going on around them. Loving a man was a new feeling for Arnessa. She knew that she cared for Butta, but never having had a boyfriend before him, she was confused about how to express her love. By nature, Arnessa was nurturing, and it felt good to have someone to take care of. Every day she cooked, cleaned and took care of all his personal needs. Little by little, Arnessa had gone from a hustler to a housewife. She enjoyed her new life, but for the most part found it dull. Arnessa missed the rush of the hustle, the day to day grind.

It had been so long since Arnessa had given any thought to what she wanted to do outside of hustling. Watching Kisa run her own businesses was making Arnessa want to become a legal entrepreneur. Quietly, she spent her days on the internet researching the most profitable businesses in the country. She wanted something with long-term potential, so she decided she wanted to get into the real estate market. Being an agent was out of the question, but Arnessa loved the idea of buying a property, fixing it up and then selling it. The whole idea seemed real familiar to her. She figured if she could flip weight ... she could flip properties.

On one of those rare nights when Butta made it home before midnight and wasn't exhausted, he and Arnessa lay in bed watching *"The First 48,"* Arnessa's favorite program. She thought it was the perfect time to tell him about her business venture. Sitting with her back against the headboard and her legs folded Indian style, Arnessa looked down at Butta, whose head was resting on her thigh. "Butta, remember how I was telling you that I wanted to start my own business?"

"Yeah, I remember."

"I've decided to open a real estate investment company."

"You wanna buy buildings and rent the apartments?"

"No, well maybe that, too, but mainly I want to buy properties, fix them up and sell 'em."

Butta sat up attentively. "It's a lot of paper in that type of business if you do it right. Let me get in on it."

"Wow, this is too funny," Arnessa laughed.

"What?"

"You're the second person who I've told about my business, and just like the first person, you want in."

"Who's the first person?"

"Kane."

"I should've known, that girl has an ear for a good business deal."

"Plus, she already plugged me to some good connections to help get me started."

He wrapped his arm around her and pulled her down. "That's what's up. I think you will be a success."

"You do?" Arnessa gushed at his encouragement.

"Yes. You're smart, ambitious, and we both know you're capable of running a business."

No one, besides her brother Deon, had ever paid Arnessa such nice compliments. Inside, Arnessa was beaming as her eyes scanned his face and her fingertips caressed his chin. She simply smiled at him.

"What you smiling at?" Butta asked.

"You, I—" she hesitated. Although they'd been together a little over six months, she still found professing her feelings aloud difficult.

"I what?" Butta nudged.

Looking toward the ceiling, Arnessa searched for the correct words. "I'm still getting use to the whole relationship thing. Lately there have been times when I wanted to tell you … I love you."

"I love you, too, baby."

Danielle Santiago

"Do you really?"

"Yes, I love you. I love you very much; it's something about you." He began kissing her. He just adored her sumptuous lips. Before getting with Arnessa, he didn't care too much for kissing, but when it came to her he couldn't kiss enough.

Tossing her leg atop his body, she straddled him and nibbled his earlobe. She'd learned him very well, and knew exactly where to kiss, massage and suck. Butta's dick stiffened beneath her. "Hmm, what's that?" she purred, moving from his ear to his neck, then down to his bare chest, circling his nipples with her moist tongue. Lying back, Butta enjoyed the immense pleasure that Arnessa was giving him. With his guidance, she'd become a superb lover. Arnessa pulled his boxers off and wrapped her hand around his dick, steadily jerking it up and down. While looking up at him, she licked her lips teasingly.

"Stop playing, girl, let me get some of that mouth."

Arnessa licked the head. "Tell me you want it."

"You know I want it."

Clasping her mouth around the head, she sucked firmly as she took more and more of him in. Bobbing her head up and down, she tightened her jaws while jerking him with her hand. Arnessa had become a professional, courtesy of the skills Kisa had shown her.

"Umm, baby," he moaned as she began to deep throat him, all the while performing swallowing motions which created intense pressure and extreme satisfaction. It felt like she was making love to him with her mouth. He removed the clip from her tresses. His body shivered in delight as he grabbed a fistful of her hair. Arnessa knew he was about to explode, so she pulled back, letting him fall from her mouth slowly.

"Why you stop?"

"Now, now, I can't just let you lay back and have all the

fun." She smirked as she crawled onto him and began riding him. Butta was elated that Arnessa was becoming less inhibited. He was even happier that it was with him. He had awakened things in her, mentally and physically, that she never knew existed. Picking up the pace, she rode him 'til they both climaxed.

Butta slapped her ass. "That was good, lil mama."

"I know," she said as she rolled off of him.

"What you mean you know? Come here." He pulled her body close to his, squeezing her tight. Her back was against his chest and he rested his chin in the crease between her neck and shoulder. As they both began to doze off he told her, "I really do love you, Arnessa. You do know that, right?"

"Yeah, I know ... but do you know you're the first and only man that I've loved?"

"I do now," he responded with a little sarcasm.

"Now that you know, don't hurt me."

* * * * *

The next day, Arnessa lunched with Kisa and Mrs. Spencer, a client from the spa. Along with her husband, Mrs. Spencer owned a successful contracting firm that had locations in six states on the East Coast. Arnessa observed while Kisa did most of the talking on her behalf. Using her most proper voice, Kisa effortlessly negotiated a deal to only use Mrs. Spencer's company for all projects, in exchange for a modest discount. Watching Kisa spew out numbers without blinking or stumbling only reassured Arnessa that she'd made the right decision by going into business with her.

Arnessa glanced down at the vibrating cell phone that rested in her lap. It was the fourth phone call from an unfamiliar Atlanta number. *This can only be Cenise or Nomie,* she

Danielle Santiago

thought, since she knew no one else in Atlanta. But, where were their cell phones? Excusing herself from the table, she answered the phone as she entered the bathroom. "Hello?"

"Arnessa," a tearful voice spoke.

"Nomie?"

"Yes ..."

"What's wrong, why are you crying?"

"It's Cenise ..."

Arnessa's heart dropped to the pit of her stomach. "What happened to my sister, Nomie?"

"She got knocked."

Breathing a little easier, Arnessa asked, "For what, fighting? I told y'all not to go down there with that rowdy shit."

"Nah, Nessa, they got her for trafficking."

"Trafficking what?"

"Cocaine," replied Nomie.

In an instant, pain shot through Arnessa's head. "Wh-what you mean *cocaine?* What the hell y'all into down there?"

"*I'm* not into nothin', Nessa, I swear. It's that dude Black that Cenise be messing wit'. I told her after she made the first couple of runs not to do it no more."

"What run?"

"From back home to down here."

This was a lot for Arnessa to process, plus too much was being said over the phone. "That's enough talking on this line. Where they holding them at?"

"Cenise is the only one who's locked up, and she's in Greenville, South Carolina."

"So where this Black nigga at? He better be on his way to fucking bond her out, I know that."

"I tried calling him, but every number Cenise gave for him is disconnected."

Arnessa was becoming more pissed with each answer.

Allure of the Game

"What's his real name?"

"We don't know," Nomi answered truthfully. "Everybody down here call him New York Black."

"That's every dark skinned, New York nigga name when they outta town. How come Cenise didn't call me?"

"She said she been calling the house, but she couldn't get you. I had her on three way the first few times I called you. I think she had to get off the phone."

"The next time she call, hit me. If for any reason I don't answer, make sure you tell her to keep her mouth closed."

* * * * *

"Are you okay, dear?" Mrs. Spencer asked upon Arnessa's return to the table, noticing the sweat stains on her beige silk blouse and her smeared mascara.

"I'm okay, my food just didn't agree with me." She smiled weakly.

Instinct told Kisa that Arnessa was lying, not to mention the fact that her hands were trembling. "Mrs. Spencer, I know you have another meeting. I'll take care of the check," Kisa suggested, wanting her to leave quickly so that she could find out what was really up with Arnessa.

"Thank you, Kisa," Mrs. Spencer said, getting up from the table. "Arnessa, I hope you feel better, talk to you soon, ladies."

"Bye," they said in unison as they watched her walk away. As soon as Mrs. Spencer was out of hearing range, Kisa turned to Arnessa. "What's up wit' you?"

Still in disbelief, Arnessa shook her head. "That was Nomie on the phone, she said Cenise got knocked for trafficking coke."

"Are you serious?"

Danielle Santiago

Arnessa nodded.

"We can go to the airport and get a flight to Atlanta and get her out."

"She not even in Atlanta yo, she some place I've never heard of called Green something, South Carolina."

"*Greenville?*" Kisa's eyes widened, hoping that she hadn't heard correctly.

"Yeah, that's the place."

"Oh no!"

"Why you say it like that?"

The waiter walked over to return Kisa's credit card. She signed the receipt, giving him a generous tip. "I don't want to scare you or jump to any conclusions," Kisa told her as they got up from the table, "but that is the absolute worst state to catch a drug charge in. Niggas be getting ten years for an ounce of blow," Kisa told her as she dialed a number. They walked out of the restaurant and across the street to the parking garage.

"What it do, mama?" Kennedy answered.

"You in Charlotte?"

"Yeah."

"You still cool with that bondsman chic?"

"Who, Dreann? Yeah, we straight. Why?"

"Hold on, Ken," Kisa said as she fished through her purse for the parking stub. Once she located it, she handed it to the young parking attendant who was openly admiring her.

"You gorgeous, yo, what's your name?" He moved in close, something he shouldn't have done. Kisa couldn't stand for strangers to get in her personal space. That type of thing made her extremely uncomfortable. "I'm telling you now, get out my face and go get my fucking car before it be a problem," she said, staring him down. Sensing her seriousness, he walked away mumbling obscenities. Kisa returned to the phone to hear Kennedy laughing. "What's so funny?" Kisa asked.

"You," Kennedy replied. "You always breaking on people."

"Whatever, that bum-ass nigga was all in my face drooling. Anyway, I need you to check with your girl and see if she do bonds in South Carolina."

"Who in the world got locked up down there?"

"Cenise, Arnessa's little sister."

"The one that was at my wedding?"

"Yeah, her last name is Binds. Find out what her charges are and the amount of her bond, and we'll put it in your account."

"I'm on it."

* * * * *

A half hour later Kisa was sitting on a stool in Butta's kitchen when Kennedy called back. "Kane, Cenise's charge is felony cocaine trafficking, 200 to 400 grams. Her bail is 150 g's. I already gave Dreann the ten percent. I'm going to ride down there with her to pick Cenise up."

"I'll probably fly down with Arnessa tonight to pick her up."

"You know Chaz and I are flying back tonight. I'll see if I can get her on the flight with us."

"That will be good. Hit me back and let me know, so if you can't, we can go ahead and make arrangements." Just as she was hanging up the phone, Butta came in, followed by Sincere, Mannie and Shawn.

"What's the word on baby girl?" Butta asked.

Kisa told him everything that she'd gotten from Kennedy.

"This shit is crazy," Butta sighed, after hearing the update. "Where Nessa at?"

"She went up to take a shower. This is stressin' her."

Danielle Santiago

93

"I already know. Cenise is her life," Butta said, heading for the stairs.

Shawn walked over to Kisa all smiles. "Sis, what up?"

"What do you want, *Shawn*?"

"You remember back in the day, how all of us would be in one place like this and you'd whip up one of them bangin' meals."

"I remember vaguely," she joked.

"Come on, Kane, cook something for us."

"I don't cook no more, ask Sin."

"Picture that," Mannie chimed in as they all laughed.

"Shawn, that chick you call your girl still won't cook for you?" Kisa asked, smiling mischievously as she hopped off the stool. "If my husband will accompany me to the store, I'll throw a little something together." Without waiting for Sincere's response, she grabbed her purse and his hand and walked toward the door.

Upstairs, Butta pushed the bedroom door open a little and peeped inside. Arnessa was lying in the middle of the king-sized bed with her back to the door. She was wearing a white terrycloth robe. Her freshly shampooed hair was wrapped in a white towel. A small duffle bag was at the foot of the bed, already packed. Butta lay down behind her and wrapped his arm around her. "You okay, baby?"

When she didn't respond, he peeked over her shoulder to see if she was awake. Arnessa stared blankly at the wall. Her heart ached miserably for her sister. "How could she do this to me, Butta?"

"I don't know, Nessa."

"This feels so crazy, it's like I don't even know my little sister. I can't believe she let some piss-ass nigga gas her. Now, *she* sitting in a cell and he in the fuckin' wind." Water filled Arnessa's eyes. "I know she scared out her mind."

Allure of the Game

"It's gonna be aight," he assured her, kissing the back of her neck. "Kane said Kennedy already paid Cenise's bond and is on the way to pick her up."

Arnessa sat up. "I need to get dressed so we can get to the airport."

"Nah," he pulled her back down onto the bed, "Cenise is gonna fly up with Kennedy tonight. You need to relax." He turned her around so that they were facing each other. Her face was streaked with tears. Butta removed the towel from Arnessa's head. Her damp hair fell across the pillow. Using the end of the towel, he wiped her face. Arnessa slipped one arm beneath him and the other around him. She planted her head firmly into his chest and wept silently until she fell asleep.

* * * * *

Later that night, Arnessa woke to the laughter and music that was coming from downstairs. Butta was no longer next to her. She slipped on a white tank and a pair of gray sweats and went downstairs to see what was going on. She found everyone sitting around the massive dining table. Eisani had also joined the group. In the center of the table were the remnants of what Kisa had prepared: king crab legs, jumbo shrimp, rice and seafood salad, along with a few top shelf liquor bottles.

Butta rose from his chair when he saw Arnessa. She waved him back down and sat on his lap. "You feeling better?" he asked her.

"A little. Has Kennedy or Cenise called?"

"They'll be here soon. You ready to eat? Kane fixed you a plate. It's in the kitchen."

"Maybe later, I don't have an appetite right now."

Butta's phone rang. "Let me up, Ness." He walked through the kitchen and out to the garage. When he came back in,

Danielle Santiago

Kennedy, Chaz and Cenise were with him. Cenise stood off in the distance while everyone else exchanged greetings.

"Thanks for getting her out," Arnessa told Kennedy as they embraced.

"You don't have to thank me, it was no problem. Baby girl is shook up, though, especially since she can't get in touch with ole dude."

Cenise walked over to Arnessa, expecting to receive compassion and comfort from her big sister. Unfortunately, when Arnessa looked at Cenise, all she felt was anger and rage. Neither sister said a word; they just stared at one another. Unable to match Arnessa's stare, Cenise looked away first. Suddenly Arnessa slapped Cenise, knocking her to the floor. As Arnessa advanced toward Cenise to hit her again, Butta grabbed her from behind. "Nessa, what's wrong with you?"

"What's wrong with me?" She tried unsuccessfully to free herself from his grasp. "Ain't *shit* wrong with me! What's wrong with this little ignorant bitch?" she demanded, pointing at Cenise, who was being helped up by Kisa. Everyone else looked surprised at the way Arnessa was handling her sister.

No one was more shocked than Cenise though. "Why'd you hit me, Nessa?" she cried. "Why?"

"Why? Why? Why were you on the highway with that nigga's coke?"

"'Cause I love him," Cenise sobbed.

"You can't be serious. You don't even know his name, *stupid*."

"And he paid me."

"Paid you what?"

"Two g's a trip."

"What the fuck is two g's to you, Cenise? That was your monthly allowance in high school. You not talking to no dummy, aight? All this is about is trying to impress a bum-ass nigga."

"You don't even know him," Cenise countered.

"Apparently, you don't either, and if he gave half a fuck about you he wouldn't have left you for dead. You can't tell when a muthafucka is using you?"

Already embarrassed, Cenise was now pissed at Arnessa for going at her in front of everyone. Mustering up some nerves and twisting her neck, she told Arnessa, "I don't know why you all in my shit, just six months ago you was moving more coke and dope than Jeezy rap about."

Hmm, let me get out the way 'cause she 'bout ta beat the shit out this girl, Kisa thought, just as Arnessa broke away from Butta's grasp and rushed Cenise. Arnessa grabbed her by the neck and slammed her into the wall. Cenise's slanted eyes became wide as golf balls as she tried to breathe. Arnessa tried to fight off the tears, a battle that she quickly lost, as they spilled from her eyes. "What I did, I did for us. I hustled every day for you so that you could have the best. I put myself on the line for you. Now you might've thrown it all away for a *boy*."

Realizing that she was choking her sister, Arnessa stepped back. Sobbing and gasping for air, Cenise crumpled to the floor.

Arnessa looked down at Cenise. "Everything is a wrap for you now."

"The police said that I could cooperate."

"*Cooperate*! Ha!" Arnessa laughed insanely. "Did you go to the academy? Do you have a uniform in your closet?"

Scared, Cenise shook her head. "No."

"Well then you don't work for the fuckin' police! Yeah, you done jumped in this game feet first wit' out a damn clue, and like it or not, it's rules to this shit. Rule number one, no snitchin'. Now if you want to break that rule I suggest you pack up the little bit of shit that *I didn't* buy and get the fuck

Danielle Santiago

out. I don't support no rats."

Cenise sat there with a hurt expression on her face. The only person she had in the world had just given her a harsh ultimatum. Arnessa knew her delivery was cruel and rapid, but so was the game. She also knew that the game didn't give a fuck about nobody. The room was so quiet, if a piece of tissue would've dropped, they would've heard it.

Arnessa watched Cenise as she contemplated her limited choices. "I bet the game don't look so good from the inside, do it, lil sis?" Arnessa chuckled. "It's a major decision, ain't it?"

Reluctantly, Cenise agreed by nodding her head.

"Well, what you gonna do?"

In a low whimper she answered, "I'll let you handle it."

Chillingly, Arnessa replied, "You made the right choice." She turned to go upstairs, but stopped and looked back at Cenise. "Welcome to the game, lil mama."

Allure of the Game

Danielle Santiago

THE FINK

By

Quentin Carter

Triple Crown Publications presents . . .

The Fink

Chapter 1

"Mr. Mitchell? Do you see the defendant, Stacy Landis, in the courtroom today?"

Phelix Mitchell sat motionless in an uncomfortable chair upon the stand in front of a packed courtroom. His family, friends, ex-friends and enemies were all in attendance and were anxiously awaiting his response, waiting to see if he was actually gonna testify against his long-time friend, or tell the prosecutor to go to hell.

The prosecutor, Mrs. McGilvery, was nervously watching him and becoming very impatient with her witness. The verdict depended solely on his testimony, and his hesitation made Mrs. McGilvery feel as if the man sitting in front of her had gotten a cold tongue.

"Mr. Mitchell?" Mrs. McGilvery spoke a little louder this time. "The court and I are waiting to hear from you. Now I'll ask again, do you see the defendant, Stacy Landis, in the courtroom today?"

Finally, he raised his head until his glossy eyes were facing the crowd. His mom's lips moved rapidly, as if she were uttering a silent prayer. Shania, his girlfriend, shot him a look of encouragement while nodding her head slowly. His friends were doing just the opposite. One of them mouthed the word "snitch," or it could have been "bitch" for all Phelix knew. Whatever was said, he felt like both of them. The fucked up thing was that that person was his younger brother.

Quentin Carter

Lastly, Phelix's eyes rested on the defendant. Stacy returned eye contact, but did not give any hard glares, nor did he mouth any profound words. Stacy had not yet lost faith in Phelix. He was confident that his friend would find the courage to take his own weight like a man without bringing him down with him.

Phelix licked his lips, and before he knew it, the word "yes" had escaped through his lips.

"And was this man, Stacy Landis, the leader of a controlled drug ring in which you served as an under boss?"

Even though his lips were trembling, he still managed to repeat the word, "Yes," just as clearly as he did the first time.

All sorts of oohs, ahhs and foul comments were shouted by the onlookers. The judge banged her gavel to restore order.

Prosecutor McGilvery proceeded without hesitation. They had practiced his testimony several times before the trial started.

"Could you please point him out for the record of the court?"

Phelix didn't move. Suddenly, after he heard Shania's voice inside his head saying, "Stacy tried to fuck me," he raised his hand and pointed toward the face of Stacy Landis, sealing his fate. Stacy sat back in his seat and closed his eyes, trying hard to hold back his tears and remain strong for his family.

His wife's cries could be heard echoing in his ears. His mother had not been able to attend. After receiving the news that her son had been picked up by the feds, she had suffered a minor stroke. It also sickened her to learn that his best friend, who was also her godson, had

The Fink

taken him down. Phelix was like her second child and was always welcomed with open arms whenever he would visit.

"In your own words," Prosecutor McGilvery said, "could you go into detail and describe a typical day for the defendant?"

"A typical day for him would be ... "

Stacy jumped up and shouted, "You bitch-made-ass nigga!" His lawyer tried to pull him back down into his chair. "How you gon' do me like that?"

Army Major Melvin Landis, Stacy's father, saw the tears on his son's face and stood quickly. "Hold back your tears, son! Take it like a man! Don't let them break you! Don't you let 'em."

Stacy followed the Major's orders by sitting back down and trying to regain his composure.

Mrs. McGilvery peered at Phelix and saw a sympathetic look on his face. Then she quickly said to the judge, "Your honor, the prosecution requests a five-minute recess."

Chapter 2

[2006]
Three Years Later

On May 28, Phelix Mitchell was released from prison. He wasn't sure what he was gonna do with himself now that it was all over. One thing he knew for sure was that he was gonna put the past behind him and leave it there.

His reality wasn't like the movies shot in Hollywood, where the feds relocate their snitches to unknown locations around the world and protect them with new identities. Snitches from the hood got thrown back into the pit after it was all over and they had been milked for all the information they had.

There was no woman waiting for Phelix at the front gate, although Shania had promised him that if he got a time cut for his cooperation, she would ride the bid out with him. After a shaky year and a half, she had disappeared without a trace. Which was really fine by him. He had long grown tired of her calling him a snitch every time she felt like starting some bullshit.

The cab dropped Phelix off at his mother's house, back in his old neighborhood. He had dreamt about the place a tad too often throughout his bid. It did not feel good to be there. For all those years, he had been anxious to come home for nothing.

The Fink

His mother was standing in the doorway, waiting to greet him with a big hug. Tears and a lifetime of stress made her eyes appear sad, even when she was not. When they embraced, he could feel her heart thumping on his chest.

"Hey, lady," he said with a smile.

"I'm glad you finally made it out. I wanted to come—"

Phelix held his hand up, silencing her. "I know, Mama."

He heard footsteps coming from the hallway. In the front room appeared Chop, standing behind her. He had grown a lot during the three years that Phelix had been away.

At twenty-one, he was over six feet tall and built like he had been to prison, too. He wore a frown instead of the expected smile. Something about the evil glare in his eyes told Phelix that his brother was not at all happy to see him.

The streets had gotten to Chop. It was written all over him, in the way he wore his pants, the expensive sneakers and the bulges in his front pockets. One concealed a small caliber pistol, and the other his bankroll.

Their mother turned toward her youngest son. "Chop, come over here and hug your brother. You haven't seen him in three years."

"That should have told him something."

"Told him what?" she inquired.

"He knows what I'm talking about."

Her eyes narrowed as she placed one hand on her hip. "Boy, you…"

"That's alright, Mama," Phelix assured her, "he's a man now."

Quentin Carter

"Goddamn right, I am. A stand-up man." Chop kissed her on the cheek. "Be back when he ain't around."

She clutched his arm. "Boy, don't think my arthritis disables me from knocking yo' big head clean off your shoulders."

"Sorry, Mama." His cell phone vibrated. "I gotta run."

Phelix and their mother both watched him walk away, pants sagging down to his knees.

"Lawd, help guide him in the right direction," she prayed.

"He'll be alright."

"He was hurt when you took the stand on that boy," she informed him. "The other kids around here were teasing him, so you can't blame him for acting a little different. But you're his blood. He should always love you, no matter what."

Home less than an hour, and the past was starting to resurface.

~ ~ ~ ~

Phelix took a long, hot bath, enjoying something that he had once taken for granted. For the first time in years, he didn't have to wear shoes while he washed his body.

He sighed. "Shit, I wonder where I'll be in five years." He had a vision of himself in a coffin. "God, I hope not."

Another problem he faced, besides being a snitch, was that he now had to live a life that didn't include aid from the distribution of cocaine. How would he survive now? He promised himself that since he had snitched, he would never sell drugs again. He didn't deserve to

The Fink

be able to use the game as a stepping-stone to financial freedom.

~ ~ ~ ~

Night had fallen. Phelix had dressed in some new clothes bought by his Mama. He was sitting out on the front steps when he heard loud music blaring from a distance. From down the road he could see headlights coming over the hill.

A bright red F-150 stopped in front of his house. The chrome wheels it flossed were about as tall as he was old. Seconds later, his old friend Sam emerged from the truck. His jewelry was gleaming, even in the dark.

Damn, Phelix thought. Last he heard, Sam had gotten caught with a few bricks and had snitched on a Mexican. But here he was, looking as if he had the entire city on lock.

"Sammy the muthafuckin' Bull," Phelix said as they shook hands.

Sam smiled, flossing his iced-out grill. "Playboy. How ya been?"

"Sheeit, you know how I been."

"Yeah, I heard. But sheeit, I know you heard about me, too. It is what it is. C'mon, let's go shoot a few games and have a drink so I can fill you in on what's going down."

They hit up a place out in Grandview called Max's. It was a small club, not really what you would call classy. But in the past, Phelix had spent enough change in there to get the whole building remodeled.

Sam had to literally fight off a few bitches on his way to the bar to order their drinks. Phelix smiled at a couple of females who he knew from way back. Instead

Quentin Carter

of embracing him, they turned and went the other way.

Juvy could be heard through the speakers, pumping, "Get ya hustle on ... get ya hustle on ... get ya hustle on." Girls in their teeny shorts and low-rise jeans, showing their thongs, were on the floor dancing and sweating all over each other.

Everybody seemed to look at Phelix with cold stares. Some he recognized, some he didn't. That made him afraid to relax. He had forgotten that he was once a big name around town. Everybody within the city limits was up on game about him.

People weren't tripping on Sam like they were with Phelix. He pranced around the club with his hat to the back like he was a real stand-up dude. He had snitched, too, but for some reason everyone seemed to accept what he had done.

Sam had a huge grin on his face as he walked the drinks back to their table. "Here, nigga. Get fucked up on me." He took a seat.

Phelix peered upside Sam's head, somewhat fascinated by the way he was handling himself. Quickly, Sam's head snapped in his direction like a chicken that had sensed danger.

"What the fuck you staring at me for, Phe? Don't tell me 'I see that lust in your eyes' bullshit. Three years wasn't enough time for you to have been on ass and shit."

"Nigga, I don't wanna fuck you," Phelix checked him. "You pretty, but not that damn pretty."

"Why you staring at me when I ain't lookin' then? You got narrow eyes like a fuckin' predator."

"Fuck you. Nah, man, on the real though, shit seems kinda funny."

The Fink

Sam sipped on his drink. "Funny how?"

"I mean, sheeit ... everybody in here grittin' on me, but they treatin' you like a king. Let me in on what I don't already know."

Sam smirked. "Last time a nigga let you in on something, you told on him."

"C'mon wit' that shit, dog. That ain't funny. Stacy fucked around and got twenty-eight years for that shit." He shook his head regretfully. "I hoped he would've pled out."

"Man, fuck these niggas," Sam said. "He would've done the same thing to you if they would've caught him first. Believe that shit. Man, look around you."

Phelix did. Every dude in there was smiling and drinking expensive drinks, wearing new gear and sparkling jewelry.

"Every nigga in here has given up some kinda information to the elroys at some point. When a nigga's car stash spot gets popped, that makes it easier for the next man with a stash spot in his car to get popped off. Or when a nigga calls the police on a drug house in their hood because it's takin' up all the money. What about a nigga that got caught with dope in his ass? Every nigga that keeps dope in his ass is gonna get caught up after that. How you think all these young niggas are getting away with wearing $10,000 chains? Driving $50,000 trucks? Living in $100,000 cribs?"

Phelix shrugged.

"'Cause they're all tellin'. If you ride past all the custom body shops in the city, I'll bet you every dude that you see pull out of that garage after spending more than $10,000 on their ride is an informant. Hell, the people who own the shops are informants, too, 'cause they're

Quentin Carter

reporting all the cash receipts for over ten grand. It's the way of the game now. They're giving up too much time for a nigga to stand strong. And the few who do are up in there now wishing that they were out here with us.

"Take Stacy for instance," Sam continued. "He's holding strong now. Just wait until all of his appeals have failed. Then that twenty-eight years sets in on him. He's gonna be looking for a way out. I hope he ain't got no dirt on you that the feds don't already know about ... or you're hit."

Phelix ignored Sam's last comment. "So that's why you're accepted?"

"Nope." Sam hit his drink again. "I'm accepted because I got something to offer. I got that work. As long as I got the goods, niggas could care less if I told on my mama." He laughed. "They're so thirsty, some of them got it programmed in their heads that me turning snitch was only a myth. You know why? 'Cause I snitched on a Mexican, not a black dude," he emphasized, "that nobody knows. It's ugly, but it's the way it is."

Phelix tasted his strong drink. "All that tells me is that our generation is not cut out for the game. So why are you back in it?"

Sam smiled mischievously. "'Cause ... I got a get outta jail free card."

No matter what Sam said, Phelix refused to let himself believe that what he did was cool ... and not the act of a poltroon. And he vowed to never do it again. Sam was sitting across from him bragging about just snitching on a Mexican like they're not human beings with families.

Everybody's doing it.

A large group of youngsters bailed up in the club,

The Fink

stopping at the doorman. One could tell they were already fucked up on some kind of narcotic. They checked their IDs one by one.

The last man to walk in wore a long, black T-shirt that read *Stop Snitchin'* in big white letters. The doorman was giving him shit about wearing it up in there. It was dark, but that didn't stop Phelix from recognizing his face.

It was Chop.

It was as if Chop could feel his sibling's eyes on him, because he looked across the room, dead at Phelix. Phelix nodded. Chop turned his head and kept on strutting like he didn't see him.

It felt like he had been cut to the bone with a dull knife. Phelix had been lonely in jail, desperately yearning to be with family. Now that he was free, his only sibling was giving him the cold shoulder.

Whatever happened to the days when Chop used to imitate my every move? Phelix wondered. Chop used to run around bragging that Phelix Mitchell was his big brother. Now he was all grown up and no longer walked around in Phelix's shadow. Chop despised his brother, who had balled hard, enjoyed fine food, fine women and good cognac. And what did he do to the game for being so good to him? He went against the rules. THOU SHALL NOT SNITCH!

"Sam?" Phelix asked. "Wha'sup with Chop?"

"He's doing a'ight for himself. Cops a brick or two from Mike every week. He don't fuck with me ... and I don't fuck with him."

Sam peered over Phelix's shoulder. "Somebody's bitch is up in here tonight ... as usual."

Phelix spun around on the stool and saw Shania

Quentin Carter

standing before him. He hated to admit it, but damn, she was hot. Too goddamned hot. Hot enough to make him go against his word.

Before he was released from prison, he vowed, by putting it on his unborn child, that he would never touch her again. Not after all she had taken him through. The letters and visits had stopped suddenly. Then he called her home one day, only to be confront-ed by some nigga that she was sucking and fucking. He thought that he could never forgive her. Hoped that he would never forgive her. Prayed that he would never see her again.

But there she was, in the flesh. Tall, a fresh tan, C-cups, a nice round ass, and smiling big, showing off her near perfect teeth. Since he had no one else to lay, he would probably end up going against his word. It was not like he hadn't done it before.

"Phelix Mitchell," she said in her loud, high-pitched voice. "Boy, get up and give me a hug."

Hesitantly, Phelix stood and complied. The warm feeling that her body produced relaxed him for a brief spell. Her breath reeked of chewing gum and alcohol and tickled his neck hairs. A tingling sensation started in his nut sack. He tried to control the upcoming erec-tion, but it was useless. He could tell by the way her body shifted that she felt the bump coming through.

"So, who you been fuckin'?" Phelix asked bluntly.

"You still mad at me?" Shania asked, ignoring his question.

Phelix knew that by her ignoring him, he had caught her off-guard, thus giving her no time to create a lie. So it must be somebody that he knew hitting it. Probably Sam's slick ass.

Phelix said, "Right now, I don't know how I feel. Ask me in the morning, 'cause tonight, I'm in love all over again."

Shania smiled, but he didn't see it. While Phelix was away, she had been through the wringer. She was fine, true enough, but the type of brothers she chose to bed down with were not looking for love or commitment. It was as simple as wam bam take this money and get on Shania. And as long as they were paying ... she was laying.

She had long been ready to put the fast life behind her. Now that Phelix was home, and if she could win his heart back, she might get that white picket fence and dog that she dreamed of having. Maybe even a child.

"Let's get outta here," Shania whispered in his ear. "I've got some love making up to do." She tugged at his sleeve.

Phelix looked at Sam. "You gon' be a'ight?"

"Eh, I'm cool, brother. Hit it for me, too." Sam winked at her.

"Let's go," Shania persisted.

Phelix got up and started for the door. Out of the blue, some big black dude bumped into him.

The man spun around with a frown on his face. "Eh, you hot-ass nigga! You almost burned a hole through my fuckin' shirt."

Phelix turned around. Shania kept tugging at him to follow her.

"Baby, c'mon."

"Fuck that," Phelix hollered as he tried to snatch away from her.

"Let his hot ass go, baby," the man barked.

Quentin Carter

Sam snuck out the front door and out to the car. With all the commotion going on, it would be easy to sneak back in with his gun.

In the time it took Phelix to blink, six more dudes had come to the man's aid. Including Chop.

Chop said, "Look Phe, just get yo' rat ass up outta here. Last time I checked, they didn't serve cheese."

Laughter came from the crowd of onlookers.

Phelix scowled at him. "You're supposed to be my brother, muthafucka! And you sidin' with these niggas over me?"

Chop's look was cold. "You're a rodent," Chop stated calmly, "and I'm a human being. So how could we possibly be related?"

By the time Sam had returned, security had already arrived. "All of you leave immediately!"

Chop laughed. "You hear that, Shania? It's time for you to take Phelix the rat back home to his cage."

"Let's go, baby," Shania urged as she clutched his arm. "Come on."

Phelix turned and stormed out the door.

The Fink

Chapter 3

"You bitch-made-ass nigga!" Phelix remembered Stacy shouting at him.

Those words kept echoing inside his head.

"Why I do that?" he asked himself. Phelix sat on the sofa inside of Shania's house, smoking a square. His first day out of the joint had been a disaster.

He glanced around the room. Everything inside her home was nearly new. Something about it, though, had the feeling of a man's presence. It was either the X-Box hooked up to the TV or the vicious water sharks that were in the huge fish tank, torturing the goldfish. That wasn't Shania's style at all.

There were about seven pictures on the wall. One was of him and Stacy dressed in Armani suits at a fashion show. Then there was a huge portrait of him and Shania back when they were in love.

Phelix could imagine just about how many different niggas had run up in her since then.

Shania came jogging down the stairs, singing, "I'll be lounging wit' Phe-lix." She wore a short, red sheer robe and slippers. His knees shook just thinking about touching her.

She was the prettiest piece of shit that he had ever laid eyes on. The three years of tension that had built up inside him was ready to release, with or without her aid. Sometimes bodily functions were uncontrol-

Quentin Carter

lable.

Phelix pointed at the fish tank. "I used to know somebody that had some of those. I can't remember who it—"

"We were so in love back then," Shania said, cutting him off. She was looking up at their picture. She made a mental note inside her head that she did not look like the twenty-five-year-old in the picture anymore. At twenty-eight, she was already beginning to feel thirty. The streets and club life had taken a toll on her body.

"I was in love," Phelix replied. "I don't know about you."

She frowned as she folded her arms across her chest.

"I needed to be held, Phe. I needed something ... someone ... to make me smile. I wanted a life outside of seeing you in that visiting room."

Anger was boiling inside Phelix. "Bitch, I told you from jump, if you're gonna benefit from me hustling, at least you can do the time with me. Otherwise, what did I need a fuckin' woman for?" He pulled on his cigarette. "I snitched on my best friend trying to hurry back home to yo' sorry ass."

Her chin fell to her chest. "I know," she said in a low voice. "And I am so ... so sorry. I fell weak and was only thinking of myself." She lifted her head again, shaking her bangs out of her face. "Now I'm begging for forgiveness."

"Because I'm out?"

"Because ... I love you. I had to bump my head a few times to realize that no one will love me like you will."

The Fink

Phelix stood and gestured for her to come to him. She did. While staring down at her face, he couldn't help but think, *damn, she look pathetic.* He untied her robe. She was completely nude underneath. Her nipples became erect. His eyes probed her body, down her swan neck, to her flat belly where he would plant his seed. His mouth watered when his eyes rested on her bald pubic mound.

She peered up at him, watching him admire her body. "See something you like? Huh? Touch something." She allowed her robe to fall to the floor. "What? I gotta make the first move? Okay."

Shania unbuttoned his pants. She stuck her small hand inside, massaging his cum stick. Phelix nearly lost control of himself.

"Want me to suck it?" She smiled. "Huh? Tell me what you want me to do with it, baby."

It was hard, but he remained in control of himself. While she stroked his Johnson, he just stood there looking stone-faced. Suddenly she caught the hint and stopped. Letting her hands fall to her sides, she stomped one foot, pouting.

"Baby, what's wrong?" Her tone was a whine. "I don't turn you on no more?" No response came from Phelix. "Phe, speak to me. I already said I was sorry. What else I gotta do?" She sighed. "I'll be in the bedroom if you should decide that you want some." She turned all the way around to bend over and pick up her robe. Her butt cheeks spread wide, exposing her pink vulva.

That had done it.

She knew after one good look at her from the back, it would be a done deal. She felt his strong hands grip

Quentin Carter

her waist. When she looked back between her legs, she saw his pants down and around his ankles. Shania smiled as she anxiously awaited penetration.

It felt like it was his first time all over again. Seven inches deep, he traveled inside her womb. His eyes were squeezed shut. For a second he just sat there and let it marinate and got reacquainted with an old friend.

Shania placed her hands flat on the floor, bracing herself for the pleasurable punishment that she was about to receive. No, Phelix wasn't the best when it came to making love, but he could fuck the hell out of a bitch.

"C'mon, baby," she begged. "Take it out on this pussy."

He pulled his shirt back behind his neck and proceeded to do what he had dreamed of doing for three years.

"Ooh, shit, Phe," Shania shouted when he sped up. "Ahh! Ach!"

Savagely, he plunged in and out of her while making angry faces and grunting noises only his own. He was trying his best to inflict pain upon her, but it only seemed to give her more pleasure.

"That's ... it ... ba-by," she coached. "Get guerilla wit' it. Fuck me, you animal."

After a couple of minutes of hard pounding, he shot a thick load of hot cum somewhere in her belly. Shania felt him go limp, but she was too far gone to call it quits.

She turned around on her knees, used her robe to wipe off his dick, and then proceeded to work his love muscle back hard by tickling it with her tonsils.

"Get guerilla wit' it," Phelix urged, as he peered

down at the top of her bobbing head.

Shania worked her lips and tongue like they had been in a dick sucking training camp for three years. When she looked up at him through seductive eyes, and a mouth full of his swipe, he looked into her eyes and saw her past.

He could see visions of her performing oral sex on somebody else's nut sack. He also saw a man hitting her from the back like he had done seconds earlier. Then he imagined that he was the other man, and the phone was ringing, and it was him calling from prison.

"Forget about the phone, baby," he imagined her saying. "It's only Phe. Ain't nothing he can do for me locked up. He's weak anyway. You know he snitched on Stacy."

His throbbing manhood brought him back to reality. Shania had successfully sucked another load out of him. A strange sound escaped his mouth when he shot his juices onto her neck.

Shania pulled him down on top of her and inserted the head of his penis into her pussy for a second helping. She worked her hips while he got his rhythm going. Soon they were moving in sync, meeting each other thrust for thrust, both enjoying the intense feeling the other gave.

Any grudges that were between them had temporarily been set aside for the night.

~ ~ ~ ~

The next morning, while taking a shit and smoking a cigarette, Phelix thought of Shania. She had sexed him up all through the night. Not all of her performance was what he was used to. She had definitely learned some new tricks.

Quentin Carter

He saw a card slide across the floor. After dropping the cigarette between his legs, he picked it up. It read,

> *Dear Phe,*
> *Sometimes life's responsibilities keep us from showing someone how much we love them.*

Shania was standing on the other side of the door. "People make mistakes, Phe. But mistakes can be repaired." She heard him fart. Even though it stunk clear through the door, she enjoyed it anyway, because it was his scent.

She was standing in front of the kitchen stove cooking sausage when Phelix embraced her from behind.

"How do you feel this morning?" she asked.

"Relieved."

Shania dropped the spatula. "Not how you *feel* feel. I meant about us. You said you would know in the morning."

"Oh, that feel." Backing away from her, he said, "I still don't know. I had a lot of bad thoughts about you last night."

After a long sigh, she pushed her hair back out of her face, spun around and walked over to the sink where he was standing. She leaned her back up against the counter.

"Look Phe, I'ma be honest with you." She paused to gather her thoughts. "Real life isn't one of those gangsta novels that you read in prison, where the hustler has some super-bad, down-ass, ride-or-die chick. Sorry. While you were away, yes, I had sex with more than a couple dudes. Some I liked, some I didn't. I didn't dog you. I just wanted to move on with my life, and I

The Fink

couldn't do that and continue to lie to you. So I broke it off. And just because I had sex doesn't make me a bad person, or a whore. It makes me human. I'm just a woman, Phe. Not bionic. Not super. Just lil ole Shania Freeman. Now you wanna dog me. Just remember this … I took a case for you. Wiped your funky ass when you were paralyzed for that year … and you forced me to abort my baby. Only this particular procedure wasn't carried out by a doctor. It was performed by you putting your big-ass size 11 in my stomach. Through all your fuck ups, I'm still willing to forgive you. Now I'm asking you to do the same."

Phelix pulled her to him and held her.

"I'm the only friend you got right now," she mumbled into his chest.

He picked her up. When she wrapped his waist with her legs, he carried her back to the bedroom.

The smoke detector would soon go off.

Chapter 4

[1995]

Phelix was sitting in his '83 Chevy Caprice listening to 8Ball & MJG's *"Coming Out Hard."* Stacy came out of the house, stormed out to the car and slammed the door closed.

"What happened?"

"He said if I'ma deal with you, then he don't wanna deal with me," Stacy replied.

"Why?"

"He didn't say," Stacy lied. What he really said was that Phelix was weak and would fold under pressure.

"So what happened?"

"I said, 'fuck it.' Ain't no dealing with me without you."

"What? Man, you better forget about me and get yo' money."

Stacy waved his hand. "Fuck some money if my nigga can't share it with me. You gotta understand what real friends is, Phe. If we come up, we come up together. If we gon' struggle, then it's gon' be together. See what I'm sayin'. If the shit hits the fan, I don't know them niggas. You're the only one I can trust ... I can trust ..."

~ ~ ~ ~

The Fink

Phelix opened his eyes. The Metro bus that he was riding on approached his stop. He exited the bus and headed up 41st toward Brooklyn Boulevard. On his way to his mom's crib, he saw a black BMW coming his way. It pulled over beside him.

When Phelix saw the face behind the wheel, he instantly remembered who it was who used to have the water sharks at home in his fish tank.

"What's up, Mike?"

Mike smiled deviously, displaying a small gap between his two front teeth. "You ... sometimes me."

A long silence passed between them. Mike had been the third man in Stacy's drug ring. He was an unindicted co-conspirator. Phelix could have taken him down, also, but he chose not to since Stacy was who they were most concerned about.

Phelix broke the silence. "I see you're still doing ya thing."

Mike shrugged. "So you say. Eh, get in real quick."

"Nah, I'm cool." Phelix did not shield the fact that he no longer trusted him.

"Ah, man, ain't nobody gon' hurt you, nigga." Mike leaned to his right and opened the passenger door.

"A'ight." Phelix got in. "Where we going?"

"Just ride, nigga." Mike made a left onto Prospect Boulevard. "How long you do, Phelix?"

"Three years."

"Three years," Mike repeated. "How much were you supposed to get?"

"What you mean?"

Mike shot him a knowing look.

"Twenty-five."

Mike whistled. "Goddamn!" He made a right onto

Quentin Carter

39th. "So that's what it took to break you down like a bitch, like your partna Sam. I know about him, too. Y'all like two singing-ass canaries. Birds of a feather ... flock tofuckin'gether." He chuckled as he made another right at Indiana.

Suddenly, Phelix became nervous. He reached over and touched Mike's shoulder. "Turn off, man."

"Why? I'm just turning a few corners."

"Turn off!" Phelix barked.

While Mike was making a right turn on 40th, he glanced up Indiana. "Eh? Didn't you use to have a bitch who lived up that street?" Phelix didn't respond. "Didn't she come up missing?"

Phelix still said nothing.

Mike peered at Phelix suspiciously, then snapped his finger and pointed it at him. "That's right. The little chick's boyfriend said that you came over there and ran him off, and started fighting with the broad. They investigated you for that."

"They didn't have nothing on me."

"That's a guilty man's response, Phe," Mike said. "You know what? I bet you know what happened to her. And you know what else I think?" Phelix shot him a questioning look. "I think Stacy knows, too. If he does, and with all that time he got, it won't be long before yo' lil secret comes out."

"It won't," Phelix slipped and said.

"I know. Not because I don't think you did it, but because I know Stacy ain't no filthy rat. There's a difference. A rat is something that gets scared when the man puts too much pressure on him and makes him fess-up. A filthy rat is the one who planned on snitching from the word go. He'll snitch on his mother, father,

The Fink

brother, friends ... because he ain't got no morals. That kinda rat deserves to die a thousand deaths.

"In order to kill him, you gotta trap him," Mike went on. "You have to use something sweet and sticky, like a pussy. Even a filthy rodent loves pussy. The pussy will lure him right into it. When he gets it, he'll get stuck and won't wanna pull out. By the time he realizes that he's been set up ... death will already be upon him."

The car stopped and Phelix realized that he was in front of his mother's house.

"Watch ya back, and these hoes, Phelix," Mike warned him. "Because there's such thing as a killa pussy."

As Phelix was walking up on the porch, he thought about the water sharks in the tank. He then remembered what Mike had said about using a pussy to catch a rat.

That's when Shania's name came to mind.

[Greenville F.C.I.]

"Eight ... nine ... ten," Stacy growled as he placed the heavy barbell back on the rack.

Standing up from the weight bench, he checked his body out in the mirror. Three years of crunches, incline presses, barbells, dumbbells and a lot of push-ups had his upper body more defined than a word inside a Merriam-Webster dictionary.

When he felt highly stressed or frustrated, he would come into the weight room and take it out on the weight pile. After his workout expired, like it had now, the harsh reality would come back and hit him in the face:

Quentin Carter

he had three decades to do there.

Sometimes he would sit alone at his bunk and wonder what was going through Phelix's head. Stacy walked back to his unit, where he stripped, then jumped in the shower.

Unlike most guys his age who entered the system with more than a dime to do, Stacy did not switch faiths by studying Islam. He still believed that Jesus Christ was his Lord and Savior.

As always, when he needed strength, Stacy closed his eyes and bowed his head in prayer.

"Dear Heavenly Father. Thank you for waking me this morning. Forgive me for all my sins. I pray that you will bless me by releasing me from prison one day soon. Keep me strong and healthy, Father. And don't let me fall weak and belittle myself like my brother who put me in here. Before that happens I pray that I catch amnesia and forget all the useful information that's stored in my brain. In Jesus' name I pray ... amen."

Yes, Stacy had avenues that, if taken, could lead to a lesser sentence, and would also put Phelix back behind bars. But doing so would make him just as much of a coward as Phelix. Back in '96, they'd both taken an oath that no matter what the circumstances, one would never tell on the other.

Stacy meant it.

[1996]

"Where we goin', man?" Stacy asked.

Phelix said nothing as he sped up Indiana Avenue.

"You know it's raining, don't you?" Stacy reminded

The Fink

him.

Without uttering a word, Phelix cut on the wipers. It was dark out. Stacy and Phelix were about to go chill with a group of women, until Phelix called his girl's home and did not receive an answer. Right away he made a sharp U-turn and headed back south.

Stacy hit his blunt. "You want some of this?"

Phelix ignored him. Rage was all in his face. When they neared 43rd and Indiana, Stacy knew where they were headed.

"Man, I know we ain't going to Kitana's house." Stacy shook his head. "That's fucked up. We gotta house full of freaks waiting on us in north Kansas City to get fucked up and fucked. But nah, you wanna …"

"I knew it," Phelix finally said. "Bitch gon' make me kill her muhfuckin' ass."

There was a white K5 Blazer parked backward in Kitana's driveway. All the lights were off inside the house. Phelix's car came to a halt in front of the house, blocking the driveway.

Phelix hit the blunt one good time, and then downed a gulp of cognac. He removed his .380 from under his seat and tucked it under his shirt.

"You need me?" Stacy asked.

"Nah, I can handle it." Phelix slammed the door shut. He began to hear slow music coming from inside the house as he approached the front porch. He knocked on the door until he heard footsteps.

Thinking that it was her friend Janice returning from the liquor store, Kitana made the mistake of opening the door without first asking who it was.

Her smile froze and her eyes flushed with fear when she saw Phelix step inside the living room.

Quentin Carter

Minutes later, Stacy was sitting in the car looking up at the house when some dude bolted out the front door. Phelix came out shortly after with his gun drawn, firing shots at the fleeing man.

The rain had covered the windows to where he couldn't see clearly. He was about to open his door when he heard the back door of the car open up.

"I'm sick of you threatening me, Phe!" Kitana yelled outside the door. "It's over between us. I mean it."

"Bitch, you'd better get yo' ass in that fuckin'," he pushed her onto the backseat, "car."

Kitana kicked and screamed. "That's kidnapping, Phelix! I'm calling the police!"

Phelix struggled to get her legs restrained, then climbed into the backseat with her. "Drive off, Stacy."

Stacy sighed, then slid over into the driver's seat. "Where?"

"Just drive, nigga!"

"Don't do it, Stacy. He's crazy. They gon' take you down for kidnapping, too."

Phelix drew his arm back and said, "Shut up!" as he struck her in the face. When she screamed out from the pain, he struck her two more times.

"You can't hurt me!" she yelled as she continued to claw at his face. "I hate you! I hate you!"

Stacy drove away while the two people behind him continued to fight.

"I loved you, girl," Phelix growled. "You hear me?"

"I ... don't ... love ... you."

Four blocks later, Stacy heard Phelix holler, "You think I won't do it? You think I won't do it?" Then he heard two blasts that echoed so loud inside the car that he temporarily lost his hearing. The only sound he could make out was his heart thumping against his chest.

Stacy turned onto a side street before he pulled over. He stuck his index fingers into his ears, jiggling them around until he heard the popping sound that restored his hearing. Not a moving car was in sight. Luckily, it was raining, which would make it hard for any passersby to see inside the car.

Phelix's deep, heavy breaths filled the car. Stacy turned around to see what had happened. Kitana was lying up against the back door with her eyes closed and mouth agape. Blood soaked her shirt and the seat beneath her. Phelix was sitting up over her with the gun clutched tight in his hand, staring down at her. Though Kitana only appeared to be sleeping, it was quite obvious that she was dead.

"Fuck did you do, Phe?" Stacy asked.

Phelix's head slowly turned toward Stacy. He had fear in his eyes. "It … it was an accident. I … I swear it was, Stacy, man. She tried to grab the gun. It was her own fault."

But Stacy had heard two shots instead of one, and he knew that it could not have been accidental. Phelix had just shot and killed that young eighteen-year-old girl in cold blood.

Stacy couldn't believe it. "Goddamn, Phelix! How could you kill that little girl, man?"

Phelix looked at him with disappointment in his face. "You don't believe me?"

"Fuck nah!" Stacy turned back around and rubbed his face with his hands. "I … do not … need this shit."

"What we gon' do, Stacy?"

Shaking his head, he answered, "All we can do is

Quentin Carter

find a nice spot to bury her at. But you diggin' the fuckin' hole."

"I ain't diggin' no hole by myself with all that goddamn rain comin' down."

"Okay." Stacy put the car in drive. "We'll just go to the police so you can explain to them how yo' gun accidentally went off two times and killed an eighteen-year-old girl in your backseat."

Phelix placed a hand on Stacy's shoulder. "You right. I'ma dig the hole by myself." As Stacy was pulling away, Phelix peered down at Kitana's body and thought, *How you gon' have that lil nigga's baby? Dead bitch.*

It was almost sunrise by the time they finished getting Kitana's body completely buried. Phelix patted the dirt down with the shovel, then followed Stacy back to the car.

Inside the car, Stacy said, "Let's make a pact. No matter which one of us does what … if the other gets caught up for it … we take the weight and do the time, like a man, without mentioning the other. Whoever's on the outside takes care of the man on the inside. Deal?"

"Hell yeah," Phelix agreed. "That should go without saying." Without a warning, Stacy swung his fist, striking Phelix in the chin. "Damn, nigga, what you hit me for?"

"I was aiming for your damn mouth."

"For what?"

"That's how we're gonna seal the pact. Now hold still."

Phelix flinched when Stacy raised his hand. "Fuck that shit," he protested. "I get the message. It's my turn to hit you in yo' shit, nigga."

The Fink

"A'ight." Stacy braced himself. "Go."

Phelix hit him in the mouth hard enough to swell his lips. Stacy wiped the blood away with his hand. "Now the deal is sealed."

~ ~ ~ ~

Stacy opened his eyes. "I didn't seal his lips," he said. "I missed. But he sealed mine."

At that very moment, Phelix lay in bed, at home, thinking of the exact same thing. Over the years, he had trained himself to forget about Kitana and that night. Now it was haunting him like every other memory that he had almost forgotten about.

He knew that even though he told on Stacy and put him away for twenty-eight years, the man would never tell on him about Kitana because, "I sealed his lips," Phelix said to himself. Minutes later he rolled over on his stomach and fell asleep. He didn't know that he was in for a long nap, filled with nothing but bad dreams.

Quentin Carter

Chapter 5

Monday Morning

"Several inner city crime fighting organizations and the Kansas City Police Department have teamed up with the FBI in hopes of coming up with a possible solution that will help solve some of the many unsolved murders in the city's metropolitan area," the Channel 9 anchorwoman reported.

"Our news correspondent, Joseph Ramsey, is here with us to tell us more."

Joseph Ramsey's face appeared on the screen. "Well, Debra, according to the city police captain, Bryan Pherson, only a mere 20 percent of the murders that have taken place this year have been solved. When asked what the problem was, he answered, 'Nobody's talking.' So in an attempt to help solve some of these crimes, they're offering immunity to anyone with a drug case who has information that will lead to an arrest for a homicide violation. Like I ..."

Chop shut off the TV. "That's fucked up. Now the feds are all on TV begging people to snitch. Fuck this world come to?"

He chewed on the last spoonful of cereal left in his bowl. Then he reached for the box. Empty. "Fuck!" he exclaimed as he threw the box onto the floor. He stood.

The Fink

"Ain't no more cereal, the world's fucked up and my brother's a bitch."

"Charles!" Their mother yelled from her room. "I'm not gon' tell you again. Shut the FUCK up!"

Chop mumbled under his breath while he bent over and reached for the box. As soon as he touched it, a mouse flew out of it, over his hand and scurried away.

"Ahh!" Chop screamed as he snatched his hand away. He saw the tail of the mouse when it dashed down the vent.

"Ain't that about a bitch? I done got scared by a goddamn rat."

"Fuck you call me, nigga?"

Chop spun around and saw Phelix standing there. He had just come out of the bathroom and walked in on Chop's two last words.

"Nigga, I didn't say shit about you!" Chop yelled as he walked toward him. "Matter of fact, fuck you, ole snitch-ass nigga." He grabbed his crotch as if it made him look tough.

That had done it for Phelix. "See if you can whoop this snitch then, bitch-ass nigga."

Chop frowned. "Bitch? Man, you got me fucked up. I ain't little no more. I ain't little no more."

"Why you hollering all loud, nigga?" Phelix said as he eased closer to him. "Why you ..." He threw a punch, striking Chop on the side of his jaw. Chop ducked his head and rushed him.

All the yelling and stomping had awakened their mother. When she walked into the room, she saw that Phelix had Chop in a headlock with one hand and was hitting him with the other.

"Oh my lord," she said as she rushed to Chop's aid.

Quentin Carter

She clutched Phelix's arm. "Get yo' hands off my baby, Phe, before you kill him."

Phelix was too far gone and would not release his grip. In his mama's eyes, he looked as if he was going to really kill him.

"Unt un. Unt un!" Mama released her grip and scooted back to her bedroom as fast as she could.

Her sudden departure brought Phelix back to his senses. Her just up and leaving like that could only mean one thing. She was going to get "Gangrene." Gangrene was an old, rusty .32 revolver that, when fired, spat fire three feet in each direction and released enough smoke to choke a nigga.

It was no secret whose side she was gonna take when she returned. So Phelix pushed Chop back toward the table and sprinted to the door. Shania was on the other side, just about to ring the doorbell when he came dashing out the house.

"Phe, wha ..."

"Let's go! Hurry up!" Phelix fumbled with the door handle until he finally figured out that it was locked. "Girl, hurry the fuck up! Shit!"

"Okay! Okay!" Shania said as she hurried down the steps, fumbling with her car keys. "What's going on?"

"Girl, hurry the fuck up! Shit!"

By the time Chop recovered and made it outdoors, Shania's Jeep was pulling away. "You dead, nigga!" he shouted. "You dead!"

Chop heard the front door open and saw Mama coming outside, still in her gown, and ole Gangrene down by her side.

He rushed over to her. "Mama, everything's cool. Go back in the house." He managed to turn her around.

The Fink

"Y'all not gon' be the death of me, Chop," she stated.

"I know Mama, I know."

~ ~ ~ ~

"Phe, what happened back there?" Shania inquired.

Phelix's legs were trembling. His eyes were as red as his T-shirt. "I'm already fuckin' tired of this shit," he growled, more to himself than to her.

She saw a small, bleeding scratch on the side of his neck. He was clenching his fists like he was ready for a fight.

"Phe, were y'all fighting in your mama's house?"

He didn't answer her. It was like she wasn't in the car with him. Shania's cell phone rang. She peered at the caller ID and saw Mike's number displayed. In a real slick way, she eased her thumb over the power button and turned the phone off.

"I should've just ... man," he said. His head was down between his legs, resting in his hands. "Muhfuckas out here think I'm some kinda bitch now. I ain't no bitch."

Shania gently placed her hand on his shoulder. "Baby, don't go feeling guilty and beating yourself up. If you're guilty of anything, it's because you loved me."

Phelix's head snapped in her direction. His nostrils flared and his eyes narrowed. "You the one to blame for this whole mess. You talked me into doing that bullshit. 'Your mom. Think about your Mom, Phe,'" he said, mocking her. "'And me. You need to be out here for us. I need you, Phelix Mitchell. He would do it to you. Hell, Stacy tried to fuck me, Phe.'"

"He did," she said through tight lips.

"Then what took you so fuckin' long to tell me? You

Quentin Carter

lying bitch."

Shania could not hold back her tears. "I never lied to you about that. He did! Stacy did try to fuck me."

Phelix smiled bleakly. "You never lied about that. What about the baby that you were supposed to be pregnant with?"

Shania looked at him with her mouth hung open. His look was so bleak that she quickly turned and faced the front window. Suddenly she pulled the car over, put it in park and began to sob.

"What happened to it!" he yelled unsympathetically.

Shania knew that if she lied to him, things would probably turn out bad. But if she told him the truth ... then she probably wouldn't leave her Jeep alive.

She lifted her head as she sniffled. "There ... there never was one," she lied.

The pussy will lure him right into it, Phelix remembered Mike saying to him. "I must be a filthy rat," he said to himself. "Phelix the rat. He goes cuckoo for the pussy every time."

Phelix opened the door. Shania stared at his back through teary eyes, seeing him pause halfway out. She wanted to say something but she knew at the moment, it would do more harm than good. So she remained quiet.

"Are you and Mike in any way in cahoots?" Phelix asked in an ever-so-calm voice.

Shania's lips quivered as she said the word, "No." And of course, it was a lie, too.

Phelix exited the car, closed the door behind him and walked away.

When he disappeared from her view, Shania turned

The Fink

her cell phone back on and called Mike.

He answered on the second ring. "Hell-OO," he sang.

"I need to see you, now!"

They met up at Blue Valley Liquors on 43rd and Cleveland. Shania parked her Jeep and stepped into Mike's car, slamming the door shut.

"Whoa! Whoa!" Mike exclaimed. "Damn, baby, watch the wood grain."

She pointed her finger at his face. "You told Phelix about us, you bastard!"

Mike put his hands up in mock surrender. "Baby, I done no such thing."

"Then why did he ask me if there was anything between us?"

Smiling, he said, "I may have said a lil something that would've made a paranoid nigga like him think that, but I never said anything about you and me."

Shania calmed down. "Why did you call me?"

"Because I heard that y'all were fucking around again, and I wanted to confirm it." She said nothing. "Is it true?"

There was so much guilt in her face when she looked at him, that she didn't have to say anything. He already knew the answer.

Mike turned toward his window. "I thought you said that it was over between you two."

"It was. I mean, I thought that after the way I treated him when he was on lock down that he would never even speak to me again."

Mike snarled, "Speak to you again? Shania, when have you ever known Phelix to turn down a shot of cat?"

She peered at him. "Mike, why are you tripping, for Christ's sake? Remember those two little boys of yours? Let's not even talk about that stuck up black bitch that you call a wife you got living out in Lee's Summit in that big-ass house of yours. You ain't never had nothing like that planned for me. All I was to you was a good fuck and some great head, so save the bullshit for somebody who don't know no better."

"Why did you even fuck with me then?"

"Because I thought that eventually it would lead somewhere. That, plus you got me so drunk and dirty macked Phelix so hard, I couldn't help but drop my drawers."

"Oh, so that's why you let me talk you into aborting his baby? 'Cause you thought that we would eventually lead somewhere?"

Shania looked out her window as a tear started a stream down her face.

"What do you think he would do if he ever found out about that?"

Shania shook her hair out of her face as she looked over at him. "Why don't you tell me, since you know so much, Michael."

"Sit tight. I wanna show you something." He drove three blocks around the corner to 43rd and Indiana. There was a little brick house in the middle of the block that had boards nailed over the windows.

Mike pulled into the driveway and parked.

"What's this?" Shania asked.

"It's a house."

"I can see that. Look Mike, stop playin ga—"

"About ten years ago, a family used to stay here. They had a little girl who was about eighteen. Phelix

The Fink

was going with her at the time." That really got Shania's attention. "One night she just up and came up missing. The little dude who saw her last said that Phelix had showed up while he was over there. Said that Phelix shot at him and fought with her. No one ever reported seeing her again."

"Did they investigate Phelix?"

Mike nodded his head. "Yep, but they never found a body, so they had no case. Now that I think about it, they never found the blue Chevy that the little dude said Phelix was driving that night."

"Why are you telling me all of this, Mike?"

He turned toward her. "Because I want you to know who you're getting yourself involved with. If he finds out I made you abort that baby ... "

"You didn't make me do a damned thing."

"Whatever. There ain't no telling what he might do to you. I can protect you."

"Look, I don't need your protection. Just take me back to my car."

"A'ight."

Mike faked like he was reaching for the gearshift, then quickly clutched her jaws and pulled her toward him.

"Mmm!" she tried to scream. "Wa ... ahhh!" She felt him bite into her neck and start sucking as hard as he could. "Ah! Ahhh! Ah!" Her body had tensed so much that she couldn't move.

Mike removed his lips and sat back in his seat, taking deep, slow breaths. Shania hurriedly wiped his saliva from her neck where he had left a big red hickey.

"Show that to yo' man," he said in between breaths.

Shania peered at her neck through the mirror. When

Quentin Carter

she saw the big round mark on the side of her neck, she almost panicked.

"You hating-ass bastard!" She turned and started swinging at him. The first two hits caught Mike off-guard, striking him in both eyes. "I hate you! I hate … you!"

Mike used his powerful right arm to lock both of her arms up, then used his free hand to bitch slap her across her face. She hollered, but to him it wasn't effective enough. So he hit her a second and third time.

"Don't you ever put yo' hands on me, bitch!" he shouted at her.

While she sat there crying, holding her face and trying to recover, he checked his face in the mirror. His left eye had a bruise starting to form under it.

"Goddamn bitch."

Shania finally shook off the shock of the blows. She quickly exited his car and started running down the street.

"Eh, Shania!" she heard him call out.

She wanted to turn around and scream, "Fuck OFF!" but her face hurt too badly. So instead, she took out her cell phone and dialed three numbers.

"9-1-1 emergency," the operator prompted.

"I'd like to report a case of domestic violence."

The Fink

Chapter 6

[1999]

Phelix shook his hand, then threw the dice. It seemed like they rolled for minutes before they finally landed on lucky number seven for the seventh time in a row.

"Yes!" Phelix could not believe his luck. "Give me my goddamn money."

One-eyed Rico peered at his brother, Porky, who nodded his head.

"I ain't givin' you nathin'," Rico said.

"Me either, dog," Pork added.

The rest of the small group of people backed up, because they knew there was about to be some trouble.

Phelix stood up. "Wha? Man, you niggas better pay me my goddamn money. I shot and you two suckas lost, fair and square."

Rico spoke. "Nigga, ain't no way in hell you gon' sit there and roll seven no seven fuckin' times in a row without cheating."

"You ain't lying," Porky replied. "Matter of fact, just give me all my money back right now, bitch-ass nigga."

"Maaan, you niggas got me fucked up—" Phelix hadn't finished his sentence when he swung and

Quentin Carter

cracked Rico in his good eye. Then a shot to his chin made him stumble backward.

Phelix seemed to have forgotten about Porky until he saw the gun he produced. Phelix gasped just before he saw the flashing light as the first bullet entered his body. He was already numb when the next two shots followed.

Phelix woke up in the hospital room. He peered at his arm and saw needles and all types of tubes coming from him. The slow beeping sound the heart monitor made was giving him a headache.

"You back?"

Phelix recognized the voice, but had not yet seen the face. Suddenly Stacy appeared, standing at the foot of his bed. He looked anxious.

"Yo' mama and Chop outside. I was hoping you woke up while they were gone. I need to know—"

"Where's Shania?"

Stacy frowned. "Nigga, I ..." he stopped to take a breath. "You almost died and all you can think about is that bitch?"

Phelix closed his eyes.

"A'ight then. Now tell me who did this shit to you, dog, 'cause I'm at they ass tonight."

Shaking his head, Phelix licked his lips. "W ... wait for me." Stacy put his head down. "What? What's wrong man?"

"I'ma let ya mama explain it to you," he said regretfully. "But it's worse than you think."

Phelix looked down at his legs and was scared to attempt to wiggle his toes. Chop busted into the room, followed by their mother.

"He woke, Mama!" Chop said gleefully. He tripped

The Fink

and fell toward the bed onto Phelix's legs.

Phelix didn't feel a thing.

~ ~ ~ ~

Phelix stood in front of Stacy's mother's house, looking up at the front door. He had promised himself that when he got out he was gonna go by Regina's house and give her some sort of explanation, if there was one.

Regina opened up the front door, looking much older than she had three years ago. It seemed like ten years had passed. Upon sight, she regarded Phelix with a curious frown on her sagging face.

"Phelix?"

"Hi, Mrs. Landis," he said timidly.

Regina closed the door and stepped out onto the porch.

"Why you here, son?"

"Because I know how angry and confused y'all must be, wondering why I did what I did. I know it don't make it right, but I thought that I could at least … I really don't know what I thought, Mrs. Landis."

Without showing any sympathy for him, she stepped to the edge of the porch and looked out into the street.

"I can remember when y'all used to play touch football out in the street." She giggled. "Y'all two used to go at it, you hear me? And Stacy was an ugly child, I'll tell you. I'd catch him out there beating up on you, and I'd tell him, 'Stacy, God don't like ugly.' And he'd say 'Well, God must hate me then.'" She laughed hard.

Regina's laughing stopped. She cocked her head in Phelix's direction. "As bright and athletic as you two kids were, I don't understand why y'all got into the

Quentin Carter

drug business. You two could have been so much more. I was always told that God had a plan for your life, no matter which road you took. But you die the same way no matter what."

"You always did have some deep religious quotes to discipline us with," Phelix reminded her.

Regina smiled. "Yes, I did. I remember the time you got caught stealing at the mall. You were so mad you got caught that you told me Stacy had stolen something, too. A pair of ... no, it was a cap gun, think it was."

"Yep," Phelix said with a sad smile. "You told me, you said, 'Nobody likes a tattle ... tale.'"

Regina just stared at him.

~ ~ ~ ~

Mike pulled up to Chop's house. Chop got in the car with him. Mike was in the mirror checking out a scar on his face.

"Wha'sup, boa?" Mike said without looking at him.

"Shit."

Mike sat back and peered over at Chop. He had a few fresh bruises on his face.

"What happened to your face, lil homie?"

Chop shook his head. "Nothing happened that I can't handle."

"See, that's why I fucks with you, Chop Sticks. You're a real stand-up nigga and I know that you'll hold your own in a dangerous situation." He clutched the gearshift.

"Where we goin?"

"I can't cook the shit up here, can I?"

"Hell naw."

"A'ight then. I got a spot out south where I do all

The Fink

my chefing at. We can do it there."

"That's cool."

~ ~ ~ ~

Phelix slowly looked up until he was facing Mrs. Landis. She had a tear in her eye. "I've asked myself why a thousand times. All I can say is that ... the truth is I was trying to get home to my woman."

"A woman," Regina said as she looked away. "Where is this woman now?"

Phelix looked down.

"I'm disappointed in you, Phelix. But I forgive you. God forgives you. The thing is ... will you ever be able to forgive yourself? If not, the guilt will consume you. It'll tear you apart hour by hour and day by day until it drives you crazy."

The phone started ringing from somewhere inside the house. "Let me get this phone 'fore it wakes my husband." She hurried into the house.

A little while later, she returned with the cordless phone up to her ear, speaking into it.

"Yes, everybody's doing okay out here." She listened. "Un huh, forget about us. How are you holding up in there, Stacy?"

Phelix's stomach stirred after he heard Stacy's name. It was almost like a feeling of excitement. He didn't understand it. He wondered had he subconsciously hoped that Stacy would call while he was over there? Or did he feel that rush because Stacy was once his best friend ... and he missed him?

Mrs. Landis looked over at Phelix while she listened on. "Guess who's here? No. Phelix Mitchell. Okay, hold on." She held the phone out to him. "It's for you."

Quentin Carter

~ ~ ~ ~

Mike whipped into the driveway of one of his cribs. Chop exited the car, peering at his surroundings.

"I left the money at the house," Chop informed him.

"That's cool. After we're finished here, I can pick it up when I drop you back off."

"Good lookin' out man."

"Ain't no use in riding around with the money and the drugs anyway." Mike opened the door, and Chop followed him inside.

~ ~ ~ ~

Phelix took the phone and placed it up against his ear but did not speak.

"I hear you breathing, nigga," Stacy said. "You ain't got nothing to say to ya boy?"

"Wha'sup?" Phelix said in a low voice.

"Shit. Trying to give back those three decades that I got. Shit's becoming stressful, ya know?"

Phelix was quiet.

"Look, dog, I know you fucked up about what you did to me and you should be. I don't have to sit on this phone and explain to you how close we was. I know your deepest secrets, but because we took an oath, and because I'm the man I am, I stood strong on my end. I loved you, man. Obviously, the feeling wasn't mutual. I did all I could out there trying to duck the feds and I had a Fink up under me the whole time." He snorted. "I guess I was only fooling my damned self."

"I'm sorry," Phelix said, too low to be heard. "I'm sorry, Stacy, man. I don't know ..."

"Save it, man." There was a long pause. "Damn,

The Fink

Phe, man. I told you not to mess with that dude, too, man. Remember?"

Phelix quietly nodded his head.

[2003]

"Them niggas is too thirsty, Phe," Stacy told him. "Niggas that thirsty always got some shit wit' 'em."

"Ain't no question," J-Ron said in agreement with Stacy. "You got enough money to let some money go by, Phe. All money ain't good money."

"I'on't know, man," Phelix said as he rose from the couch. "Them niggas is willing to pay top dollar for them thangs. Sheeit, and I need to get rid of a few of 'em."

Stacy grabbed his jacket from off the couch. "If you need some cash, I got you. Just for me," he held his hand up to his chest, "don't fuck with lil Baby or none of them niggas that he rolls with."

Phelix thought about it for a moment. "A'ight man, you probably right. I don't need that money. Good lookin' out."

Stacy shook his hand. "Good. A'ight, dog, I gotta get outta here. Me and wifey gotta go to the travel agency and book this trip for her birthday next week."

"A'ight. I'll be here," Phelix stated. He patted J-Ron on the back on their way out.

"Yo, stay up, cuz," J-Ron shot back.

"You, too."

Stacy and J-Ron hadn't been gone five minutes before Phelix called lil Baby and said, "Yo, come through. I got them thangs over here at my crib. Bring

Quentin Carter

ya money. A'ight."

Thirty minutes later, Phelix was lounging on the couch, talking to Shania on the phone when he heard his front door come crashing in. At first he thought it was a robbery until he heard a man shout, "FBI Search Warrant! Don't fuckin' move!"

That's when he thought about the sixteen bricks of dope that he had in his bedroom closet.

~ ~ ~ ~

"You fucked with him anyway, Phe. As a result, I'm sitting in prison for three decades because of yo' hard head. You didn't have a wife, kids ..."

"Believe me when I say I'm sorry, man. I'm fucked up out here. I can't even fuckin' think straight. Ain't no me without you. Remember?" Phelix sounded sincere.

Stacy remained silent for a moment, then continued. "You can't cut my throat, then apologize for doing it, Phe. It's too late. I'm already dead. Dead to the world ... to my wife ... and my kids. So let's keep it how it's been ... and make like I'm dead to you, too."

The line went dead in Phelix's ear.

Phelix clutched the phone tight and squeezed his eyes closed. Then the tears started to fall.

"Stacy's dad is dying, Phelix," Regina said in a low voice. "He has terminal cancer. The doctors say he won't make it to see Christmas."

Phelix stared up at her through tear-filled eyes.

"Does Stacy know?"

Regina shook her head. "Haven't figured out a way to tell him yet. I ..." Her voice cracked. "I don't know what I'm gonna do without either of them in my life." She began to cry.

The Fink

Phelix went to her and tried to console her by attempting to embrace her.

"No," she said, pushing him away. "I said that I forgive you, but you're still at fault." She sniffled. "You need to leave now."

Instead of protesting her decision, which he knew would have been useless, he put down the phone ... and walked away.

Chapter 7

Mike and Chop came walking out of the house, talking and laughing. Mike threw the black bag of drugs onto the backseat before he got into the car.

He was about three blocks away from the house, traveling down Cleveland Avenue, when a police car jumped behind him.

"Be cool, Chop," Mike said when he spotted the car. "The elroys are behind us."

Chop tensed up. "What they doing?"

"Looks like he's running my plates. Don't worry, my shit is all the way legit."

"I'm cool." Chop tried to disguise the fear that he felt.

"Let me see something." Mike made a left at 68th then drove a few blocks and made a right on College Boulevard. The police car continued to trail him.

"What they doin' now?" Chop asked nervously.

"Just chill out." When Mike reached Meyer Boulevard, there was another cop car blocking the intersection, forcing him to bring his car to a halt. Before he could figure out his next move, the policeman from the car behind him was tapping on his window.

Mike let down the window. "What's going on?"

"You need to step out of the vehicle. Now. You have a warrant for assault and battery out for your arrest."

The Fink

"Assault and battery? Against who?"

"Some young woman. I don't know all the details."

There were about thirty-six ounces of crack inside the bag on the backseat. Being that they were two young black males in an expensive car, there was no way in hell the police weren't going to search it.

"Remember," Mike whispered to Chop, "that stuff was for you, so it's yours."

"What?" Chop said, but the policeman had snatched Mike out of the car before he had a chance to respond.

~ ~ ~ ~

"Damn!" Shania said to herself. She had just taken the ice pack off her neck and was looking at the now purple hickey inside the mirror. "That nigga's a hater, man. How in the hell am I gonna explain this?"

The bruises on her face would not be a problem to explain. She could just say that she got into a scuffle with some hoodrat bitches. The hater mark on her neck was a different story. She opened the medicine cabinet and took out her make-up kit. When she closed it back, she saw Phelix's reflection in the mirror.

"Ahh!" she screamed as the kit fell from her hands. "Phelix, how did you get in?"

"The door was unlocked." Although he was just looking at her, Shania naturally assumed that he was looking at the red marks on her neck and face.

She turned away. "I can explain."

"Ain't no need to." He stepped over to her, bent down and started kissing her lips.

"You're not mad at me?" she asked, shockingly.

"For what? You were probably just doing what Shania does." She tried to speak, but he covered her mouth. "No arguing. Right now I want you to make love

Quentin Carter

to me like it was our last time."

It hurt for her to smile, but she managed to produce one anyway. "I can do that." She jumped into his arms and began to caress his face with her lips.

~ ~ ~ ~

"I'm Special Agent Tim Gainer," the man said to Chop in a raspy voice. "Before I sit down and speak with you, Mr. Mitchell, I have to ask you, would you like to retain counsel first?"

Chop nervously said, "No."

"Good." The agent took a seat across from him. "Look, Mr. Mitchell. I'm not here to play games with you. I'll be frank. With the amount of crack that we found in Mr. Fluker's backseat, you could spend a minimum of twenty years in a federal prison."

"Twenty years?" Chop shouted.

"That's right. The bright side of this is that you're only twenty-one with no record and Mr. Fluker is twenty-eight with a record a mile long. Speaking frankly, the world would be a better place without him."

The agent took a minute to let Chop digest what he was saying. He could tell by the childish quiver in his voice that the kid was scared out of his mind.

"Like I was saying," he went on. "We wanted Mr. Fluker three years ago when your brother agreed to roll over on Stacy Landis. But ... our bosses were so happy to get Mr. Landis that they basically forgot about Fluker. Now that we got him, we want to get rid of him. We have a bag full of crack ... and hopefully a witness who's willing to testify."

"So, what you're asking is ..."

"What I'm asking is for you to be smart like your brother was, and save yourself. Everybody's doing it,

The Fink

Mr. Mitchell, and I know from experience that rats travel in packs. So don't try and play tough guy with me. You'll lose." He placed a piece of paper and pen in front of Chop, and then stood. "I'm confident that this statement will be signed by the time I return with my coffee." With that said, he turned and walked away.

Now Chop knew what it felt like to have twenty years worth of pressure on his back. But just like with every drug case, there was an emergency button he could press to help ease a lot of that pressure.

All Chop had to do was press it.

~ ~ ~ ~

"What's on your mind, baby?" Shania asked. They were lying in bed together. Her head rested safely up under his arm.

"Thinking."

"'Bout what?"

"I got something that I gotta do."

"I don't want you to go away again."

"I might not have a choice."

Shania sat up and shot him a questioning look. "Phelix? What are you talking about?"

He looked at her. "I'm a snitch, Shania. And there's nothing I can do to change that. I used to be somebody to a lot of people. Now I'm a rat to everybody." He shook his head. "I don't think I can live with that. I tried, but I can't."

"Phe ... what are you gonna do? Kill yourself?" Her breathing accelerated.

He snorted. "Nah. I'ma try to make it right." He removed the covers and stood. "I gotta call my Mama."

"Phelix!" She yelled at his back. "Please don't walk outta my life again. You don't know what I've been

Quentin Carter

through without you here." She buried her face in the sheets and began to sob.

The Fink

Chapter 8

[2003]

"Get a picture!" Stacy hollered over the loud voices singing "Happy Birthday" to his three-year-old daughter. "Get a picture."

Stacy and his wife both stood behind their daughter as she prepared to blow out the number three candle that rested on top of her cake. Everyone inside the room had smiles plastered on their faces.

"On the count of three," his wife said, with a big smile. "One ... two ... thrrrr ..."

The four huge Federal Agents that barged in on their fun turned everyone's smiles into immediate frowns. When Stacy saw that they were all staring at him, he knew immediately what they had come for.

When his daughter saw her daddy being handcuffed, she busted out into tears, locking into her memory her worst birthday ever.

[2006]

Inside the interrogation room, downtown, Phelix sat in the exact same chair that he had been sitting in when he agreed to help the feds take down Stacy. Only this

Quentin Carter

time he was there for a different reason.

To help take himself down.

Two men sat across from him. One was the federal court prosecutor and one was his attorney.

The prosecutor cut on the recorder. "Mr. Mitchell? For the record, why are you here?"

"Because I'm confessing to a crime that I committed about ten years ago."

"And were you promised anything in return?"

"Yes."

"Which was?"

"I made a deal with the government to give my friend, Stacy Landis, who is currently serving a twenty-eight year sentence for narcotics, a twenty-two year time reduction. In return, I will confess about my involvement in an unsolved homicide that I committed ten years ago."

"Okay, Mr. Mitchell. You do know that in order for us to proceed, we have to first verify your claim. Right now, we need to know where we can find the body. Then an autopsy has to be performed so we can determine the identity and cause of death."

"I buried her body ..." he paused and took a deep breath, "behind the school, located on 42nd and Indiana. She's resting on the east ..."

After the confession, they took Phelix upstairs and booked him. Then he was led to a holding cell where he would remain until the autopsy report came back.

There was already a man sitting inside the cell. He had his face resting inside his hands. The man looked up when Phelix entered.

"Chop?" Phelix said, surprised. He waited for the door to close behind him before he spoke again. "What you doing here, man?"

"I got caught up on some bullshit fuckin' with Mike," Chop explained. "They said I could be looking at twenty years."

Phelix peered at his face. "Did you?"

Chop scowled. "Did I what? Tell? Yeah, I told. I told 'em to suck my dick." He looked away. "Fuck it. They say I got twenty to do," his voice cracked, "then that's what I gotta do."

Phelix put his arm around him.

"Get off me, man," Chop demanded. "You still a rat to me, nigga. I'm holding mine." He looked at Phelix curiously. "What you doing here anyway?"

Phelix explained his situation and what he had done for Stacy.

"Damn, man," Chop said after he finished. "I would never have thought you killed that girl."

Phelix looked away.

"But that was some real shit that you did for Stacy," Chop told him. "I guess we gon' have to do all this time together … brother."

Phelix looked over at his little brother and smiled. Even though he probably was gonna get forever for his confession, it sure felt good to be respected again.

Chapter 9

[2002]

Shania was sitting at the bar inside of the club, working on her fifth glass of Vodka and cranberry juice. She wasn't tipsy. Baby girl was drunk, and she had to be in order for her to work up the courage to do what she was planning on doing.

"How do I look?" she asked her friend Mandi.

"You look great, but why are you doing this?" Mandi asked.

"I love Phelix. But right now, I'm lusting after Stacy. It's something about him that just seems … I don't know … powerful, and I wanna feel it all up in me." Shania finished off her drink. "Now hold down the fort. I'll be back."

Shania walked into the men's restroom, then closed and locked the door. Stacy was standing in front of the stall pissing. She smiled and wobbled over to him.

"Hi, Stacy," she said in a seductive tone.

Stacy looked over at her, then winced. "Girl, what yo' crazy ass doing in here?"

She looked down at his impressive-sized organ while he shook it off. As soon as he finished, she reached down and grabbed it.

"Ahh!" Stacy hollered as his body tensed up.

The Fink

"Shh! Don't scream," she whispered. "I have to entice you first, otherwise you might not accept what I'm offering." She had a tight grip on it. "Step back a few steps."

Slowly, Stacy took three steps backward. Shania held it tight while she kneeled down.

"It's only gonna hurt for a little bit, baby," Shania said. She cleaned any excess pee away with her thumb. Then she completely covered the head of it with her lips. When she mistakenly took his grunt for a moan, she released some of the pressure from her grip, and then took him in even further. That's when Stacy drew his arm back and smacked the shit out of her. She fell backward on her ass.

"You drunk, nasty-ass bitch!" Stacy hollered as he put his dick up and zipped his pants.

Shania got up, wiping her mouth with a devilish grin on her face. "Nasty-ass bitch, huh?" She shrugged. "Can't blame a woman for trying to get her fuck on."

Stacy looked at her in disgust. "And you say you love him."

"I do. And he loves me. So go 'head and tell on me, Stacy. I'll just flip the script, 'cause he loves his baby, Shania, more than he loves you." She caught her breath. "That's the power of the punanny."

Shaking his head, he said, "You's a trifling-ass bitch. Even if I don't tell on yo' punk ass, the truth'll come out, 'cause a ho can't keep a secret." He unlocked the door and walked out.

"Nigga, you won't tell because you really want this pussy!" Shania yelled at him. "You think he loves you? That nigga will turn his back on you for me. You watch."

Quentin Carter

~ ~ ~ ~

Shania remembered that night well. As she sat up in bed inside a hotel room, she thought about Phelix. How brave of him to sacrifice his own self in order to get Stacy out of prison. In all honesty, Stacy was worth it. She knew it.

He was always there for Phelix, and even after she lied to him about Stacy trying to fuck her, Stacy never mentioned what really went on inside the restroom that night. He kept it to himself because he knew that eventually time would tell it for him. Shania had to respect him for that.

"What're you doin'?" Sam asked as he sat up next to her in bed. "You thinking about Phe?"

"Yep. I can't believe he did such a dumb-ass thing like that. He finally chose somebody over me."

"That's why I told you to persuade him into telling on Stacy three years ago. 'Cause I knew he was gonna listen to you." Sam reached over and pinched her long, pink nipple.

"Ouch! Boy! You know us white people bruise easily."

He kissed her shoulder. "If I had known that white pussy was this good, I would've gotten some a long time ago."

Shania pushed him back down. "Not all white pussy." She straddled him. "This pussy." She inserted him inside her. "It'll make a black man do strange thangs."

There was a loud knock on the door.

"Get that, baby," Sam said.

Shania frowned, sighed and smacked him on the thigh. "Man, damn," she said as she got up. "I'ma put a

The Fink

sign on the door that says 'Don't disturb this groove. Hole drilling in progress.'" She giggled.

While she put on his shirt to cover herself with, Sam thought of Phelix. *That's one dumb fool,* he thought. Snitches didn't have to run and hide anymore. It was the cool thing to do now.

Shania had only twisted the knob when someone from the other side of the door pushed it in on her, forcing her to stumble backward.

Sam jumped up when he saw the two Mexicans enter the room. Both held shotguns in their hands.

"You told on my cousin, Hector, holmes," one of them said. "He had a family. Did you think you were gonna get away with that?"

Sam was terrified, and for the moment, he wished that he was in jail with Phelix, behind the safety of a locked prison cell.

"Hombres," Sam said in a nervous tone. "Listen, I ..."

Shania screamed as the two men started firing on Sam's body, mutilating it before her very eyes. Even after the shooting ended, she continued to scream and quiver because in her heart, she already knew—she would be next.

Quentin Carter

Cold as Ice

By T.Styles

Triple Crown Publications presents . . .

Cold As Ice

Just Anotha Day

The sweltering heat didn't stop the beat of the street in Southeast D.C. Dudes were washing their cars or moving product, while females were walking up and down the block in the hopes of being seen in their designer fits and purses. While the blood in the veins of 58th Avenue's worst project continued to move, seventeen-year-old Pepper Champagne Thomas was sitting on the steps of her house getting her hair braided, watching it all, and hating every bit of it.

Sweat ran down her back, causing the white tank top she was wearing to cling to her skin, and the black LRG sweatpants she was sporting didn't make her much cooler. Ants were circling a piece of melted candy her cousin threw on the ground next to them, and the ice in her cup had dissolved and rendered her Coke tasteless. It was hotter than a pair of opened legs.

Wiping sweat off of her face with her hand, Pepper noticed that her cousin had used an entire pack of red braiding hair in an hour, which was strange considering she was supposed to be doing micro-minis, not African twists.

"Nic … I think these are too fat," Pepper said under her breath, trying to avoid confrontation. She was rubbing her fingers over the extra large braids. She knew the moment Nic's big-mouth friend Treesy called, breaking her concentration, that she'd be too concerned with gossip to tend to her hair.

Nic hit her cousin's hand with the yellow rat tail comb and said, "Hold on Tree." With that, she placed the white cordless phone on her fleshy right shoulder and held it in place with her fat cheek. Afterwards, she gripped a fistful of her baby cousin's unbraided hair. "First off, these ain't too fat," she said, grabbing a few. "And I been braidin' hair for ten years, so if you don't like 'em, you can take yo' ass down to the African Hair Gallery and pay dem bitches five hundred dollars, instead of the measly forty yo' mother givin' me!" She pointed with the comb.

Without even giving Pepper a chance to respond, she resumed the conversation she was having with her ghetto-ass friend. Pepper's stomach turned a little when a summer breeze came through and forced the scent of Nic's corn-chip-smelling pussy in her face.

Pepper was angry about the bullshit job Nic was doing on her hair, but knew if she bucked she wouldn't get it done at all. Plus, she'd have to take out the thirty braids Nic had done so far. She wished she wasn't afraid to speak up. All her life she let people walk over her, and her cousin was no exception.

As Pepper listened to her cousin talk about everybody else except for her own fat ass, she looked around her block. She saw Khoury walking down the street with her best friend's dumb-ass brother, Jordan, and Izzy, his other friend, who was nothing but a punk.

"What up, Pepper?" Khoury waved.

Pepper placed her head down, pretending not to see or hear him. Zykia, her best friend, said she ignored him because she was feeling him. After all, he was easy on the eyes. Khoury was about 6'3" with neat dreads and light brown skin. He had them boy muscles on lock, too. Word on the street was that he wrote and sang R&B songs. He was new around the way, so Pepper didn't understand why he got up with the wrong crew so quickly.

Cold As Ice

"I told you she dumb as shit," Jordan yelled, throwing a rock her way. "Leave dat bitch alone."

"Don't get fucked up, JD!" Nic yelled, interrupting her call.

"Whateva!" he screamed, grabbing his dick.

"That lil boy is worthless!" she said to Treesy.

When they were gone, Pepper took a bite of her pickle in a bag. She glanced around and saw empty potato chip bags, beer bottles and drug paraphernalia all around her streets. Graffiti was all over the boarded up houses, yet kids played in and around them as if they were playgrounds. Even though she lived in the PJs, every other house had either a Cadillac or a souped-up hooptie on 22-inch rims sitting in front of it. Every day she walked out of her door, she dreamed of one thing ... getting away.

"Peppa, hand me another strand of hair!" Nic yelled, breaking her out of her thoughts. Pepper carefully parted a few strands of the red hair from the bundle, so that she could limit the thickness of her braids. Nic snatched it and said, "Give me some more!" Pepper parted a few more strands and handed it to her.

When she took another bite of the sour pickle, she saw her next door neighbor, and 58th Avenue's biggest drug dealer, walking to his car. Ice was dressed perfectly for the hot weather. Wearing a pair of blue Evisu jean shorts, a white wifebeater and his platinum and diamond chain and watch, it was no mistaking that he looked like money. He completed his look with the trademark original Timbs most DC natives rocked. Ice favored The Game greatly.

At 6'2", he had that jailhouse body thang going on strong. Every muscle on him was cut. He was tattooed from head to toe, but the one that stood out the most was the snake that wrapped around his neck and ended at the tip of his dick. Some people said the snake represented his personality. He never denied it.

On hot days, he'd be outside cleaning up his silver Aston Martin with no shirt on. All the females, young and old, would be outside just to catch a glimpse of him.

His mother, "Dip," was right by his side, sporting a brown Birkin bag. They called her Dip because even though she was thirty-six, she had been stripping and dipping up until a year ago. She even looked like Ronnie from *"The Players Club"* movie. Dip was wearing tight blue Seven jeans, a brown tank top and brown Prada sandals. Her waist was still small and her ass was beyond fat. She had a hell of a body to be 5'2", with a bigger mouth to go with it.

As always, Dip sported a blond, bone-straight weave that hung down her back. Even though nothing was natural about its color, her hair was always fresh. Plenty of dudes would kill for a chance to fuck Ice's mother, because she was beyond sexy. But since they valued their lives, too, these same dudes left her alone.

Dip's high heels clicked as she walked toward the car. They stepped over Deadman, now the neighborhood drunk, who had shown up out of nowhere about two months ago. Dip waved with her extra long, red nails when she saw Nic and Pepper sitting on the steps. When Ice saw who she was waving at, he opened the car door for her and yelled, "What up, Nic?!" The passenger door remained open as his mother slid in. The thick black hair under his arms was showing.

"Hey, baby!" she screamed over Pepper's head. "Hold on, Tree. Ice out here."

Nic was just like the other girls in the neighborhood when it came to Ice, always on his dick. As much as Pepper hated his guts, she could see why. He was *fyne*!

Ice let his mother inside the car then slammed the door

Cold As Ice

shut. He gripped the top of his pants, pulled them up, and strolled in their direction. The shoestrings on his Timbs were untied and dragged against the ground. The snake on his neck moved when he did.

He winked when he saw Pepper staring at him. She turned away. Nic jumped up, knocking Pepper over with her fat ass cheeks, just to hug him. The entire back of her grey sweat pants was filled with sweat. Pepper lifted herself up and found her hand had been pressed in the candy the ants were circling earlier. *Damn*! she thought as she turned her hand over and saw bugs everywhere.

She walked into the house and washed her hands. When she came back out, she saw Ice was still there. *Shit, why don't he leave? I can't stand him.* She wasn't bold enough to say anything to him, so she rolled her eyes.

Ice and Nic were handling business until Pepper returned. They took a few steps forward, and he placed a 20 sack in her hand. Nic stuffed it in her bra, afterwards turning around to see if Pepper was watching … she was. Pepper couldn't believe what she was seeing. Nic had just taken drugs from Ice. When Nic was served, they walked back toward Pepper. Out of nowhere, Ice smacked Pepper upside her forehead, causing an immediate red bruise.

"What's up wit' yo' punk ass?!" he joked.

"Why you do that?" she said, rubbing her head, making the mark worse. "I'm not even bothering you!" Pepper screamed.

Pepper didn't understand why he insisted on treating her like a kid. If he wasn't slapping her upside her head, he was clowning her in front of everybody on the block.

"Girl, shut up and stop trippin'," Nic interrupted as she nudged her cousin in the arm. "He was just playin' wit' you."

"Yeah ... calm down, girl," Ice laughed. "It ain't like you weren't ugly to begin with."

Ice and Nic both laughed again.

"She is a mess, ain't she?" Nic continued.

Pepper wasn't considered the prettiest girl on the block, but she was thick to death. She had a little bit around the waist, but her ass made up for it. When she came into view, it was the first thing you saw. And if there was any doubt it was her, her light skin, bright red hair and pepper-colored freckles would assure you it was Pepper coming in the room. People didn't believe her real name was Pepper, but it was true. Her mother had given it to her the moment she saw the freckles on her face.

When they saw how mad Pepper was, they continued to laugh at her expense until Dip began blowing the hell out of Ice's car horn.

"Aight, Nic," Ice said after giving her a pound. "I'ma get up wit' you later." He pointed.

"Good lookin' out, boo." She smiled, taking her seat back behind Pepper. When she saw him pull off, she direct-ed her attention back to Pepper. "You need to stop actin' all funny and shit wit' Ice," she yelled, grabbing her hair.

"Ouch!" Pepper screamed, pulling away from her.

"I'm serious! It ain't like he ain't yo' neighbor," she con-tinued, pointing the comb in her face. "Plus, he just be playin' wit' yo' ass."

"So you doin' drugs now?" Pepper asked out of nowhere. She couldn't believe she called her on her bullshit, because Nic would fuck her up.

"You ain't see shit," Nic said, staring at her. "If my momma tell me you told Aunt Grace, I'ma beat yo' ass every day for a week."

Pepper looked at her cousin's face. It was weird how

Cold As Ice

much she looked like her mother. All of the women in Pepper's family had light skin with *some* freckles, but none of them had as many as she did.

"Keep yo' mouth closed, Pepper! I'm serious. And ease up on Ice. He just a man."

"Well I don't like him playin' wit' me like that!" Pepper advised. She spotted her best friend walking into her house a few doors down with her mother, who was strung out on crack. "I just want him to leave me alone."

"Keep actin' like dat and see where it gets you, Pepper." She grabbed her hair and told her to turn around. "All dem A's and B's ain't gonna change the fact that you still live in the PJs! So *pllleeeeassse* believe, you ain't no betta than the rest of us and you gonna always be here, so get use to it!" After she finished chastising her, for what Pepper didn't know, she got back on the phone and ran her mouth until the battery ran dead.

Pepper was relieved because she wanted a chance to think. So what, she wanted something different with her life? And so what, she wasn't sweating Ice like the other girls on the block? Her dreams extended beyond the hood. Still, she thought about what her cousin said over and over again.

All dem A's and B's ain't gonna change the fact that you still live in the PJs! So pllleeeeassse believe, you ain't no betta than the rest of us and you gonna always be here, so get use to it!

"I might not be better than everybody, but I am getting out of here," she said to herself. "I don't care what I have to do."

And The Beat Goes On

"They want more DVDs, Ice. You got any?"

"Naw, but what I tell you bout callin' me on dis line?"

"Sorry ... I called you on the other one but you didn't answer."

"Next time wait till I call you back!" he said firmly, looking at his mother, who was shaking her head. "Look, tell them perverted-ass mothafuckas they gonna get their movies. Just make sure they wire my money."

He ended the call and placed his Palm Treo cell phone back in the belt clip.

"Can you trust her?" Dip asked as she sat in the passenger seat, applying her MAC makeup. When she was done she said, "'Cuz I don't like a whole lotta of people in my business." She turned up the radio the moment she heard Ciara's *"Promise"* playing.

"She got the connections we need," Ice said as he sipped on the Captain Morgan rum and Coke in his Ravens cup. "And so far she hasn't proven me wrong."

"I sure hope you right, Ice," Dip said, pointing her extra long, red nail in his face. Dip never cut her fucking nails and because of it, they grew real long and began to curl under. "You trust too many people, and one day that's gonna bite you in the ass."

"I got this," he said, putting his hand on his chest. "Let me worry about this part of the business. You just make sure the hoppers are supplied with everything they need on the streets," he continued as he placed his right hand on the

Cold As Ice

steering wheel and leaned toward his window.

"Yeah, whatever," Dip said, waving him off and popping a piece of gum. "Just be careful."

Ice hated when Dip ragged on him about handling business. Hell, it was because of him she didn't have to strip anymore, and as far as he was concerned, she should be grateful. To hear Dip tell it, it was her skills that made him who he was today, and anything he earned was as much hers as it was his.

"Like I said, Dip, let me handle it. You just keep the camera rollin'."

The Price of Curiosity

Grace Thomas was throwing down in the kitchen. The two bedroom row house smelled like fried chicken, rice, string beans and blueberry cornbread. Although Grace worked three jobs, one as a waitress, another as a maid and her latest job as a security guard in a Downtown D.C. federal office building, she still managed to cook for Pepper every night.

When dinner was ready, Pepper rushed to the table with a *"Home Buyers"* magazine in hand. Her fresh new braids sat in a ponytail on top of her head. Her scalp was still sore, but she didn't mind because the more pain she was in meant the longer they'd last. Sitting at the table, she turned around when she heard the anchorwoman on the news say,

"And the search for a masked serial rapist continues."

Pepper listened attentively as the anchorwoman continued the story.

"He has kidnapped and raped at least six young women in the Southeast D.C. area. The perpetrator is apparently meeting these young women on the internet. The attacker sets up a meeting location with the women, then jumps out of his vehicle wearing a mask and abducts them. Afterwards, all of the victims have been drugged, rendering them unconscious. Although no accurate description of the subject can be given, witnesses do say he is an African American over six feet tall, with a muscular physique. Crystal Hyatt, who has been missing for two months, is believed to be one of his latest victims. She was last seen

Cold As Ice

walking toward Addison Road subway station in Capitol Heights, Maryland. If you have any information about this case, please contact authorities immediately."

Hearing about murders and crime wasn't new to Pepper. What was new was the idea of a serial rapist roaming so close to her home.

"You and Zykia be careful out there," Grace said as she entered the living room wearing her black security guard uniform, no weapon. Out of all the jobs Grace had, Pepper hated the security one the most, because she was charged with defending others, without a gun. "I don't know if they're gonna ever catch that bastard."

"I don't understand it, mama," she said as she stood up from the table to help bring over the large white plates from the kitchen. "Why can't they catch him?"

"I don't know, but if they don't, someone else will. Rape is horrible."

"That's why I'll be so glad when we move from around here," she said as Snoop and R. Kelly's *"That's That"* video played in the background. Setting the plates down, she grabbed the magazine and flipped to the folded page. "Why can't we move into a house like this?" she pointed.

Grace glanced down and saw the three hundred thousand dollar home she was pointing to.

"Because we don't have *house like this* money."

Pepper closed the magazine and flopped down into the kitchen chair.

"It's not fair! People like Ice get to buy whatever they want and we have to struggle just to have a nice place to live!"

"Pepper, we only need two thousand dollars to bid on one of those new homes in Virginia. With all the overtime I'm doing, I'll have that by next month."

T. Styles

"Yeah, but the houses may be sold by then."

"Pepper," Grace said, exhaling. "You're too anxious. Don't *ever* let people or situations change who you are. Everything will happen in time. God's time."

"Okay, ma," Pepper said, ignoring everything she said.

"So what's going on with you and that young man?"

"Jai?"

"Yes."

"He's okay," Pepper said in a low tone. He was the reason she had plans later on that night.

"Are you two still fighting?"

"Ma!" Pepper said, embarrassed by her pushiness.

"Okay," Grace laughed, grabbing her car keys. "Whatever you do, don't stay up late."

"Aight, ma."

"I'm for real! I want you in bed by ten. Not a minute later."

The minute Grace hit the door, Pepper ran to the phone.

"Who is this?!" Zykia's brother screamed into the phone. Ludacris' *"Grew Up a Screw Up"* blasted in the background, so Pepper knew their mother wasn't home.

"It's Pepper. Is Zykia there?" she asked carefully.

"Girl, do you know what time it iz?!" he yelled. "It's fuckin' 11:00 at night."

"I'm sorry, Jordan," she whispered, wishing she could give him a piece of her mind without being afraid. "I just wanted to holla at her right quick."

"Next time look at a clock before you call here, bitch!"

Pepper heard the phone drop and thought he hung up, until she heard her best friend's voice.

"What's wrong with your brother?" Pepper asked. Whenever she saw or spoke to him, he had something smart to say out his mouth.

Cold As Ice

"You know how JD is. What's up?"

"I want you to go with me to Jai's house tonight," she said, looking at a few pairs of jeans in her closet. When she couldn't find the ones she wanted, she remembered that she'd worn them yesterday, and they were in the hamper. She ran to the bathroom, opened the lid and smelled the jeans. She lifted them out, concluding they were good. "I think he messin' with Diamond or somethin'."

Zykia took a deep breath and said, "Stop trippin', Pepper! You know he hangs with her brother."

"Tell Pepper I said 'hi,'" Khoury said in the background, interrupting the call.

Pepper smiled when she heard his voice.

"Khoury told me to tell you 'hi,'" Zykia teased.

"So what!" Pepper yelled.

"You over there worryin' about Jai when Khoury tryin' to get wit' you. He fine, girl!"

"He just tryin' to hit. Anyway, I'm not trippin' off that boy," Pepper dismissed. "Back to Jai, why she keep hangin' up when I call to talk to him? Everybody at school think they together now. You got to roll with me over there."

"I can't. Jordan will have a fit!"

She placed the jeans on her bed and put a white D.C.'s Finest baby T a few inches over them, to see how they'd look if she rocked them together.

"Zy, please!" she whined. "Yesterday at school she told Caramel she wanted him."

"Aight, Pepper," Zykia gave in. "I'll meet you in front of Old Lady Howard's house in fifteen minutes. I have to think of a way to shake JD's ass."

Old Lady Howard had the most fucked up house on the block. The fence was broke. The trees in her yard were overgrown and extended beyond the fence. People couldn't

T. Styles

even walk past her house without knocking into branches. It was a perfect place to be incognito, as long as her barking dog wasn't outside. Many a drug transaction went down right in front of her property.

"Thanks, girl!" Pepper yelled.

"Don't thank me yet. You know since ma's sick, JD think he's my father, so he's goin' to trip."

Zykia could never admit that her mother was on drugs. She always said she was sick instead.

Pepper couldn't stand Jordan's ass. He was the meanest nineteen-year-old she'd ever met. He'd done everything from robbery to assaulting elderly people for money. But the thing that really caused her to hate him was the night she stayed over their house. Pepper woke up at 1:00 in the morning because Jordan was pressing his body on top of hers, tugging at her panties. He was pulling them so hard to the side that she cried out in pain before he even entered her virgin womb. He told her over and over to be quiet, but she didn't listen. The only reason he stopped was because his mother was home and he didn't want to get caught. Jordan threatened to hurt her if she told anybody, and as violent as he was, she knew he meant it.

"Okay, do what you can."

"And bring me a Coke, too!"

"Got it!" Pepper said, jumping up and down. She didn't know what she was going to do once she saw him, because for real, she was scary-hearted. She was going to think of part two of her plan as they walked the four blocks to Jai's house.

Pepper put on her outfit with her favorite red Old Navy thong sandals. Afterwards, she grabbed two Cokes, one for herself and the other for Zykia. It took her fifteen minutes to get dressed, so she was sure Zykia was already waiting in front of Old Lady Howard's broken fence.

The moment she twisted the doorknob, she heard a lot of commotion outside. When she opened the door slightly and peeped outside, she saw four men rushing from Ice's house. One of them looked toward Pepper's house and she slammed the door shut, cutting the lights off, too.

She didn't want to be a witness to what she knew was going down: robbery. When she thought it was safe, she kneeled on the couch and moved the yellow curtains slightly to the side. She saw two men quickly carrying a safe to a van.

"Hurry the fuck up!" one of them yelled as they placed the safe in a black van and slammed the door shut. "That nigga may be on his way."

"Nigga, shut the fuck up and bring the rest of that shit in here!" the second replied from the van.

"You got everything, right?" a third man questioned, placing two pillow cases full of drugs in the van.

"Everything we need," the fourth replied. A DVD dropped out of the pile of things he had in his hand.

"Let's roll!" the second yelled.

They were in the van when the second man said, "I think somebody was lookin' out the window in that house." He pointed at Pepper's crib.

"So," the first said, shrugging his shoulders. "Why should we give a fuck? We out!" They sped off.

Pepper didn't move for five minutes. She couldn't believe someone had the nerve to rob Ice's house. She looked out of the curtain one last time to be sure they were gone, and to be sure no one was watching *her* watching. The streets were clear. She looked at his house, and heard the screen door swinging back and forth, making a screeching noise. She saw something lying in his grass.

Pepper jumped up and slowly opened her door. She squinted and saw what appeared to be a white DVD case. Something told her to mind her own business, but curiosity got the best of her.

Pepper slowly stepped out the door and ran to his yard. *Go back in the house, Pepper,* she tried to tell herself as she ran barefooted from her grass to his. But it was too late. The case was in her hands. She dipped back inside and locked the door behind her. She pushed up against the door as she slid to the floor, examining the case. Her breaths were heavy.

The phone was in reach, so she picked it up to call Zykia.

"Where you at?!" Zykia yelled. "I was waiting at Old Lady Howard's fence and her dog started barking and stuff. JD heard that shit and came outside looking for me. I had to go back in."

"I'm sorry, Zy, but something came up."

"Like what?" Zykia asked, thinking her friend was bluffing.

"I just saw Ice's house get robbed!"

"You lying!"

"I'm not! I have to call you back, too."

"Why?"

"They left something on the ground. It looks like a DVD or CD."

"It's probably music," Zykia laughed. "Who cares?"

"You're probably right."

"You better be careful, Pepper. Ice will kill you if he finds out you got somethin' that belongs to him. CD or not."

"I know. I'll call you later."

Before she could finish talking, Pepper hung up. She opened the case and discovered it held a DVD. *If it's a home*

Cold As Ice

movie or somethin' I'll just give it back to Ice. Maybe he'll give me a reward, she thought.

She stood up, walked toward her player and put it inside. Just when she hit play, her phone rang. "Hello," she said, uninterested in whoever was calling.

"You busy?"

It was Jai.

"Actually, I am," she responded, no longer caring about where he was or who he was with. The DVD was loading.

"Diamond said you called over here fifteen times. Now you don't wanna talk?" he asked, breaking her concentration.

"Why didn't you get the phone then?" she blurted out. She was surprised at herself.

"What?"

"I mean, can I call you back?"

"Don't call me, I'll call yo' ass," he said with attitude.

Pepper didn't care. The phone dropped out of her hands and onto the floor. She couldn't believe her eyes. She was watching the most brutal thing she'd ever seen in her life. So brutal that tears fell from her eyes. If only she would've left the DVD where it was, she would never have known.

T. Styles

The Blame Game

Kris was sitting on the floor with his dick in a dog's bowl. His penis was covered with fresh ground beef ... Crunch's favorite. Crunch was an orange-colored Pit Bull who was salivating. Kris couldn't move because his hands were tied behind his back and he was duct taped to a radiator.

"So let me get this straight," Ice said, standing over Kris as Dip held Crunch's black leather leash firmly. The dog was barking loudly and moving crazily, trying to get at his meal. Dip kicked him and he yelped loudly and lay down. "It just so happened da moment dese niggas run up in my crib, you at the fuckin' carryout."

"I swear it's true, Ice! I would neva play you like that!" Kris cried. He was covered in sweat. "We go way back, man! Don't do this to me!" he continued, looking at the dog, which was waiting for Ice's patience to run thin.

"Fuck this nigga, baby," Dip yelled, begging him to release Crunch. She looked at him and talked calmly. "He just tryin' to play you. Don't be no fool. If you let him go you might as well give a pardon to the rest of these mothafuckas out here!" She paused. "I'm tellin' you straight up, this nigga was in on it!" She pointed at Kris with her curly nail.

Ice was furious. As he stared at Kris, sitting naked on his living room floor shivering, he wondered how much of what his mother was saying was true. He wasn't worried about the money or the drugs they got into him for. He never kept

Cold As Ice

more in that house than he could afford to lose. Ice was more concerned about the DVD that was missing. He kept it under the safe, beneath a floorboard.

"Hold up, Dip," Ice said, looking at his mother, who was pleading with him to let his dog go. "Let me hear this fool out." Dip shook her head in disgust and reluctantly remained silent. She got off on violence.

"I'ma ask you again. Do you know who ran up in my place?" he questioned as he stooped down to face him. "'Cuz if you don't know somethin', I'ma let Crunch loose and you'll be *dickless*. You best be telling me somethin', man," he continued.

Again Kris cried and denied any knowledge of the robbery. The messed up part was that he was telling the truth. Without even waiting for Ice's approval, Dip released the Pit Bull onto him. Crunch tore into the meat—all the meat.

Ice turned around angrily. He didn't give the okay, but now it was too late. Kris cried in pain as the dog feasted on him.

"You couldn't wait, huh?" Ice asked.

"No," she smiled. "Waiting's for fools."

Pepper was walking by Ice's house when she heard screams coming from inside. She stopped in her tracks. The cries were followed by bullets ringing. She quickened her pace, leaving Jai, who was walking with her a few steps behind.

"What in the fuck was that?" Jai asked upon hearing screams and bullets.

"I don't know," Pepper responded, even farther ahead of him. "I'm not trying to find out."

When Pepper passed Ice's car she took a quick glance. It wasn't fair that people like him got to live the *life* while she and her mother struggled. Pepper was aware of the four

T. Styles

car garage house he owned in Virginia. The house in D.C. was nothing more than a business location, to stay close to his dough and the niggas on his payroll.

"And why in the fuck are you rushing?" Jai continued, noticing she had been on edge ever since they left school earlier.

Jai didn't believe in rushing. Everything with him had to be cool, smooth and slow. They called him Lil Jay-Z at school. His relaxed attitude was one of the reasons Pepper fell for him. Although he was two inches shorter than she was, standing 5'5", he had a huge personality. His honey-brown skin and low hair cut with a connecting goatee made him look older than sixteen. Wearing black sweats and a white T, with red, yellow and black Bapes, he walked as if he didn't have a care in the world.

"I'm not rushing," Pepper smiled, trying to be cool. "Can we just hurry a little? I don't want my mother coming home with me out here," she continued, knowing that if her mother came home, her being outside would be the least of her worries. Jai would.

Jai took his time walking up Pepper's stairs. She opened the door and he followed ... slowly. She threw her red book bag on the couch and locked the door. Once completely inside, she did a quick run through to be sure her mother wasn't home. Normally she never was, but with what she wanted to show him, she had to be sure sure. While Pepper busied herself with a few details, he sat on the couch, grabbed the remote and turned on the TV.

"So I heard that nigga got robbed," he said as he scanned through the channels.

Pepper stopped in her tracks, her eyes two sizes larger.

"W ... wha ... what are you talking about?"

"Stop playin'," Jai laughed as he turned on "*MTV Jams*"

Cold As Ice

and dropped the remote. "You live right next to this nigga, so I know you know somethin'."

"Oh," she laughed. "You talkin' about that. Uh ... yeah ... I heard somethin'." She picked her book bag up off the couch.

"So did you see anything?" he asked, screwing his face up at her.

She sat down beside him, thinking about her lie.

"Naw ... I was 'sleep."

"How you gonna be 'sleep when you was calling me all night?" he continued.

"I can't remember," she said, clearing her throat. "But I want to show you somethin'." She paused. "I'm kinda scared though."

"Pepper, I told you I'd be easy on you," he said, turning off the TV. Now that he thought she was *finally* going to let him hit, he was suddenly interested in what she had to say.

"I'm not talking about that, Jai." Pepper exhaled as she unzipped her book bag, removing the DVD. She looked at him again, trying to determine if she should show him or not. "I found something the night Ice's place got robbed."

"So you *were* up?"

"Yes," she continued as she stood up to place it in the player.

Jai knocked it out her hand and said, "Man, I'm not tryin' to see no fuckin' DVD! I'm tired of you playin' games wit' me, Peppa!" he yelled. "Are we fuckin' or not? You been holdin' out on me for six months like I'm some sucka-ass nigga!"

She picked the DVD up off the floor and placed it on the glass living room table, keeping her eyes on him the entire time. He'd blown up at her before, but never like this.

"Jai ... I really have to show you something," she said

real low, trying not to upset him.

"You know what?" he said, getting up. "My boys told me not to fuck wit' yo' ass! I shoulda listened. You ain't nothin' but a mothafuckin' tease! I'm out of here." He walked toward the door.

"Don't leave, Jai," she cried, grabbing his hand. "I don't have anybody else to talk to about this."

"Get the fuck off me," he continued, pushing her to the floor. She bumped her head on the glass table, causing it to bleed a little. "Don't call me no more eitha! I'm fuckin' wit' Diamond now."

Jai walked out the door and Pepper stayed on the floor, crying.

Ice had a few dudes pick up Kris' bodily remains, which were packed inside of three Glad bags. He and Dip watched from the couch. After the dog ate his penis, they put him out of his misery by putting three bullets in his head.

"We have to find that DVD," Dip said when the pick up boys were gone. Ice and Dip were sitting on the couch smoking a blunt. Dip glanced over into the kitchen, looking at Pipes and Dro, Ice's friends. "And quick!"

"Ain't nobody watchin' no DVD," Ice responded as he sipped on the beer and looked toward the kitchen, too. Dro, who had been slinging for him for ten years, was playing dominoes with Pipes, his cousin. "Think about it. They came for the money, not a DVD. Don't nobody but me, you and them mothafuckas in Cali know what we got goin' on with them DVDs."

"How you know?" she whispered, pointing her blunt at him. "Think about it. Why would they take it out the floor-board if they didn't want it?" She blew smoke in the air and passed the blunt to him. "You have to be smarter than that."

Cold As Ice

"I *am*," he confirmed, accepting the hand off. "That's why I think we're good. If they do find it, they gonna think it's a porno or some shit like that. Chill out."

"Listen," she yelled, forgetting they had company. This time Dro and Pipes looked in their direction. "You got a problem?" she asked them. They shook their heads. "Well turn the fuck around then!" When their attention was totally off of her, she continued. "Like I said, you have to be smart about this shit. That bitch they lookin' for is on that DVD. That means if it gets in the wrong hands, we're through. And I'm not going to jail for no murder shit, Ice."

Ice tried to hand her back the blunt, but she waved him off. Instead she grabbed her purse, searching for something else. When she found a rolled up napkin with tiny red pills inside, she got exactly what she wanted … "E." Realizing she didn't have anything to swallow the pill with, she snatched Ice's beer can and tried to swallow the pills. It wasn't enough. "Dro, bring me a Coke from the fridge!"

Dro stood up, wanting to tell her to get the fuck out of his face, but thought better of it. "Aight," he said, opening the fridge and walking the drink to her. Dro was white and black and very tall. He was loyal to Ice, but hated Dip's ass with a passion. After handing her the Coke, he walked back to the table.

"And how you know his ass ain't have nothin' to do with it?" she questioned, pointing her red manicured nail at Dro as he returned to the kitchen table with Pipes.

"'Cuz dem my niggas, that's how I know," he responded, putting her back in her place.

"I don't know if you had a chance to look, but them ain't no niggas. They half breeds, and they'll roll on you in a heartbeat."

"They ain't have shit to do with it," he said firmly. "You

always comin' down on me like I don't know how much shit can kick off if that DVD shows up. Right now it's out there and until it shows up, we have to deal with not knowing."

"Ice, you betta have this shit under control!"

"I do … I do."

Cold As Ice

Another Kind of Criminal

Pepper and Zykia sat on the edge of the bed, eyes glued onto Pepper's TV. Zykia wore pink pajamas and pigtails. She was a cute, short, thin girl who looked as if she was mixed with Indian and black. Pepper was right beside her wearing a long T-shirt with sweat pants. They couldn't believe what they were seeing. Pepper had watched it ten times and it felt like the first time, *every* time.

"Pepper, y'all ready to eat?" Grace yelled from the kitchen, waking them from their stupor. The sound was completely down on the TV.

"Uh … no, ma," she said, wiping the tears from her face. "We'll eat later!"

"Don't let it get cold," Grace continued. "Y'all have been in there all day."

"Okay," Pepper replied as she got up to lock the door, just in case her mother got the urge to bust in on them. Pepper turned the sound back up a little.

When she returned to the bed, she saw the part where Ice was with a young girl. Her naked body was tied to the bed. He repeatedly raped her. In the background they heard a woman's voice. And since Dip was always with Ice, Pepper was familiar with her voice. When a portion of her long nail appeared in front of the camera, it was confirmed.

"Just smile, sweetheart," Dip said. "This DVD is going to be seen around the world." She laughed. "You'll be a star."

"Damn, this young bitch's pussy's tight as shit!" Ice

responded as the girl cried out, begging him to stop.

The scene was extremely violent and had both girls cringing. The girl was clearly around their age and this made the act all the more real to them. The sheets were covered in blood. Ice placed his entire mouth over hers and kissed her harshly. His jeans were at his ankles and his body was sweaty. What gave him away was not his face, because it couldn't be seen. It was the snake tattoo that ran from his neck and down his back, but this time they could see the head of the serpent ending on his penis.

"Pepper ... this is serious," Zykia said, wiping the tears from her face again. "We have to tell somebody." She looked at the TV once more.

"Who we gonna tell, Zy?"

"Uh ... how about the police?" she replied sarcastically. "Look at what he's doing to her? We have to say something now," she continued, reaching for the phone.

Pepper stood up and pressed pause, and the video stopped on the part in which Ice was licking between the frightened girl's legs.

"Calm down, Zy," she responded, slowly taking the phone from her hand. "I'm fucked up about this, too. But I have a plan."

"You have a what?" Zykia repeated. "What are you talking about?"

"Do you know why my mother is still here?" Pepper asked as her face turned red. "She here because she lost her third job today! That means we can't get the new house. That means I can't leave this fuckin' place, Zy! I'm tired of being around here."

"Pepper, what are you talkin' about?" Zykia asked as she stood up. "You livin' around here ain't got nothin' to do with that DVD! At least your mother ain't all strung out and shit like mine," she added.

"I want more!" Pepper said, ignoring her comment. "A lot more."

Silence.

"What does that mean?"

"I say we get paid for this shit," she said, pointing and looking at the TV.

"What?!" Zy yelled.

"I say we get paid! Think about it for a minute," Pepper continued as she paced the room. "He knows the DVD is missing, *so* ... he'll probably be looking for it."

"But he won't be able to find it because the police will have it," Zykia advised.

"And then what, Zy? He pays some high-priced lawyers and gets off easy. You know how shit works. How many niggas been locked up for doin' shit only to get out two days later? And guess what will happen when he finds out who snitched? He'll kill us!"

"Pepper, what is going on in there?!" Grace yelled as she knocked on the door.

"Oh shit," she whispered, clearing her throat. "Nothing, ma. We're just talking."

"Well talk a little lower," Grace responded. "I can hear y'all all the way out here." Pepper knew that wasn't true, because she'd be in there asking a whole lot of questions instead of yelling at the door.

"Aight, ma," Pepper responded. "Like I said, we should get paid," she continued, whispering. "I'm tired of seeing Ice wit' diamonds and new clothes while we're walking around here lookin' a hot mess!"

Zykia shifted her weight from one foot to the other, studying her friend's gaze.

"So I propose," she continued when she felt Zykia was-

T. Styles

n't buying in, "we blackmail him."

"Pepper ... you sound crazy! I don't want no part of this."

"Don't you want your own money for a change?! Ain't you tired of relying on JD?"

Zykia shook her head.

"Look at your shoes, Zy!" she said, picking her Nikes up off the floor. "They run down! Don't tell me you want to roll like this. You get messed wit' at school more than I do."

Zykia was no longer rebellious. She thought about having to wear the same banged out clothes day after day and having to wash them in the sink by hand. She shared her panties with her mother, and who knew where she had been. Suddenly, the idea of getting a little something for nothing started to sound good to her.

"Pepper," Zykia said, breathing heavily. "What will stop Ice from killing us? I mean ... if he finds out we're blackmailing him, he will kill us. By hand, too!"

"No, he won't."

"How do you know?"

"Because he won't know it's us."

Cold As Ice

The Ultimate Disrespect

"Y'all get from around my house," Grace said as she came home early to find three knuckleheads drinking on her steps, playing dice. They had liquor bottles spread out everywhere. "I'm serious! Leave!" she yelled as she pushed past them with her purse in one hand, a brown paper bag filled with groceries in the other.

"Man, we leavin'!" one of them yelled back, clearly intoxicated and not budging.

"Yeah, old lady bitch," another responded. They all laughed. "I'm 'bout to break these fools real quick, give me five seconds," he continued, holding up five fingers.

"I'm gonna call the cops!" she continued. "I don't want my daughter seein' all this!"

"You talkin' bout Pepper's fine ass?" the third man asked. "She look like she been eatin' real good lately," he laughed, smoking a Black & Mild with one hand, stroking his dick with the other. "What you feedin' her?" he asked, looking in her brown paper bag.

"What's wrong with y'all?" she asked, snatching the bag away from him. "I changed half of y'all Pampers."

"You ain't change my Pampers," the first man laughed, giving the second one dap.

"Everything okay, Ms. Thomas?" Khoury asked, seeing what was going on. They looked at him and stood up. He pulled his cap down and took one step forward, clearly ready to back his question up despite being outnumbered.

"Everything alright, lil nigga," Ice said, walking over to

T. Styles

him out of nowhere. Removing Khoury's cap, he replaced it, sideways.

"I'm talkin' to Ms. T," Khoury bucked. He looked at Ice, placed his cap on right and then waited for Grace's response. "Are you okay, ma'am?"

"Yes, son," she smiled. "I'm fine. Go on home."

Khoury looked at Ice once more and walked off.

Ice smirked, making mental notes to check his lil ass later. "What y'all doin' out here on this lady's steps?" Ice continued. When they didn't respond he said, "I ask y'all a mothafuckin' question! What y'all doin' out here?"

"Nothin', man," one of them said, picking up their things. "We're leavin' now."

"Well get from the fuck around here!" When they didn't move quick enough, due to being scared, he yelled, "Move!"

They hurried down her steps. When they were gone, he directed his attention to Grace. She looked him over and noticed he looked especially *Icey*, with his diamond watch and platinum chain. He was also wearing a red button up shirt which exposed his white wifebeater.

"Sorry bout that, man. These youngins today don't know the first thing about respect," he continued, wiping his mouth with his hand. "I'll make sho dat don't happen again, wit' you bein' my next door neighbor and all."

He went to help her with her grocery bag, but she snatched it away and said, "What you want with me, Sherrod?" She was one of the few people alive who knew his full name was Sherrod Davis. His evil presence made her extremely uncomfortable.

"Damn, Ms. T," he said, approaching her as she stood in front of her door. "I'm not the enemy." He smiled.

"I've been knowing you since Dip got ahold of you," she

Cold As Ice

responded, slowly and carefully. She was trying her best not to let him see her fright. "And you ain't never known me to play games, so I'm not goin' to start now."

"I can respect that," he continued, smiling. "I'ma be straight up wit' you. Did Pepper mention anything to you bout last week?"

"No," she responded quickly. "I don't know what you talking about, but Pepper's a good girl. She don't get involved in all of this mess out here. If she woulda seen anything pertaining to you, she woulda told me."

"I sure hope you right," he continued. "'Cuz I like Pepper, but I'd hate to find out you're lying to me."

"Are you threatening me?" she asked, her entire body trembling.

Ice took two steps closer to her. She could smell his cologne.

"Naw, Ms. T. I would *never* threaten you," he said calmly. "I would fuckin' kill you and your daughter, too. Remember that," he ended, walking off.

She couldn't say anything. Grace just backed up, walked in her house and closed the door, locking it behind her. She made up her mind that she had to get Pepper out of there, if it was the last thing she did.

"Hey, Ice."

Ice looked out his peephole and opened his door.

"Did we do everything right?" one of the guys, who was just at Grace's house harassing her, asked.

"Yeah," he said, looking at her house and then back at him. "But why you come straight ova here? I told you to wait a minute before you came."

"Sorry, man. They wanna get somethin' to eat from Lenny's, and we ain't got no money."

"Yeah, whateva," he responded, waving them off. "But

y'all not finish yet."

"What you mean?" he asked confused. "You told us to sit on her steps and fuck wit' her when she got home. That's what we did."

"But that wasn't the whole deal. You s'pose to be cleanin' my car, too."

He looked at Ice with disgust. He knew he didn't say anything to them about cleaning his ride, but he wasn't bold enough to challenge him on it.

"Aight, Ice, what time you want us here tomorrow?"

"Tomorrow? I want you here tonight," he said as he looked him up and down. "And make sho you get the rims, too."

After Ice was sure he understood, he handed him fifty dollars to split amongst the three of them. It was seventy-five dollars short of the agreement.

"And hurry up."

As Ice walked back in the house and slipped into bed with a young thing he picked up at the bus stop earlier, he thought about Pepper.

"Is everything okay?" she asked as she wrapped her thick tender legs around him.

"Yeah ... finish doin' what you were doin'."

She slid under the covers and wrapped her mouth around his penis. As she went to work on him, he thought about Grace. He knew Pepper didn't know anything about the robbery, but he had to cover all angles. He'd never had anything against Pepper. As a matter of fact, he had plans to fuck her, but Grace played her too close for his taste. But business was business, and whoever got in the way had to be dealt with.

Cold As Ice

Plan into Action

"Zykia, this got to be right! You can't be actin' all scared and shit!" Pepper said as she looked out of her window, waiting for Ice to appear. Instead all she saw was Deadman lying on the ground.

"I don't think he gonna go for it," Zykia responded hesitantly. "He too smart for this shit."

"How you figure?" Pepper asked, releasing the curtain to focus on what she was saying. "If he was real smart he woulda put the DVD somewhere safe. Now say your lines again." Pepper sat on the edge of her bed, listening attentively to be sure Zykia got the lines correct. She got Ice's number from Nic's phone when she was over her house the night before.

"Can I speak to Ice?" Zykia said, quoting her lines.

"This him," Pepper responded. "Who dis?"

"Don't worry about that," Zykia replied. She sounded more confident than the other times they rehearsed. She sounded seductive. "I got something you want, really bad. You might even be willing to pay for it."

"And what's that?" Pepper said.

"A DVD. *Your* DVD. And to get it back, it's gonna cost ya."

"I'm listening," Pepper continued.

"I want you to pack twenty-five large into a McDonald's paper bag. Then I want you to take it to Addison Road subway station and buy a pass. When you get the pass, I want you to go to the section upstairs by the trains and place the

T. Styles

bag in the trash can next to the map. After that, I want you to walk your fine ass back outside, get in your car and go home. Got it?"

"Perfect!" Pepper yelled, jumping up. "You don't sound nothin' like yourself. He won't know who you are! Just remember to tell him when he makes the drop, his DVD will be at home. Make sure he don't try to follow, 'cuz it'll make the news instead."

"Okay, Pepper," Zykia responded, breathing heavily. "I hope you're right about this."

"Just trust me," she replied. "But look … he's outside now! Call him in five seconds," she continued, rushing for the door, phone still in hand. "I have to throw him off our tracks."

Without waiting for Zykia to respond, Pepper rushed out the door. Before she walked down her steps, she took one deep breath. Ice was outside putting car cleaning supplies in his trunk.

"Hey, Ice," Pepper said softly.

Ice turned around and slammed his trunk closed.

"Aw shit," he joked. "Look at lil-big-head-ass Pepper." He went to smack her upside the head, but she pushed his hand away. "I see you quick today," he laughed. "What's up?"

"Have you seen my mamma?"

"Have I seen your mamma?" he repeated, placing his keys in his pocket. "Who I look like? Your papi?"

She was standing in front of him, procrastinating, wondering why Zykia hadn't called yet. *I hope you didn't chicken out on me, Zy,* she thought. If the plan didn't go through, it never would, because she couldn't see holding a conversation with Ice's ass again.

"I'm just askin' because she was supposed to be home

Cold As Ice

by now to take me to the store."

"I'll ride you," he said, licking his lips. "Would you like that?"

Thoughts of the girl he raped entered her head. Before she could respond, he threw his index finger up in her face when *"It's Okay"* by The Game rang from his phone. Stepping a little to the side, he answered the call.

"Who dis?"

Silence.

"Yo, what you just say to me?" he asked, walking farther from Pepper.

Silence.

Pepper's heart began to thump. Suddenly she realized there was no turning back. Maybe she was out of her league after all. What made her think she could blackmail one of D.C.'s most notorious dealers? Ice had murdered at least six people that she was aware of. She started sweating and wiped her face with her hands, hoping Ice didn't see her. And as if that wasn't enough, suddenly she felt faint.

Still on the phone, he turned around and faced her. Pepper tried to maintain the innocent look he'd known her for, but it was difficult.

"I see," he responded slowly, still eyeing Pepper. "And if I don't?"

Silence.

"You'll get your money," he replied. "But you betta hope I never find out who you are."

With that he hung up, still staring Pepper down. She knew it was over, so she started saying the Lord's Prayer in her head. Her only wish was that she was able to tell her mother goodbye. For some reason, she looked down at Deadman as if he could save her, but he could barely save himself.

T. Styles

"Listen, shawty," Ice said, as if he was madder than the devil himself. "I can't take you to no store. I got some shit to handle. Layda."

And just like that ... he walked off. *Did I actually get away with it?* she thought as she watched him walk into his house. She didn't waste any time. She had to be sure Zykia was okay. She rushed inside and called her, but she didn't answer the phone. Pepper called five more times and got nothing. Suddenly the phone rang, and Pepper snatched it up.

"Pepper, ask your mother if I could wash two loads of clothes over there," Nic said.

Click.

Pepper didn't have time for her shit. She called Zykia again, and it felt like forever until she answered the phone.

"Are you okay?" Pepper asked, out of breath.

"No," Zykia responded as if she had been crying.

"It's gonna be alright," Pepper consoled. "If he knew it was us, he would've said something to me."

"That's not it, Pepper," Zykia continued.

"Then what is it?"

"Somebody knows."

Silence.

"Somebody like who?" Pepper asked as her heart began to race.

"P ... pe ... Pepper, just come over. And bring the DVD."

Click.

Zykia was gone, and Pepper was shook.

Cold As Ice

A Whole Different Game

"What's up, Pepper?" Lil John, a neighborhood youngin, asked as she stood outside of Zykia's door.

"Nothing ... why?" She turned around nervously.

"Just askin', damn," he said, walking away shaking his head. "Reds actin' crazy today."

When he was gone, Pepper knocked softly on Zykia's door. She took one last look behind her to be sure Ice wasn't there, ready to smoke her. When she saw he wasn't, she knocked harder. Instead of Zykia opening it, JD did.

"Uh ... hey ... is Zy home?" she stuttered.

"Now why you actin' all scared and shit, girl?" he responded, nicer than normal. "Me and you cool," he said, opening the door fully. "So it's time we start actin' like it."

Pepper paused, not knowing what to say. She glanced inside and saw Izzy, one of his friends, trying to play hard, and Khoury with him. Zykia appeared from behind them, still crying.

"You gonna come in so we can get down to business, or what?" JD asked.

———

"You can't go!" Dip yelled. "This ain't nothin' but a set up!" she continued, pacing Ice's living room floor. "The cops probably gonna be there waiting."

"Dip, what are you talkin' about?" Ice asked as he sat on the couch with his face in his hands. "What you want me to do? Not go?"

"I want you to wait."

"For what? The bitch said she got the DVD! Ain't shit to wait on."

"I think it's the cops, Ice. They probably didn't even know it was you until you admitted to it."

"Dip," he paused. "If it was the cops, they'd be in here already. Now I say we pay dese mothafuckas and get it over wit'. We'll get the DVD in our hands and find out who had the nerve to fuck wit' me. For real, for real," he continued, standing up. "What's twenty-five G's? I'm gettin' off easy."

Dip threw herself on the couch and went through her purse. Ice knew exactly what she was looking for, another "E" pill.

"You need to stop poppin' dem mothafuckin' pills! They fuck wit' your head and we need to be thinkin' straight right now," he continued as he poured himself a glass full of Captain Morgan, straight up.

"And you don't need to be tellin' me what to do when you drink that shit like it's water. I shoulda neva got caught up in this porno DVD bullshit," she yelled, spit escaping her mouth. "We were gettin' money already, movin' the package around here. Why you had to go and fuck shit up?"

"You wasn't sayin' that shit when I bought you them purses and diamonds you sportin'. With the money them mothafuckas pay us for them DVDs, we ain't neva got to sling again!"

"But you murdered that bitch, and they still lookin' for her."

Ice jumped and wrapped his hands around Dip's throat.

"Don't you ever say that mothafuckin' shit out loud again! I had to kill her because she could ID me. You know that shit. You got a nerve, considerin' how you did Kris."

When he removed his hand off her throat she said,

"How *we* did Kris," correcting him. "You sure you ain't in this just to fuck young girls?"

"What you say to me?" he asked slowly.

"I mean ... you always liked 'em young, Ice. How old is that girl you fuckin' now?" she paused. "Seventeen?" she laughed. "You fuckin' twenty-two years old, Ice, start fuckin' wit' girls your own age."

"She twenty, and who I'm fuckin' ain't none of your business. Matta fact," he continued as he snatched her purse and emptied its contents on the floor, "since you got a problem with me and my biz, give me everything I bought yo' ass." She tried to get her purse back, but he pushed her away. Her 130 pounds were no match for his 190. When everything was on the floor, he stripped her of all her jewelry, diamonds and all. Then he tore off her red Edun blouse, exposing her breasts. She covered herself with her arms, and he grabbed her by the hair. He opened the door, tossed her out and slammed it shut.

"Fuck you!" she yelled, banging on the door. "I don't need yo' mothafuckin' ass! I don't need you fo' shit!" she continued, crying uncontrollably.

Everyone in the neighborhood pointed as they witnessed Ice's mother outside of the door, naked.

"If I was yo' real motha," she continued yelling, "you wouldn't be treatin' me like this! I shoulda left your ass on the streets! I shoulda never took you in!"

Ice heard what she was saying but didn't know if it was true. The truth was, she wasn't his biological mother, but up until now, he never treated her any differently.

He remembered when Dip fed him in the dressing room all those nights, while his mother danced at Louis Rouge, a strip club in D.C. Jasmine always forgot to feed him, and sometimes could care less if he ate or not. Dip looked after him and even picked him up from Jasmine's from time to time. She couldn't have kids, so she always had her sights on taking somebody else's and one day, for five hundred dollars, she got her wish. Sherrod was only five years old.

—From that point on she looked after him, doing everything she could to make him cold as Ice. Dip would do things like slap him if he cried and tell him that only suckers showed emotions. She even introduced him to Canyon, one of her regulars at the club, and he in turn introduced him to the glamour of the drug life. When he had it down pat, Dip nicknamed him Ice, disposing of the birth name Jasmine had given him.

But Ice had a taste for something different. He got off on raping high school girls. He'd lure them in from the internet and release them when he was done. He'd hide his video recorder and place clips of his actions on the internet under the screen name *Biggerthanitlooks*, never showing his face.

Out of nowhere he started getting requests for the entire DVDs. He sold them for two hundred dollars a pop on the black market. Before he knew it, Marcella, a Spanish broad from L.A., introduced herself by sending him her personal information. Ice was hesitant at first, but she offered to wire him money in an offshore account he set up. From that point on, it was organized. He now had a *reason* to do what he always loved—rape. And with his mother holding the camera, it seemed he could get away with it all, until *she* snatched off his mask and saw his face. That girl didn't make it home for dinner.

Knock. Knock. Knock. Dip knocked softer than before.

"What?!" Ice yelled on the other end of the door.

"I'm sorry, baby," she said, letting her guard down.

"What?" he repeated as if he didn't hear her.

"I said, I'm sorry. Don't do this to me. I raised you. I was

Cold As Ice

wrong for talkin' to you the way I did. Let me in … *please*."

He won. He'd broken down the one woman who taught him everything he knew. Ice opened the door slowly and pointed to the floor. Not knowing what he meant, she walked in until he stopped her in his tracks. "Crawl."

"What?" she cried, shirtless.

"I said get on the fuckin' floor and crawl."

She did, and he smiled.

———

The phone rang just when Jordan was about to tell Pepper what he wanted. Instead of talking to her, he answered it.

"Aw shit!" Jordan laughed. "Stop lyin', nigga!"

"What? What, man?" Izzy asked, grabbing his arm. He was ear hustling and being nosey as shit.

"Shut up, mothafucka!" Jordan said to him before getting back on the phone.

Zykia and Pepper sat on the couch while he amused himself with whoever was calling.

"I wish I coulda seen them fat-ass titties!" he continued. "But look, I'ma get up wit' you layda. I got business to handle over here. One."

When he hung up, he told his boys how Ice threw Dip out on the street, shirtless. JD and Izzy laughed. Khoury didn't.

"Where's the DVD?" Jordan asked straight up.

"The DVD," she laughed. "I don't know what you're talkin' about. What DVD?"

"Man stop fuckin' playin' wit' me before I go down there and tell Ice what's really good!" JD yelled. "Now where's the fuckin' DVD?"

She had to show him because she ain't want it with Ice.

T. Styles

She was more afraid of him than Jordan. Pepper looked at Zykia.

"You told him?"

Zykia nodded.

"He heard me on the phone when I was talking to him."

Pepper glanced over at Jordan and his friends again. Khoury was looking away, while Izzy and Jordan looked her dead in the eyes. They had larceny in their hearts. Jordan rocked back and forth in the beat up leather recliner he was sitting in, waiting on her response. She reached into her book bag and pulled out the DVD. Jordan jumped up and snatched it from her hands.

"Go get my PlayStation, Zy."

She went in the room and hooked it up to the TV, afterwards placing the DVD inside.

"Oh shit!" Jordan yelled as he saw the same gruesome scene. Instead of being disgusted, he and Izzy were cheering Ice on. Khoury looked away. "That nigga's a beast!" Jordan continued.

"He killin' that pussy!" Izzy added.

After watching the complete DVD, he turned it off and said, "Whoa! This shit is major! When I heard babygirl over there on the phone, I didn't think what y'all had was this good. At first I ain't even know it was her, sounding all sexy and shit," he joked.

Zykia held her head down, while Pepper grew so angry she felt like spitting in his face.

"It's like this," he continued. "After seein' that shit, I come to a realization."

"Did dis nigga just say *realization*?" Izzy laughed, looking for Khoury to cosign. He didn't.

"You know what I mean?" Jordan asked, looking at Izzy's fat ass. "Like I said, y'all ain't askin' for enough

Cold As Ice

money. So I'm uppin' the ante. We want fifty G's instead of twenty-five and we splittin' it—forty for us, the rest for y'all."

"Fuck you, JD!" Pepper yelled, standing up. She was through with his fucking ass. She needed that money so she and her mother could leave the projects, and here he was, taking it all.

"Who you talkin' to?" he asked, stepping toward her. He grabbed Pepper's arm and pulled her closer. Whispering in her ear, he said, "You don't want to fuck wit' me Reds. 'Cuz next time I won't be tryin' to slide in from the front," he continued, rubbing his fingers between her legs. "I'll be hittin' that shit from the back." He released her.

"What you doin', man?" Khoury asked, mad at how he was feeling her up.

Pepper looked at Khoury and then back at JD.

"Chill out, man," he laughed. "I'm just having a little fun wit' her." He paused. "*Now* ... call him back, sis. Tell dat nigga the plan is still on for tonight, but pack twenty-five more."

Zykia didn't move.

"Move, bitch!" he screamed. "Time is of the essence." He laughed, looking back at Pepper and licking his lips.

She stared him down, trying to determine if she could take him or not. "Whenever you feelin' yourself," Jordan warned, sensing her anger. "Make a move."

Just as Pepper was ready to smack him and deal with the consequences later, someone knocked at the door. Everyone scattered.

"Oh shit!" Izzy's scary ass yelled. "Dat nigga know!" he continued, hiding behind the recliner. "He know."

"Yo, shut yo' bitch ass up, Tenderheart!" Jordan responded, embarrassed by how Izzy was acting. "Now everybody calm the fuck down!"

When he felt he was back in control, he walked over to the door and saw two plain-clothes officers through the peephole.

"It's the cops," he whispered. "Let me quarterback this shit! Chill out!" he advised as he raised his hand. When they were in order, he opened the door. "Can I help y'all?"

"Yes," a female officer said. She resembled Vivica Fox. "I'm Officer Roberts, and this is Officer Deville. Are your parents home?"

"Naw," he responded as he stepped outside, closing the door behind him. "But what's up?"

"You seen this girl?" the white officer questioned. She looked like Rosie O'Donnell.

Jordan took the picture out of her hands. Without even looking he asked. "Why? She dead or somethin'?"

"That's a hell of a question to be askin'," Officer Roberts replied, looking at her partner.

"I don't know why," Jordan responded. "Y'all don't never come around here unless somebody's dead."

"She's missin'," Officer Deville said. "Now have you seen her or not?"

JD looked at the picture and his mouth dropped open. The officers looked at one another.

"Well?" Roberts replied.

"Uh … uh … naw. I ain't seen her."

"Well, if you do," she continued, "call us." She handed him a business card. "Keep the picture."

"Sure thing," he nodded, still looking at the photo.

When they got in their cars and drove off, he entered the house, slowly. Everyone was waiting on him to say something.

"Well?" Izzy said. "What they want?"

Cold As Ice

"They lookin' for that girl."

"What girl?" Khoury questioned.

"The one on the DVD."

"Oh shit!" they both responded.

Can't Turn Back Now

It was two hours from the time they were supposed to pick up the money from Ice at the train station. Pepper sat in her house, nervous and afraid. With JD involved, she saw only one outcome—death. She thought about what her mother said last week: *Don't ever let people or situations change who you are. Everything will happen in time. God's time.*

If only she'd listened, she wouldn't be in this predicament now. She decided to call her just to hear her voice.

"What you doin', ma?"

"The same thing I was doing five minutes ago when you called, silly," Grace laughed. "Working."

Silence.

"*Pepper* ... are you okay?"

"Yeah ... uh ... I'm fine."

"You don't sound like it," she responded, worried at her tone. "Are you feeling alright? Go in the bathroom and get the thermometer to take your temperature."

"I'm fine, ma. I was just callin' to say I love you. You were always there for me. I wish I could've been more like you ... honest."

"Pepper, you're scaring me."

"I'm serious, ma," she said, sniffling.

"Pepper ... I didn't tell you this earlier because I hoped it would go away. But I want you to stay away from Ice, he's a problem."

"What?" Pepper said, trying to be sure she heard what

Cold As Ice

she did.

"Just stay away."

"Okay … I have to go. Bye, ma."

"You stuffed fifty G's in that bag?" Dip asked, trying to be careful with how she talked to Ice. She didn't want to risk another altercation.

"Yeah," he replied, rolling up the edge of the McDonald's bag. "You got everything you need, don't you?"

"Yes."

"*Everything?*" he asked to be sure.

"Yes, Ice."

"You remember the plan, right?" he continued, checking her for confirmation.

"Yes, but do you actually think they're gonna give us the DVD?" she continued, picking up her plastic bag.

"I don't know," he said, hunching his shoulders. "'Cuz eitha way, somebody knows, and that means somebody has to die. Crystal's on that DVD."

"I know. That's why I'm worried."

When they walked to the car, Ice saw Deadman, passed out drunk as always, in front of his house.

"Yo, Dead," Ice yelled, kicking him. "Yo, Dead!" He continued kicking him harder with his Timbs. "Get the fuck from in front of my house."

Dead barely lifted his head when he kicked him in the guts.

"I … I'm movin'," he said slowly, clearly intoxicated.

Ice was in his car with the key in the ignition when he came up with a plan.

"Stay here. I'm holla at Dead for a minute."

When he got out of his car, he had a plan that he was almost positive wouldn't work, but still, it was worth a chance. Since Dip was rolling with him to watch his back,

T. Styles

nobody he trusted would be at the house to see the drop off. But Dead would.

Ice called Deadman as he was trying to pull himself from in front of his house. *Damn! Dis nigga been drinkin' too long*, Ice thought.

"Yo, Dead!" Ice yelled.

He turned around.

"What you sippin' on tonight?"

"Sh ... shit," he stuttered. "Whatever you buyin'."

Ice reached in his pockets and pulled out fifty bucks.

"Here ... the next round's on me."

"What's the catch?" Dead asked, snatching the money before he had a chance to change his mind.

"No catch," he replied, wiping his goatee. "And there's more where that came from, on one condition."

"What's that?!" Dead responded.

"I need you to keep a lookout on my crib. If you see anybody pull up, write the tag number down."

"Okay," he laughed. "I'll put it in my planner." He continued laughing harder. He was so dirty, Ice couldn't see his face. "I don't know if you took a look, lil man, but I ain't got no pen or paper."

"You know what the fuck I mean, nigga!" Ice yelled, trying to take his respect back. "Rememba as much shit as you can."

Dead nodded a little and Ice slapped him upside his head.

"You gettin' this fool?!" Ice was starting to wonder if this drunk would even remember what he said five seconds from now, let alone a few hours.

"Uh ... yeah ... sho ... I got it," Dead responded, swaying from side to side just to keep his balance. "But what you do?"

Cold As Ice

Realizing he was wasting his time telling him anything, because Dead was nothing more than a worthless drunk who wouldn't remember shit, he said, "Fucked and murdered a young bitch. You gonna remember that?" he laughed.

With that he pushed him off and walked away. "Drunk-ass nigga!"

Seconds from Greatness

"There he go," Izzy said to Khoury as they sat outside of Addison Road subway station in a stolen blue Honda Accord Jordan hotwired earlier. Both of them watched Ice pull up in his Aston and park in the lot. "Text JD and tell 'im that nigga here!"

Khoury was checking their surroundings and noticed Ice was by himself. He thought for sure that he'd have at least one person with him.

"Somethin's up," Khoury advised Izzy. He'd sent the text to JD and was waiting on a response.

"Why you say that?" Izzy asked.

"'Cuz it don't feel right," he continued, scanning his surroundings again. "Why he givin' in so easy?"

"'Cuz he's a fuckin' molester! Either way I don't give a fuck. All I want is the dough."

Khoury wasn't buying it. There was something about his surroundings that messed with him. The normal watcher would see a girl strolling a baby, an old man and woman walking toward the escalators and a chick talking to some dude at the phone booth, but he saw a set up. A few seconds later Khoury received JD's message, which read, *"Affirmative."*

"He got it," Khoury advised, placing his phone back in his pocket. "I sho hope he gets away with this."

"He will. It's a piece of cake," Izzy laughed.

Ice walked slowly to the subway map. He tried to look around without making himself obvious. But because he

Cold As Ice

was a lover of time, he realized that with patience, he'd get his revenge. With the bag in his hands, he took a few sips from a McDonald's cup he was carrying and placed it inside, and then he threw it in the trash can. Afterwards, he took one last look at the pedestrians before stepping on the escalators, fifty G's shorter. As agreed, he walked to his car and drove out of the station, without confrontation.

"That nigga's gone!" Izzy said, sliding all the way down in the car seat. "He really rolled out! Oh shit!" Without wasting time, he called JD. "He's out!" he cheered. "Grab the dough, JD!"

"I already got it, man," JD advised.

When he got off his cell he said, "We 'bout to be paid!"

"That's how it looks," Khoury said, unenthused.

"You don't sound too happy," Izzy replied.

"I'll believe it when I see it."

With the bag in tow, Jordan ran down the escalators. He had more money in his hands than he'd ever seen. When he approached the exit doors he took two steps out, looked around and darted to the car.

Slamming the door shut, he said, "Behold, niggas." He opened the bag to let them see the crumpled money. "We bout to get pussy for days on account of this shit right here! And we splittin' it three ways."

"What about your sister and Pepper?" Khoury asked as he counted a few of the bills, Izzy helping them.

"What about 'em?"

Still No Turning Back

"Okay, I'm leaving now," Zykia said. "They got the money and he wants us to make the drop."

"Aight," Pepper responded. "But I want to tell you something."

"I don't know if I want to hear this," Zykia said as she grabbed her keys. "The last time you told me somethin' you showed me that fuckin' DVD. So unless it's important, I want you to save it until this is over."

"I made a copy," Pepper blurted.

"For what?!" she asked as she locked the door. "I want this to be over!"

"I want it to be over, too." Pepper replied. "But I thought about it. If we don't tell the cops, he'll get away with this. You heard what JD said. They're lookin' for this girl. What if she dead?"

"Don't say that, Pepper!"

"It's true!"

"Whateva you do," Zykia responded as they passed Old Lady Howard's fence, "leave me outta it." When they reached Pepper's house, Zykia said, "Now you stay right here."

"Aight," she said, looking around. "Be careful."

Zykia looked around and saw a few people doing regular shit. When the coast was clear, she crept past Deadman, who was passed out next to Ice's house. When she passed him, she had a feeling he was watching her. But when she

Cold As Ice

turned around, he wasn't. When she reached the steps to Ice's house, she placed the DVD in an old, empty flower pot. Then she ran down the stairs.

"Let's go!" Zykia yelled, grabbing Pepper's hand.

Pepper was right behind her.

———

"I can't believe dis lil nigga was bold enough to fuck wit' me," Ice said as he spoke to Dip on the phone.

"Yeah, well, he did," Dip responded. She was the lady talking to the man at the phone booth at the station earlier. When Ice let her out before him, she walked up to some bum-ass nigga who was on the phone, just to cause a diversion. And because she was wearing a black wig instead of her normal blond hair, it worked.

"I'ma fuck them lil niggas up!" Ice spat. "Who was wit' 'em?"

"I'm not sure, but it looked like Izzy and some other boy. I haven't seen him before."

"He have dreads?"

"Couldn't tell. He was stooped down real low in the seat."

"Where you at now?" Ice questioned.

"Just caught a cab."

"Cool," Ice responded, relieved she was on her way back so that she could grab the DVD and he could go after his money. "Go straight to my crib and see if they left the DVD."

"Where you goin'?"

"Dro and Pipes on their way to meet me at that lil nigga's house."

"You got them involved?" Dip asked, concerned.

"Yeah, but they don't know why they helpin' me murder dese lil niggas," Ice advised.

"Aight."

"Call me when you get the DVD."

"Got it."

"I hope so," he said, hanging up.

Jordan, Izzy and Khoury made it back to his house safely.

"This shit was too easy," Jordan bragged.

"Yeah!" Izzy added, on his dick as usual. "Let's divvy this shit up real quick 'cuz I already know what I'm buyin'."

"Maybe we shouldn't spend that dough just yet," Khoury advised.

"Why not?" Jordan asked. "We earned it."

"'Cuz if we're spendin' money out of nowhere, people are gonna start suspectin' stuff," Khoury added.

"Dis nigga's dumb," Izzy laughed.

"I'm serious, Izzy," Khoury continued. "JD, no offense but your moms is on that shit. So you showin' up with loot all of a sudden is kinda hot."

"Oh shit," Izzy laughed. "Dis nigga's raggin' on your peeps!"

"Is you raggin' on my moms?" Jordan asked, standing up and approaching him.

"I'm bein' real wit' you," Khoury responded, not backing down. "Ice ain't dumb, he's gonna be lookin' at everything and everybody now that he's out of fifty G's."

"Fuck you, nigga!" Jordan yelled. "Since you got a problem wit' this, you ain't gettin' none of it." He continued spreading the money on the table.

"I'm out!" he said, walking out the door. "Just remember I warned y'all."

"Nigga, get the fuck out of my house and lock my door

behind you!"

"I guess we splittin' the pie two ways now." Izzy smiled.

"Yep, that's one unlucky mothafucka."

Pepper and Zykia were walking down the dark street when they spotted Khoury.

"Ain't that Khoury?" Pepper asked, unsure because it was dark.

"Yeah, that's him," she confirmed.

"Where's his boys?" Pepper joked.

"Khoury's cool," Zykia said under her breath. "If you notice, he ain't say shit when my brother was bein' greedy earlier."

"Yeah, he ain't say shit," Pepper responded sarcastically. "Good or bad." Pepper didn't want to admit it, but she peeped his quietness, too. "Anyway he's still cool with JD so for real, I don't like him."

"I don't think y'all want to go to your house now," Khoury advised, approaching them. "JD's on a power trip," he continued as they stopped in front of Old Lady Howard's house.

"Why you ain't wit' 'em?" Pepper interjected. "They're your friends."

"'Cuz I'm not tryin' to be involved in that," he said, waving them off. "But I'll get up wit' y'all layda."

He was walking away until he suddenly stopped dead in his tracks.

Turning back toward them he said, "Walk toward the fence real slowly and don't look across the street."

"Why?" Zykia asked, frustrated with everything. All she wanted was to go home and go to sleep.

"Yeah, what's up?" Pepper added.

"Ice is on the other side of the street walking in the direction of your house."

Asking no more questions, the three of them dipped behind Old Lady Howard's fence. Thick trees, long grass and the unattended grounds hid them well.

"Oh my God!" Pepper said, looking through the wired fence. "He must be looking for us!"

"Or us," Khoury replied.

"We're dead," Zykia said.

———

"Dem lil niggas in there," Dro responded as he peeped through the window. "How many you said we're lookin' for?"

"Two and a possible third," Ice responded. "You see my money?" Ice asked, two .45s in hand.

"Yep," Pipes replied.

"Let's move," Ice responded, giving the word.

Without discussing the details, Dro kicked down the door.

"Oh shit!" Khoury responded upon seeing them run up into JD's house.

"Oh God!" Zykia cried, trying to run over to the house. "I have to go help him!"

Khoury grabbed her while she was kicking and screaming. Pepper helped him.

"Listen, Zy!" Khoury yelled, trying to talk to her. "Listen to me." When he saw she was partially calmed down he continued. "If you go in there, he'll kill you. Do you wanna die?"

"What about my brother?" she sobbed. "They gonna hurt him!"

"I don't know," he said softly. "But I do know you ain't no good to him if you go in there now. Let's just chill and see what happens."

Cold As Ice

"I'm sorry, Ice!" Izzy cried. "This was Jordan's idea. I ain't want nothin' to do with takin' your money."

Without saying anything else, Ice took the butt of one gun and cracked his teeth out, and watched as three of them rolled out on the floor, hunks of his gums still attached. Izzy fell to his knees, holding his bleeding mouth.

"Don't say shit unless I tell you to," he warned. He didn't want jabber jaws saying too much about the DVD. As far as Dro and Pipes knew, this was a drug deal gone bad. "Is this all my money?"

"Yeah," Jordan replied, scared shitless. "It's all there."

"Man, why you give dese lil niggas shit?" Dro asked.

"Yeah, man," Pipes confirmed.

"Layda for dat shit," Ice responded.

They looked at each other and shook their heads.

"It's all there, I promise. We ain't got the DVD though," Jordan cried as his softhearted friend lay helplessly on the floor. "You can count it if you want to."

"*DVD?*" Dro and Pipes repeated.

Ice looked at them and said nothing.

"I think I will," Ice responded. "Count that shit, Dro."

Dro complied as Pipes and Ice kept the burners on them.

"I counted fifty G's," Dro advised.

"Fifty G's? Y'all tryin' to play me? Where's the rest of my money?" Ice asked as he cocked his gun.

"It's all there!" Jordan replied. "We only took fifty and every penny is there."

"Man, what the fuck is goin' on?" Dro asked, more confused than ever.

"What's goin on is this," Ice said as he let out four shots.

T. Styles

Boom. Boom. Boom. Boom.

Four bodies dropped, and Ice placed the money back in the McDonald's bag and hit the door, with no witnesses standing.

Zykia cried in Khoury's arms when the shots rang out. "Jordan!" she sobbed. "My brother's dead!"

"Ssshhh," Khoury advised.

Pepper was trying to maintain her composure. She had to deal with the fact that this was all her fault. All she'd wanted to do was get away from the projects. But she'd let greed consume her, and now it was too late. Her best friend may have lost her brother and they could possibly lose their lives.

"There he goes," Khoury replied. "Be quiet!"

———

"There he goes," is what Ice heard on the other side of the street.

When he looked around, he couldn't see anybody. This was usually the case whenever shots were fired. No one wanted to be a witness in case the cops came knocking.

But just to be sure, he moved toward Old Lady Howard's fence, since the sound came from that direction. Ice was all prepared to unload if need be.

"Who over there?" he asked, gun in hand, as he pushed some of her overgrown trees aside. "I said who's here?!"

Silence.

He moved closer to the fence and was preparing to go in until he heard, *Woof, woof, woof!*

"Oh shit!" He jumped upon seeing the dog. "Fuckin' mutt!" he continued, bouncing off.

When the dog had gone running out toward Ice, it had frightened them. They'd forgotten she had a dog when they

Cold As Ice

hid in her yard. Old Lady Howard let him out at night to keep thugs off of her property, but as filthy as it looked, she didn't have anything to worry about.

Pepper, Khoury and Zykia were distraught, but were able to get away from the scene when the dog came out. As the night progressed, things got even more out of control.

Excuses in the Face of Evil

"The cab broke down," Dip responded to Ice on the phone as he walked toward his house.

"So basically, you sayin' you ain't been here yet?" he continued, approaching the steps on his porch.

"It wasn't my fault," Dip responded.

Ice hung up, not wanting to hear excuses. All he wanted was that DVD in his hands and a chance to return to normalcy, as he knew it anyway. He searched everywhere around the yard looking for that DVD, including a flower pot he kept in front of his house that was used to stash drugs. With all of the searching, he still came up short.

"Where in the fuck is it?!" he asked out loud.

He was preparing to walk back to Jordan's house, thinking it was there, when he heard, "Lookin' for this?"

He turned around and saw Deadman holding the white DVD case in his hand, standing up straight, his speech clear, not slurred.

"Aw shit," Ice laughed. "Let me find out your bum ass looked out after all."

"Sho did," he responded, approaching him. "Now it's time for you to pay me."

"Not a problem, old man," he replied, snatching the case. "I got you."

"When?" Deadman questioned.

"When hell freezes over," he laughed. "But good lookin' out on this. It's time to celebrate."

He ran up his steps, turning his back on Deadman. He

Cold As Ice

didn't hear the footsteps that were coming his way, but he did feel a stinging sensation in his back.

"What the fuck?" Ice cried, realizing he had been stabbed.

When he turned around he saw Deadman standing in front of him, and then he felt a pressure in his stomach. Ice fell against his door.

"How does it feel?" Deadman asked, watching him slide down.

Ice tried to pull his gun, but didn't have the strength.

"What did I do to you?" he asked, looking at the blood on his hands. "I was gonna pay you, man."

"Do you remember Crystal?"

"N ... no," he lied.

Deadman stabbed him again. "Next time I'm slicin' your throat. There's still time to call the ambulance to get you some help if you come clean."

Ice suddenly noticed that Deadman was coherent.

"Now, do you know Crystal Hyatt?"

"Yeah, man, shit!" he replied, giving in to the pain.

"Did you kill my daughter?"

Ice looked into his eyes, slowly slipping out of consciousness.

"No," Ice lied.

"Even on your death bed you check in for hell," Deadman responded. "But I saw what you did to my daughter on this DVD. So the last thing I want you to see is my face. I spent two months sleeping on the streets in front of your house just to find out the truth. I lost my wife because she thought I was ignoring the rest of my family, my oldest daughter because she thought I didn't love her, and my house because I couldn't work without finding out what happened to Crystal," he continued, sprinkles of spit escaping his mouth, falling on Ice's face. "And you know what? It will finally be worth it when I see the life leave your eyes."

Not saying another word, he slit his throat.

Cold As Ice

The Calm After the Storm

"Y'all take the last of that stuff and put it in the truck," Grace said to Pepper and Zykia.

"Okay, ma," Pepper replied as Zykia grabbed one of the boxes, too.

They were finally leaving 58th. And although they weren't moving to a new house in Virginia, they *were* moving somewhere safe. Grace was renting an apartment in Laurel, Maryland. She convinced Zykia's mother to let her move with them.

"You want me to carry anything?" Khoury asked.

"Yes, baby, if you can lift those boxes that will be good." When she hit the corner he stole a kiss from Pepper.

"I saw that!" Grace yelled.

The two of them giggled and got back to business. Most of their things were inside the truck when Pepper passed Khoury with a box in her hands. She put it inside the U-Haul truck.

"Pepper."

She turned around and saw Deadman, all cleaned up and standing before her. He looked like Morgan Freeman.

"Deadman? Is that you?" Pepper questioned, not believing her eyes.

"Yes."

"Wow. You look … different," she said, staring him down, making sure everybody was in the house.

"Thanks. I wanted to give you something I think belongs to you."

T. Styles

He reached into his pocket and handed her an envelope. "Go ahead, open it."

She took the envelope, not knowing what it was or why he was giving it to her. When she looked inside, her mouth dropped open. Enclosed were sixty one-hundred-dollar bills.

"What's this for?"

"It's the money from the night Ice was killed."

Pepper looked at him in fright. Up until that point, she figured somebody robbed him for the money.

"You killed Ice? Why?"

"That girl on the DVD ... was my daughter. And I've been sleeping out here for two months trying to get some answers. I finally did the night things kicked off."

"But you was sleeping on the ground every day."

"It was hard, but I had to know the truth. I got a lead that Ice knew something. But when I saw what kind of person he was, I knew he'd never tell me. So I'd come out here night after night. Eventually I got fed up and had my nephews run up in his place looking for clues. But one of them dropped the one thing I didn't even know existed, the DVD."

"But ... I don't get it," she responded, still shocked. "How did you know I was involved?"

"I saw you and Zykia drop the DVD off. So I put one and one together."

"What is your real name?"

"Craig Hyatt."

"Oh ... thank you, Mr. Hyatt."

"I would've given you more, but the rest is going to a foundation in her name. I'm glad y'all are getting out of here," he said, looking around.

"Me, too. Thanks for everything. But can I ask you

Cold As Ice

something?"

"Sure."

"Do you have the DVD?"

"Yes ... but I destroyed it. My family's been through enough. I told them I can't say how, but I know for certain she's in a better place. I don't want them involved in the media. I've lost their trust and I'm going to spend a lot of time getting them back, so I'd appreciate it if you kept our little secret."

"I will." She smiled.

"Tell Zykia I said goodbye, and you two be safe."

"We will," she said as she held the money pack firmly. "But what about Dip?"

He turned around and said, "I pray if our paths cross, that I have enough strength not to send her to meet her son, but I can't make any promises. Goodbye, Pepper."

When she watched Mr. Hyatt get into the same van that the thieves who had robbed Ice had driven, she still couldn't believe her eyes. He loved his daughter so much that he played himself off as a bum just to find the truth. She was still thinking about him when Dip rolled up on her two minutes later.

"So you finally leaving 58th, huh?" she asked from Ice's car.

Pepper nodded, her heart beating rapidly.

"You know what they say though," Dip started, smoking a Black & Mild with the window down. "You can take a thief out the hood, but it doesn't mean they'll live. Watch your back."

Pepper kept her eyes on Dip, lifted her shirt in the back and pulled out the copy of the DVD she held.

"And you watch yours," she said, waving her copy.

"I will Reds ... I will."

T. Styles

"What she want?" Khoury asked, kissing Pepper's cheek and watching her pull off.

"Nothing, baby," she smiled, tucking the DVD in the front of her pants. "Nothing."

Cold As Ice

T. Styles

B-MORE LOVE

Leo Sullivan

Triple Crown Publications presents . . .

236

B–More Love

One

Ashley

I sat in my sixth period class at Southwestern Senior High School bored to death as my English teacher, Ms. Crabapple, an aging amicable white woman with a cherub face, rosy cheeks and a short, round body, stood at the blackboard going over the day's assignment. Suddenly, my name was called over the P.A. system. Heads turned in my direction. At first, I wasn't certain it was my name being called until the acoustic static blared again, "Ashley Gray, report to the Principal's office immediately!"

My heart pounded in my chest as a slight murmur of whispers rose in the classroom and everyone stared at me. That day, I was rockin' my new Baby Phat blue jean skirt set and opened-toed sandals. As I gathered my things and walked by Rasheed's desk, he stuck his foot out and playfully tried to trip me. I stepped on his foot and swung my book bag, barely missing his head. A chorus of laughter erupted. Just as he was about to throw his English book at me, Ms. Crabapple turned around.

"Rasheed!"

She'd caught him in the act. As I walked out the door, I wondered what the Principal wanted with me. I quickly decided it could only be about one thing—my sister, Vanessa. She was a hell-raiser. It was only her freshman year, but she had already gotten into three fights, cut a girl in the face with a razor and had been suspended twice.

Leo Sullivan

I entered the Principal's office with a feeling of apprehension and dread. Mr. Brown, our high school Principal, met me at the door with a sympathetic expression on his face as he fumbled with his necktie. I noticed the jittery movement of his hands. He cleared his throat and spoke in a deep baritone voice that sent chills down my spine.

"Your mother has just been taken to Bond Secure Hospital."

"For what?!" I raised my voice. My book bag fell to the floor. He looked at me surprised and shrugged his shoulders, weary, like a man lost for words.

Finally he answered, "Ashley, I don't know … I honestly don't know." I noticed he interlocked his fingers in front of his chest.

"Do you need any change for the bus?" he asked as he watched me pick my book bag up off of the floor.

"No," I replied, "but you can tell my sister to pick Jasmine up from school."

"Vanessa didn't come to school today," the Principal responded, knotting his brow.

"But I drove her—" the words slipped out of my mouth by mistake. Not only had I told on my sister, I let it slip that I drove a car. Even though I was seventeen, with a driver's permit, I still had to have an adult with me when I drove. Principal Brown gave me a knowing glare the way a father would. He started to say something but changed his mind. I turned and walked out of his office.

o o o o

It was a beautiful day outside, full of cotton candy clouds and a large majestic sun. I walked briskly to my car in the parking lot, a late model '93 Camry. I had saved almost two years to buy it by working at McDonald's.

Times were extremely hard for my family. I was the oldest,

with two younger sisters. Jasmine was six going on twenty-six and Vanessa was fifteen. She was in a rebellious stage where she fought constantly. We lived on Montford and Jefferson in East Baltimore, one of the worst neighborhoods in the city. It was poverty-stricken and crime-ridden, full of crack heads, prostitutes and ghetto superstar drug dealers. I was determined to make it out of the ghetto and looked forward to going to college after I graduated from high school.

I had to succeed.

I had to.

o o o o

When I arrived at Bond Secure Hospital, the emergency room was jam-packed. The stench of unwashed bodies and cheap disinfectant permeated the air. I noticed a trail of crimson-colored blood that led to the nurse's station. Somewhere in the distance, a police radio blared. A woman was cradling her baby while vehemently arguing with a nurse. A stretcher was wheeled past me followed by a host of distraught-looking medical staff. As I approached the counter, I noticed a pregnant girl around my age. "I don't know how the crack cocaine got in my system," she said innocently, trying to persuade a Vietnamese-looking doctor, but he was not buying her story. The girl began to cry. The doctor was impassive to her tears. I tore my eyes away from them.

"Ma'am, I'm lookin' for my Mama." My voice cracked with emotion as I tried my best to ignore what was going on around me. The nurse at the desk was a pleasant-looking Spanish lady. She had small hoop earrings and wore her long, black hair in a perfect chignon. Her full lips hinted at a smile as she looked up from several folders on her desk. I detected something in her face that said she'd rather be someplace else. What she didn't know was the feeling was mutual.

Leo Sullivan

"What is your mother's name?" she asked in a nasally voice. Just as I was about to answer, to my right, the woman who was cradling the baby began screaming and hollering.

"My baby ain't breathin! Somebody please help me!"

The doctor rushed over into the commotion. I had not been in the hospital three minutes and already the pain and suffering was too much to bear.

"What is your mother's name?" the nurse asked for the second time. I turned back around to face her.

"Um, Tonya Gray," I said in a small voice, shuffling my feet uncomfortably. I felt something sticky under the bottom of my shoes. I didn't want to check to see what it was. All I wanted was to find my Mama and take her home with me.

Someone bumped into me. I spun around and saw a dude with a deep gash in his forehead, like maybe someone hit him with an ax. I frowned. The nurse looked up from a computer screen.

"She's in room 511. Take the elevator over there." She pointed down the hall.

"Ma'am, uh, could you tell me what my Mama's here fo'?"

"Sure," she said brightly and looked at her computer screen again. I watched her entire facial expression change as her eyes grew wide. "Hummm, you might want to talk with her doctor."

"But you just said—"

"I'm sorry," she interrupted me, "her doctor's name is Turner," she said curtly and turned away from me. I stood there for a moment in a daze.

"Excuse you!" a prudish voice huffed from behind me. I turned around and met the angry glare of a fat chick with an attitude. She was dark skinned, blue-black, with a wave of blond hair. I turned and walked away, my sandals sticking on the marble floors. The chaos of caustic madness threatened to

B-More Love

envelop me as I tried to bridle my sanity.

o o o o

I exited the elevator on the fifth floor with a white woman. She had a box of candy, a bouquet of red roses and a ready smile for anyone who looked at her. The fifth floor was much quieter. I could hear the hum of the hospital and my shoes sticking to the floor. I walked down the hallway, checking each number on the room doors: 508 … 509 … 510. There it was, 511.

I walked inside with my heart pounding in my chest. The theme music for *"The Price is Right"* blared from a television beside one of the beds in the room. In the bed lay an elderly, sepia-complexioned woman. Her nappy hair was gray with two long braids on each side, parted down the middle. In the adjacent bed I saw a woman's head as I padded closer.

It was Mama. My legs almost buckled. My chest heaved so hard, I couldn't breathe. I raced over to her. Her eyes were closed. Her mouth was slightly opened and she had a tube running through her nose, an IV in her arm and other medical devices connected to a machine that chimed a persistent beep.

"Mama?" I said in a shaky voice that usually signaled I was about to cry. Her brown eyes fluttered open. I grabbed her hand. She squeezed tight. "Mama, what happened?" I asked with my bottom lip trembling, tears filling my eyes. She primed her lips with a dry tongue and tried to speak but winced.

"Baby … remember the past few months I had been unable to work?" I nodded my head. She cringed again, squeezing my hand harder. It was obvious she was in a lot of pain.

"Mama, what's wrong?" I raised my voice. The old woman in the next bed stirred in her sleep.

"I was having … oh umph … awful headaches. They were so bad I couldn't walk. I passed out on my way to the unemployment office this morning." Mama stopped talking and

Leo Sullivan

pinched her eyes closed. She grimaced in pain. I noticed a tear in the corner of her eye. It glistened but did not fall.

"They think … may have found something on my brain. I'ma need you to be strong—"

"Nooo, Mama, nooo! Found what?" I couldn't help it, couldn't hold it. My Mama was my best friend, my everything. I began to sob uncontrollably. The old woman in the next bed awakened and closed the divider curtain.

"They can't be certain until they run more tests." Mama winced again, causing her eyebrows to knot up. The lone tear brimmed in the corner of her eye. I kneeled, laying my head on her chest, crying hysterically like a three-year-old.

"Naw, Mama you gotta come home with us … with me. You gotta leave here!" I sobbed mournfully.

"I can't, baby," she cooed, caressing my hair.

"Why? What they talking 'bout they found on your brain?"

"They … they think they might have found cancer," she said softly.

My Mama was a strong black woman. I'd only seen her cry once and that was when her mother died, also from cancer. I raised my head off of her chest and the tear in the corner of her eye slid down her ebony cheek. She held me in her arms and cried. We cried, mother and daughter holding onto each other as if it was the end of the world and in some ways, it was.

"Awh, awh," she moaned, closing her eyes tightly as she grabbed her head like I had been seeing her do around the house lately. She moved her arm to wipe at her tears, almost toppling over her IV.

"Ashley, you'll be eighteen soon. I want … you to take care of your sisters until I come home. The rent money is in my closet on the top shelf under some clothes … rent's overdue … tell Frank to give you some money."

B-More Love

"Frank!" I frowned, dismayed. He was her no good, live-in boyfriend. I couldn't stand his ass and just the thought of him filled me with more dread. It was bad enough I had to watch my Mama lie in bed suffering, it broke my heart, but to even think about Frank made me sick.

Then she began to moan and groan, writhing in the bed. She was only thirty-seven, but in only a few hours, the ravishing pain that had seized her brain made her appear as if she'd aged ten years. It was too much to see my beloved mother suffering. I pushed the call button for the nurse.

"Mama, can you hear me?" I sniffled. She bit down on her lip with a subtle nod and more tears soaked her cheeks. I wiped at them, smearing them with my own. The nurse walked in, followed by the doctor. "My Mama is in a lot of pain. Please help her," I cried in fitful sobs.

The doctor was a tall, handsome white man in his forties. He walked over and placed his hand atop hers and spoke in a congenial tone that exuded compassion for human life.

"Ms. Gray ... Ms. Gray, can you hear me?" he asked, stroking her hand.

No answer.

The doctor gave the nurse a disturbed look. Instantly I caught on. Something was wrong, terribly wrong. I lost it.

"Mama! Mama!" I screamed at the top of my lungs.

The nurse tried to calm me and tugged at my arm. "Please step outside the room—"

"Noo! Noo! Mama wake up ... wake up!" I wailed, shoving the nurse's hands off me. The doctor began to frantically check Mama's vital signs. The doctor brushed over a tuft of blond hair that had fallen over his forehead as he spoke to the nurse in an urgent tone.

"This is a code red. I want you to prepare for emergency

Leo Sullivan

surgery. STAT!'"

As the nurse hurried off, the doctor turned to me and placed a gentle hand on my shoulder, holding it firmly. His eyes were transparent, the bluest I have ever seen.

"Your mother is not doing well. She's going to need all the support and help you can give her. Do you understand?"

"Yes," I said, swallowing hard.

"Go home, be strong and say a prayer for her. There's nothing you can do for her right now," he said, patting my back.

"But I don't want to leave her alone," I pouted ruefully, on the verge of a tantrum.

"The surgery is going to go well into the evening. Come back tomorrow. Hopefully once we go in, we can do something to stop the cancer from spreading."

"What are her chances?" I asked, throwing words at him.

He pressed his thin lips together until they formed a line. "Not good," he said with a deep sigh and wiped at the tuft of hair on his forehead, looking like this was the hardest part of his job. "Your mother waited too long to come to the hospital."

"What are her chances?" I asked again, this time raising my voice just as a group of hospital staff rushed into the room.

"Maybe ten percent," he finally said.

"Oh, Mama!" I cried direfully as they whisked her past me. I reached out to touch her hand but missed, grabbing the sheet.

"Go home, get some rest," the doctor said as he followed in the direction of the staff, his white coat billowing over his backside.

I staggered to the elevator in a fugue as I continued to cry. *This can't be happening to me, oh Lord, what about my two sisters? What am I going to tell them ... what am I going to do?*

B-More Love

Two

Jamal Lawson a.k.a. Jackie Boy

For the third time, my nigga Rock and I went over the plan as we sat parked in a stolen Chevy Caprice. We were about to rob the gambling joint The Spot Pool Hall, located on Greenmont Avenue and 25th Street. Every Friday, the pool hall was closed to the public in the daytime, but open to an esoteric group of choice niggas with long cheddar: hustlers, ballers, shot callers and the elite the of drug dealers. You had to have ten grand or more just to get in the door. The problem was getting inside the side entrance. It had two steel reinforced doors, and old man Humphrey, who didn't take no shit. He ran the pool hall with an iron fist. It took me years, but finally I had figured out how to pull the robbery off.

Ever since I was a shawty, grindin' on the corner, touchin' niggas for a livin', I used to watch all the new Lexuses and big Benzes pull up in the trash-littered parking lot and dream about laying them down, taking their shit. Oh, and I was an equal opportunity nigga, too, meaning if a nigga ain't got no muscle in his hustle, and I catch you slippin', I'm grippin'. A bitch can get it, too. Like I said, I don't discriminate. A nigga tryna eat, namean?

One day while I was on the corner daydreaming about hitting a nice lick, I watched a delivery boy pull up to the side door of the pool hall. He was delivering food. Once they identified him through the peep hole, they opened the door. That's when

Leo Sullivan

the idea hit me: food! I would disguise myself as a delivery boy. Yeah, get me a baseball hat, some dark shades and knock on that door. For me, that would be like the fox dressed in sheep's clothes.

Old man Humphrey was dangerous. He had already shot a dude who tried to rob his establishment, so I knew if I didn't pull it off right, he would "buck the jack" and that was what made the caper extremely dangerous. I had been touchin' niggas ever since I was thirteen. I was famous in the hood.

If old man Humphrey looked though the peep hole and saw me, he would bolt the locks and scream for someone to call the police, or worse, open the door and start blastin'. That was one of my concerns. The other one was the fact that no one had ordered food and that might make them suspicious about opening the door. I knew it was a big risk, but if we pulled it off, the take would be two or three hundred grand, or better; but at the time, I can't lie, I was on my dick doin' bad as a muhfa.

Me and Rock went way back to grade school, juvy and twistin' bitches' backs out, running a train on them at his ole girl's crib while she was at work. He was dark skinned with a chipped front tooth that gave him a sinister look when he grinned. At the time, he was fresh out of jail after serving eight months for a possession of cocaine charge. He needed a come up, and this was it.

"Yo, I'ma knock on the door with food in my hand and look at the ground, so whoever look out don't get a good look at my face. If they open the door, it's on and poppin'!"

"But s'pose they don't open it?" Rock asked, picking up the sawed-off 12 gauge from the floor just as two chicks passed by. It was Destiny and Nicole, both hood rats. They looked at us like they knew we were up to something.

"Bitch, wha'cha lookin' at?" Rock yelled out the window.

B-More Love

"Nigga, it ain't yo' broke ass!" Destiny retorted.

"All they finna do is try ta jack somebody." Nicole had to put her two cents in.

"Yo' funky ass need ta get a job so a nigga can rob you," I cracked on her as I watched Nicole's ass shake from side to side. "Dat ass shole done got phat since she had that baby," I commented to Rock.

"Heads up! Heads up!" A cop car was doing a slow creep headed straight for us. The guns were on the seat. I held my breath, watched as they passed and sighed in relief. They were too busy looking at all the expensive whips parked in the lot next to the pool hall.

I placed my nine in my drawers and the sawed-off under the crook of my arm, all the while feeling an adrenaline rush like I had jumped off of a building, one hundred stories high. My heart was beating fast. Rock had a .357. His job was to gather up all the money as I held everyone at gunpoint.

I knew whoever answered the door, Humphrey or a hired henchman, would be heavily armed.

"Let's do this, my nigga!" I said with vim. I pulled the cap down over my forehead and placed the shades on. With my weapons concealed, I grabbed both bags of food off the seat.

I was a young nigga, eighteen, about to take a hell of a chance fuckin' with dem ole heads. As I got out the car, I heard Rock's door close behind me, but I didn't look back. I moved forward with determined strides, those of purposeful intent.

In the hood, life was strange. I must have looked like the Grim Reaper in my disguise because people were walking to the other side of the street to avoid us, trying to get the fuck out of the way. I glanced behind me and saw Rock make a stop at the pay phone as planned. He gave me a subtle nod. For some reason, I hesitated before I knocked, but glanced up at the sky. It

Leo Sullivan

was a beautiful day with an ardent, bright sun. A light breeze brushed against my face. I realized I was perspiring. A little boy wearing threadbare, raggedy blue jeans meandered up to me, staring at the bag of food. He licked his lips.

"Man, yo' bag leakin'," he said and walked off. I looked down and some of the barbeque sauce in the bag had opened up, spilling inside.

Fuck it, I thought and knocked on the door. The shotgun was starting to slide from under my arm. Furtively, I reached under my shirt to position it just as a deep baritone voice bellowed, "Who is it?"

The voice sounded like it belonged to Humphrey. I tilted my head forward. "Delivery! Somebody here order some ribs, fried chicken, cheeseburgers and French fries?"

Silence.

I noticed my shirt moving. My heart was beating at record speed.

"Hold up a second," the voice returned. That was the last thing I wanted to hear. Whoever it was, I couldn't chance them walking away to go get somebody.

"Man, the damn bag busted. I'ma have to take it back. Y'all already had me waiting out here for an hour!"

I waited and watched the streets. My left leg started trembling and I glanced over at Rock. His eyes were wide, full of anticipation. Then suddenly, I heard steel door locks being released. My breath lodged in my throat. The door opened, making a squeaking sound and a head peered out. I went into action, dropped the bags and pulled out the shotgun all in one quick motion. I struck dude in the face with the butt of the weapon and pushed my way inside with Rock behind me.

It was on.

B-More Love

Three

Jamal

As usual in the ghetto, the streets were watching as we rushed inside, pistols in our hands. To my surprise, it wasn't old man Humphrey who had opened the door. It was an old cat named J.B. He had been getting money hustling since back in the day in the dope game, selling heroin. J.B. alone was a meal ticket. He drove a new 600 Benz, fucked a lot of young chicks and stunted, wearing too much ice. I pressed the shotgun under his chin, felt around under his waistband and found a Glock nine.

"I'ma do your fuckin' ass right here nigga if you make a sound."

Fear shown in his eyes as he nodded his head. A trickle of blood came from the open gash on his forehead. In the darkened vestibule, with my disguise on, I was certain he couldn't see my face, but I still pulled the scarf over my nose and mouth. Rock put his ski mask on. We quickly duct taped J.B.'s hands and mouth. Moving fast, as planned, we were on schedule.

The next door led to the pool hall. From this point forward, we would have to inflict as much fear as possible. On the other side of the door we heard the loud clamor of voices. I had counted at least twenty people entering the pool hall that morning. I was sure half of them were strapped, so I prepared myself for the worst.

Rock and I exchanged knowing glances as he held his pistol to the back of J.B.'s head. I took out my Glock with the sawed-

Leo Sullivan

off in my other hand and expelled a sigh.

"Let's get this money, my nigga," I exhorted. The second part of the plan was underway.

Rock turned the doorknob. It opened with a snap. Niggas inside gambling didn't notice us. I shoved a bound J.B. through the door with so much force he fell, sliding across the wooden floor on his face.

Kaboom! I let loose with the 12 gauge, firing a shot up into the ceiling, causing paint and paneling to fall.

"Everybody get da fuck down! Dis is a jack! Don't make dis a muthafuckin' murder!" I yelled, walking up. Niggas dove to the floor like it was a swimming pool. A fog of smoke hung over the pool tables. With caution, I watched, my eyes trained to spot anything that moved. I heard a few muffled complaints but all complied.

I saw a pile of money on the pool table, and watched as my nigga Rock worked with meticulous care, searching each vic, relieving them of their cash and jewelry. The pillowcase he used was already half full. It was more money than we had expected. Box Stale's old ass looked up at me from the floor as Rock took his Rolex and a wad of cash off of him. I saw nothing but seething hate in Box Stale's eyes.

Back in the day, he used to have the block on lock. I used to admire him, wanted to be like him, but the nigga was cheap—wouldn't pay his workers. He'd front crack to junkies and brutalize them. He was the kind of nigga that made it hard on the streets for a nigga to eat.

"Nigga, you must not know who you fuckin' wit'. I'ma find yo' family—"

"My family? My family?" I raved and ran over and kicked him in the face, one, two, three times. "My family?!" I jumped up and stomped on his head with both feet and blood squirted everywhere. He was knocked out cold. "How in da fuck you gonna threaten me, nigga?"

Afterward, quiet hummed as Rock continued to go from man to man. Already he had collected seven burners. A few niggas grumbled, complaining when he took their wedding rings, but we kept it moving. Finally, there was the loot on the pool table.

Rock was standing next to a door that led to a back room. Just as he bent over to sweep the piles of hundred dollar bills into the pillowcase, I thought I saw a glimmer in his eyes.

Then out of the blue, the door next to Rock swung open. I had forgotten all about the back room. Time slowed down to a surrealistic slow-motion as I caught a glimpse of old man Humphrey standing in the shadows of the doorway. His face was twisted in an evil scowl as he held a shotgun in his hands.

"Look out!" I hollered to Rock.

It was too late. As he spun around, Humphrey fired. An orange blast came out of the muzzle of the shotgun. The impact lifted Rock, propelling him over the pool table. I ran over to the door.

Boom! Boom! Boom! Kaboom! I shot wildly with both the nine then the shotgun. Humphrey had moved out of the shadows of the doorway. Blue smoke billowed as my ears rang. In my peripheral vision, I saw someone move. I shot them and a voice screamed in agony. Someone else moved. I shot them, too.

Just that fast, things had gone bad. I fought the urge to run through the door and kill Humphrey. I walked over and looked down at Rock. He had a gaping hole in his chest the size of a softball. He panted and moaned. He was covered in his own blood, more blood than I had ever seen in my life. Enraged, I shot a man trying to hide under a pool table. I aimed and fired two more shots into the shadows of the doorway to keep old man Humphrey at bay.

Leo Sullivan

I bent down and pulled up Rock's ski mask. His eyes gaunt, they fulgurated both terror and fear. He still clinched the pillowcase in one hand and his pistol in the other. As I reached to pick him up, I saw a shadow in the doorway move. I fired again.

"Come on, my nigga. Let's go," I said, reaching for Rock. He shook his head and tried to hand me the pillowcase stuffed with money.

"Gon' man. Leave me. I can't make it. Go!"

Just then I heard police sirens. "Nigga, put yo' arm 'round my neck! Dawg, you came wit' me … you leavin' wit' me!"

I hoisted him up and carried his limp body to the door, certain that Humphrey or someone was going to shoot me in the back. I heard Rock make a gurgling sound, then take a deep breath. I prayed it was not his last.

Finally, I dragged Rock out of the second steel door. The sun momentarily blinded me. The large crowd of people that had gathered outside the pool hall scattered. A police car came to a screeching halt a few feet in front of us. I let loose with the 12 gauge, shattering the windshield. I had injured one of the cops, the driver. The passenger looked to be about my age and he returned fire. Bullets whistled past my head as we exchanged gunfire. The young cop stayed with his partner and waited for backup as I dragged Rock's body around the corner thirty or so yards to the awaiting car.

I opened the car door, slid Rock in and propped his body against the door. My clothes were drenched with blood. As I got in the car, I turned the ignition, put the car in reverse and backed out. I took the back street undetected.

"I'ma get you some help. You fucked up bad, yo," I said and looked over at Rock. His eyes were open. The stench of blood filled my nostrils. Rock clinched the pillowcase with one hand and his burner with the other.

Police cars sped past us, going one direction while we went in the opposite. Suddenly, it dawned on me that Rock had not answered. I slowly turned and looked at him just as I pulled into the hospital entrance.

His opaque eyes stared straight ahead at something that neither one of us was supposed to see at such an early age: DEATH. It then dawned on me, painfully. The deep breath I had heard him take as I dragged him out of the pool hall had been his last. I killed the ignition in the parking lot and held onto the steering wheel with blood smeared on my hands. I peered out the window. I did not want to look at him like that. Not in death, not ever.

I swallowed hard. "Oh man! Fuck!" I slammed my fist on the dashboard. "I'ma ... I'ma ... make sure yo' mom and little girl get your half of the money," I said, choked up on the verge of tears. I looked in the sky and saw a low flying helicopter. I knew by now the car was hot and I needed to get moving.

I reached for the pillowcase in Rock's hand. He had a death grip on it. I had to peel his fingers off of it. I took off my shirt and dumped the contents out of the bloody pillowcase. It had to at least be over a hundred grand, not counting all of the expensive jewelry. I placed the Glock in my pocket and grabbed a towel off the back seat and began to wipe my prints off of everything I had touched. I wrapped the shotgun neatly in the towel then watched as an ambulance pulled into the Emergency section of the hospital.

I took one last long look at Rock. I don't know why, but I reached over and closed his eyes. Perfect in death as he was in life. His pistol was in his hand and he was hunched over slightly with his eyes closed ... dead at seventeen. In my world, the ghetto, that was keeping it gangsta!

Leo Sullivan

Four

Jamal

As I passed the hospital entrance, about to walk between two cops, I saw Ashley sitting on the sidewalk, crying. Her hair looked a mess; her eyes were all swollen and red as sobs racked her body. She was crying hysterically. I stopped dead in my tracks.

I had a crush on Ashley since we was shorties in sixth grade. Ashley had a phat ass just like Serena Williams, only with a much slimmer waist and a prettier face. She wore her long, silky hair straight. It cascaded down her shoulders like one of them exotic model chicks. She was pristine and sophisticated, the kind of chick that made a thug nigga like me wanna hang up his tools and wife her ass.

Ashley Gray was also stuck up as shit and couldn't stand my ass. She always said I was a bad boy. Rumor was, she was still a virgin. I wanted to hit that ass, but the only conversation I could get out of her was a heated argument. She said she hated cats who robbed for a living. I told her I was doing a community service—I only robbed drug dealers. She turned up her nose at me. A few days later, she walked past while I was robbing a substitute teacher. I knew in her eyes it made me look bad, but dude tried me with some gay shit.

"Ashley!" I called her name.

Startled, she looked up at me. The sunlight accentuated the brown flecks in her eyes and her brown skin radiated.

B–More Love

My chest heaved.

Ashley was just that beautiful, even with her face streaked with tears.

"W … what's wrong?" my voice cooed, devoid of my gangsta mentality.

"It's my Mama … they think she ain't going to make it," she muttered. I noticed two of the buttons on her blouse had come loose. I could see the vanilla silk bra and the outline of a supple brown nipple. I tore my eyes away from her as she mopped at her eyes with the palms of her hands and cried harder.

It was killing me softly to see her so distraught. I resisted the urge to reach down to hold her. Instead, I cast a weary glance back at Rock's lifeless body. What the fuck kinda day was this? I don't know what made me do it, but I reached down tenderly and helped Ashley to her feet. To my utter surprise, she stepped into my embrace like I was a pavilion. She laid her head against my chest and I caressed her back, inhaled the sweet redolence of her perfume and felt her warm tears on my chest.

"It's gonna be okay, don't cry, Ashley," I said softly as someone rushed by. "Where your car at? I'll drive you home."

She pulled away from me, sniffled and pointed with a hand with some type of bangle on her wrist. As we took off walking, I had the shotgun in a towel under my arm and the shirt with the money in it in the same hand.

"They say she only has about a ten percent chance to make it," Ashley said melancholically.

"Fuck dem crackas! They don't know shit!" I huffed. She turned and looked at me. Once we reached her car, she put her hand inside her purse and searched for the keys. Her hands were trembling badly when she passed them to me. I opened the door for her. That was the first time in my life doing some shit like that. Once we got inside the car, she thanked me as she

Leo Sullivan

continued to cry.

"It's a'ight, shawty." I couldn't help staring at her breasts with her sitting across from me. It gave me a much better view. She looked over and caught me ogling her breasts. She glanced down and realized her blouse was undone and buttoned it up fast then crossed her arms over her chest for good measure. We drove in silence for a minute with her crying softly.

I drove past the pool hall. It was a few blocks from Ashley's crib. The streets were cluttered with police cars, ambulances and medics rushing by, pushing bodies on stretchers. I turned the baseball cap on my head around backward and dipped low in the seat, incognito as possible as I zigzagged through throngs of cop cars. On the corner were the hood rats, Destiny and Nicole. They saw me and bugged out as I crept through with one of the baddest chicks in B-More. I knew they figured Ashley was my new upgrade.

"Oh my god! What happened here? Look at all the bodies," Ashley said in shock. It came as a surprise to me, too. I didn't know I had shot that many muthafuckas, and I felt no remorse. My nigga Rock was dead.

"Damn, I dunno what happened," I lied.

I felt Ashley cast a long glance in my direction just as we passed a K-9 Unit car with a ferocious German Shepherd in the back seat. The dog went crazy barking at me. I noticed Ashley's eyes travel from my naked chest to my soiled pants and bloody Timbs. She sniffed the air, crinkling her delicate nose at me with that look ... the one Black women use after they have detected you are lying.

We turned onto her street. She lived well within walking distance of where I was going. She had gathered some semblance of composure. I didn't know if that was good for me, since like I said, she normally couldn't stand my ass. She wiped

B-More Love

her eyes and checked her face in the mirror then reached over and kissed my cheek.

"Uh … umm … thank you for driving me home. Uh … I'm sorry for some of the things I used to say to you at school."

I nodded my head.

"Some of the things," I quipped. She turned and looked at me through puffy swollen eyes like "nigga, I'm tryna be nice to your ass."

"It's all good. Namean?" I said, trying my best to placate her and figuring it would be a good time to try my luck. "Dig, Ash, if you ain't doing nuttin' tonight, maybe—"

"Nope, uh uh!" she cut me off mid-sentence, giving me the sinister hand in my face the way chicks do when they dissin' you. The shit kinda struck a nerve, but on the strength of her moms was sick, I let it go. Plus, I ain't gon' front, she had me sprung. She shrugged her shoulders and sighed. A nasty-ass pigeon landed on the hood of the car.

"It's just so much I need to do, so much drama in my life. I'm about to graduate, now this."

Her voice quivered then tears welled in her eyes. She wiped them quickly with the back of her hands. I tried my best not to look at her but I couldn't help it. We were silent and still as the noise of the streets droned around us. A car passed, the pigeon took flight and I realized I wasn't about to give up that easily.

"Would it be okay if I stopped by tonight and checked on you, please?" I begged and wasn't ashamed of it.

She didn't answer, just sat there starry-eyed with tears soaking her ebony cheeks and the sun glistening off her silky black hair. Her features were enhanced by chatoyant brown eyes and high cheekbones. I reached for my gear in the back seat, making sure to keep the sawed-off concealed under the towel. I reached inside and pulled out a wad of cash and didn't even

Leo Sullivan

count it, just tossed it in her lap, where it fell in between her thick-ass thighs. I stared at her wide hips as they spread over the seat. She dug between her legs and pulled the money out and handed it back to me.

"I can't take this," her voice whined. She turned her head, her silky hair twirling over her shoulder.

"Why not?" I asked incredulously. It wasn't like I was in the business of giving chicks money anyway. I could give a fuck 'bout a bitch.

"Jamal, thank you for everything … I didn't mean to hurt your feelings," she said sweetly.

"Sheit, you ain't hurt a nigga feelings," I lied. Truth was, I didn't mind breakin' her off. She wasn't with the drama. Simply said, Ashley Gray was a bad bitch, fine from head to toe.

She leaned across the seat. I watched her short skirt rise up her thick, chocolate thighs as she kissed me softly on the cheek. I ain't gon' front … my dick got hard as a muhfa. Afterward, she looked at me a moment too long. I saw a flicker of something in her brown eyes. "I gotta go," she said and took her keys out of the ignition.

I looked up to see a black Caddy coming up the street. It was my nigga, Black Roy. I jumped out and flagged him down. They were four deep. I squeezed in the back seat between T. Kelly and K.B. All of them niggas were at least twice my age, but respected a young nigga's grind. Plus, I had a body count and a brain that was impeccable.

"I'll holla at'cha later," I said to Ashley out the window. Heads turned, watching her fine, bow-legged ass bounce from side to side as she walked and waved a hand.

"Bye."

B–More Love

Five

Ashley

I walked in the house and felt a cold draft. It felt like my soul was hemorrhaging. My heart was aching with the most unbelievable thought—I had just left my Mama at the hospital on her death bed.

The old wooden floors cracked under my feet as I walked through the house. My mind flashed back to Jamal. I knew he thought after all those years I hated him. And I did. I hated that he robbed for a living. I once walked up on him when he was robbing a substitute teacher at school, taking his shoes and leather jacket at gunpoint. Even though the teacher was gay, and had supposedly asked for a sexual favor, that was no excuse for Jamal to rob him.

But what I hated most about Jamal was how he was irresistibly fine and always well-dressed. He wore his short cropped hair in a tight Caesar fade with nice honeycomb waves. His skin was the color of pecans, roasted in a dark brown sugar glaze. Every girl at school wanted to have him, and the few who had bragged about his love-making skills and big dick. The few times he did come to school, just seeing him walk made me want him.

I always pretended like I couldn't stand him, but as he sat in my car after driving me home, I couldn't help noticing his brawny chest and six pack abs because he had his shirt off. I felt something overpowering for him. Maybe it was because of my

Leo Sullivan

mother's illness, but I wanted him to hold me, so I kissed him and to my surprise, I saw his enormous erection. I was seventeen and still a virgin but couldn't help wondering what it would feel like to have him inside of me, making love for the first time.

○ ○ ○ ○

"Vanessa! Vanessa!" I yelled for my sister. My voice carried in the old house. The sound was eerie. We barely had any furniture, just a few pastel-colored plastic chairs Mama had bought from Wal-Mart, a second hand couch with matching end tables and a rent-to-own stereo system. I walked down the hall to Mama's bedroom and stepped inside.

Her bed was unmade and her nightgown was in the middle of the floor next to her slippers. Although the room was vacant, her larger-than-life presence filled me. Again, I thought of my Mama in the hospital all alone and suffering. I began to cry. I felt a hand on my shoulder. Startled, I whirled around. It was Frank, my mother's boyfriend. I could smell alcohol on his breath. He was standing too close, causing me to take a timid step back.

"Mama's in the hospital," I said in a strained voice and wiped at the tears in my eyes.

"I know, I'm the one who drove her there." He tried to show a face of empathy, but I saw something else. Frank stood about 6 foot 4 and was very muscular, about three hundred plus pounds. He was in his early thirties, considerably younger than my mother. She said he had spent a lot of time in prison once for murder. Mama was bad at picking men, and worse at keeping them. He had a deep J-shaped scar around his neck like someone tried to slit his throat and only did a decent job of it. He took a step toward me, glassy eyes focused on my thighs. I backed into a dresser. He pressed his body against mine.

"I'ma miss yo' Mama, but the doctor said she ain't got much

chance at making it, so I'm going to need you to be really really good to me."

"Leave me alone, Frank," I said, trying to get around him.

He grabbed my waist. "You don't want nothing to happen to your little sisters, do you?"

"Naw," I answered. I felt his erection pressing against my thigh and was scared to death. All my life, I had been passive and easy to intimidate. I couldn't kill a bug. Mama said God made some people like that. She said I was born with a gentle soul. He let go of my waist and placed his hands on my neck and let his fingers trail down between my breasts. I was too petrified to stop him—couldn't if I had wanted to.

"Now, I want you to do me a little favor. If you do this, I promise I won't hurt you," he whispered low, in a guttural tone that made me shudder. I heard him unzip his pants and suddenly it dawned on me that I was about to be raped. "Tonight, I want you to come into this room and don't make me come lookin' for you. Hear me?!"

"Yes, yes!" I shrieked, nodding my head nervously. I was pressed against the dresser, standing on the balls of my feet. I felt his hand ease up my skirt and touch the satin lace next to my vagina. "But first, I want a little sample of that virgin twang," he hissed with this teeth clinched tightly. He yanked on my panties.

Just then, the door opened. My little sister, Jasmine, skipped into the room. Frank quickly placed his penis back into his pants. He turned around and scooped my hyperactive six-year-old sister up in his arms. I'll never forget the wild look in his eyes. Almost inhuman. Vanessa came through the door and did a double take at us standing around. She cut her eyes at Frank as he held Jasmine. A Black & Mild cigar smoldered in her hand. She narrowed her eyes into tiny slits and spoke. "Where

Mama at, Ash?"

"Girl, you know you ain't s'posed to be smoking in this house," Frank admonished her.

Vanessa twisted her lips. "Nigga, you ain't my daddy. You don't even pay rent in this house," she hissed. Vanessa and I were about the same weight and height. She was light skinned with a slight overbite and short brown hair. That day she had a blue scarf on her hand and wore a G-Unit outfit—baggy jeans and a blue T-shirt. Her girls boosted clothes for a hustle. Vanessa, at such a young age, was into chicks—a full-blooded lesbian who made no secret about it. She also hated Frank with a passion. She placed the Black & Mild in her mouth, walked over and boldly took Jasmine out of Frank's arms. She looked at him daringly. Frank knew that Vanessa carried a razor in her pocket and wasn't afraid to use it.

"Yo' Mama is in the hospital and you 'round here tryna play grown," Frank said sarcastically.

"Wha?" Vanessa quipped and placed her hands in her pocket. It must have dawned on her what he said. She turned to look at me with Jasmine balanced on her hip. "Ash, what's wrong with Mama?" Her face was ablaze with shock.

"I don't know," I lied.

Frank stepped forward and folded his huge arms over his chest and glowered at Vanessa with malice. "Doctor said your Mama got brain cancer and she ain't gonna make it!"

Vanessa turned and looked at Frank with hate simmering in her eyes as her mind registered what he said. Jasmine asked with her two front teeth missing, "What is brain cancer, Ashley?"

Fainthearted, I took her out of Vanessa's arms as she shot daggers at Frank with her eyes. Her chest heaved. She breathed, panting, nostrils flaring like she was finna be a charging bull on

B-More Love

his ass.

"Nigga, wha-da-fuck you just say about my Mama?!" The cigar fell to the floor as she placed her hand in her pocket. Taking a step forward, Frank's eyes scrolled over to me with an expression like "you better get her."

"Vanessa!" I yelled. I couldn't stand the sight of blood or the fact that Frank might hurt my little sister.

Vanessa turned slowly and looked at me. Her forehead creased with dismay. Her eyes searched my face for any truth as to what Frank had just said.

Slowly, I nodded my head in confirmation. Shock registered on her face like she realized she was standing in front of an approaching train. I shifted Jasmine to my other hip while she sucked on her finger. Suddenly, I heard a piercing, gut-wrenching scream. I looked up and Vanessa's face was a ball of anguish and despair as she cried, never taking her eyes off of Frank, like he was to blame. Jasmine began to cry also.

I walked over to Vanessa to console her as Jasmine held onto my neck crying, "I want my Mommy!" Frank just looked at us. I thought I detected a hint of glee in his eyes as he gave me a warning look. Instantly a chill ran down my spine. I thought about him raping me, or worse, one of my little sisters. Something else occurred to me—the rent money.

Mama said the money was stashed in the closet. I needed to get it, but how? I had no intentions of going into her room that night as Frank had told me to. Then again, I wasn't going to let him hurt one of my sisters. I knew I damn sure couldn't tell Vanessa or anyone for that matter. I was too scared.

"Tomorrow, we goin' to go see Mama. She'll be okay," I said softly. I wasn't sure if Vanessa heard me, she was crying so hard. She ran out of the room, got in her bed and cried herself to sleep.

Leo Sullivan

o o o o

That night, Frank asked me to cook dinner. The first thing that went through my mind was to poison him. I was just that terrified of him. As usual, there wasn't much food in our refrigerator. I found some pork chops, so I took my time cooking them. I also found a box of macaroni and cheese but the roaches had found their way inside of the box first. I cooked it anyway.

It seemed like Frank strolled into the kitchen every five minutes with a beer in his hand, telling me to hurry up. It felt like every second he was looking over my shoulder. As I continued to cook, he walked in wearing a wife beater and jeans with his zipper undone. I pretended not to see him and held my breath with my back to him but felt his burning stare boring through me. My legs trembled badly. He walked up and rubbed his thang against me. It was hard. My hand trembled noticeably as I turned the pork chops over in the hot grease. He began to grind on my butt then whispered in my ear, "Don't make me wait all fuckin' night long fo' yo' ass, 'cause if it ain't you, one of yo' sisters will do."

A shiver ran down my spine.

"Pah ... pah-leese don't hurt my sisters. I'ma come to the room as soon as I'm finished," I said, panic-stricken. My hand was on the handle of the skillet. The hot grease popped and crackled and suddenly it occurred to me that if I doused his face with the hot grease, he'd leave me alone ... leave us alone. *Throw it on his ass. Throw it!* a voice chanted. *Oh God, forgive me for what I'm about to do. Lawd, help me!* I prayed, and closed my eyes. His lips were against my ear. More threats. I picked up the skillet and turned around ...

B-More Love

Six

Jamal

As we drove to my crib in West Port Projects, I listened as I sat in the backseat of the Caddy, wedged between T. Kelly and K.B. I tried to listen as they talked about the robbery. Humphrey's pool hall got laid down. It was a big caper that went bad. The robbers ran off leaving a half a million on the pool table. Lots of gun play with bodies being dropped.

Of course, them niggas was talking about me indirectly because like I said, in the ghetto, the streets is always watching. Jay-Z's joint, *"Dig a Hole"* was banging through the speakers while smoke permeated from several big blunts being passed. I just stared out the window as the world passed me by.

We passed by a building where prostitutes stood out front. Rock and I used to skip school and hang out there. The big Caddy passed another cut where Rock used to smoke at.

As I sat there with blood on my pants, someone passed me a blunt. I inhaled deeply, blew smoke out my mouth and nose and then talked slowly. I wanted these niggas to feel me. "My nigga, Rock, got kilt today."

Silence.

Then a low ripple of voices stirred in the front seat. Niggas whispering. I looked up and thought I detected someone passing a burner. The driver looked at me through the rearview mirror as smoke hovered like we were trapped inside of a cloud.

"Cuz, it might be that nigga Humphrey, but somebody got

Leo Sullivan

a fifty thousand dollar hit out on you."

I leaned forward to hear him. Just then, I realized he was about to make a wrong turn and the thought hit me like a ton of bricks. For fifty g's, a nigga couldn't trust his own mama. In a car full of cutthroats, I got paranoid, so I pulled out my nine and brandished it like a crazy muthafucka.

"Lemme out dis muthafucka, now!" I barked.

The car stopped. Niggas was mad buggin', but I was a young nigga and that in itself taught me a lot—don't trust nobody!

Once I was outside the car, niggas started mumbling, looking at me crazy. I reached into my stash and threw K.B. a stack of bloody money. "Y'all niggas split dat," I said and bounced, with my pants sagging and large T-shirt full of guns, jewelry and more cash, not including the 12 gauge in a towel tucked under my arm.

o o o o

My little sister opened the door. She was fifteen years old and six months pregnant. She took one look at me and frowned. Playfully, I knuckled her head and rubbed her basketball-sized belly.

"Stop it, boy!" she shrieked, looking like our Mama. I noticed she had on the same jeans and blouse she wore yesterday. Even though they were washed and ironed, it reminded me of just how poor we were. For some reason, she looked sad, crestfallen.

"What's wrong, Nikki?" I asked.

She shrugged her shoulders. I noticed my little sister's breasts had grown so big. Her face glowed with a youthful innocence, and baby hair glistened in a soft cascade down her shiny forehead. She had on bubble gum scented lip-gloss that exaggerated her pouting lips.

"I want to go to the mall with my girls, Kymberli and Alicia.

B-More Love

Chris Brown fine ass gonna be there signing autographs … but I need to borrow some money." She made a face.

I decided to play with her head. I reached into my stash and pulled out a knot of money.

"I'll give you two dollars if you tell me who the nigga is who knocked you up."

She clucked her tongue. "Two dollars!" she huffed with her eyebrows knotted together. Then her adolescent eyes grew wide. "Ooohh, where did you get all that money from?"

I snickered at her antics then added, "You need to tell me who the nigga is." I waved the money in her face.

She sealed her lips. At times I wondered if she even knew.

I peeled off ten one-hundred-dollar bills and passed them to her. She squealed with delight as she jumped up and down. I was afraid she would hurt the baby. "Thank you! Thank you!" She hugged me, full of jubilation. I wrestled to get her off me.

"You got on Mama's perfume," I said, holding her arms at bay. She blushed, batting her long, pretty eyelashes.

"Ah ah ah … gotta go call Kymberli." She raced off then turned and ran back to me and kissed me on the cheek. "Thank you!" She trotted off.

All I could do was smile at her crazy ass. That's the best part about a hustler's grind—being able to take care of family.

I eased into my Mama's bedroom. She was asleep. She worked two jobs. I placed some money on her dresser drawer and tiptoed out.

In my room, I counted the cash. In all, there was one hundred and six grand, not including the jewelry. Afterward, I stashed half the money. The rest I took to Rock's mom's crib to give it to her. She came to the door drunk as usual.

"Bitch, what you want?" she slurred, looking at me like she was seeing double. She hated my guts. Always said I would end

Leo Sullivan

up dead and blamed me for Rock's troubled life. I didn't know if she had learned of Rock's death or not but I abruptly turned and dipped in my whip, a '98 Buick Park Avenue, squatting on 26s with a dope, midnight-blue bowling ball paint job with metallic flakes that sparkled like diamonds. I turned on my Alpine system, bumping MIMS' joint, *This is Why I'm Hot.*

Later that day after taking a long, hot shower, I had on a blue polo shirt and some Red Monkey jeans with white Air Force 1's. With my pistol in my lap, I cruised through Dorton Court, missing my nigga Rock in the vacant passenger seat. I was checkin' Trips, business as usual, lookin' for a nigga to touch, only now, I had my ear to the street.

A cat named Ski Mask flagged me down. He was one of them ruthless niggas who couldn't be trusted. Skinny nigga with a mouth full of gold, wore his hair braided to the back with a trim beard. He looked like Young Buck.

"What it do, my nigga?" I said, lowering the window. As usual, Ski Mask was rollin high off Oxitasy—a potent drug cocktail of Ecstacy pills with OxyContin. The combination of the two drugs was euphoric; made a nigga fuck a bitch like a maniac, twisting her back out. I was addicted as well. It had been a minute since I had some.

Ski Mask wobbled back and forth on his feet. I noticed a sheen of sweat on his forehead. Behind him was a bad bitch with a big, phat ass and thick thighs. She had on tight, white shorts and a pussy print like she had a monkey in her drawers. She had a face like a camel with big-ass lips a nigga could work with. I had seen her around before. Niggas said she was a crack head. I thought about trickin' and getting my dick sucked with them big-ass, made-for-suckin'-dick lips.

"Humphrey n'em come through here in two carloads askin' 'bout you," Ski Mask said in a conspiratorial tone.

My heart skipped a beat as I tore my eyes away from the broad.

"Me? They lookin' for me?"

He pursed his dry lips. A car passed with loud music blaring.

"Yep."

"Ski Mask!" The crack head called his name, anxious to get high.

"Hol' up, bitch!" he yelled over his shoulder then continued. "Cuz, it ain't just that. Word is you got a fifty-thousand dollar bounty out on yo' head. You or somebody you love."

I felt my heart pounding in my chest. It was the second time that day I'd heard that.

"Fuck dat! I'm finna go holla at this nigga."

"Want me to roll wit' you?"

"Nawll, Cuz, I'm good," I said, burning rubber.

○ ○ ○ ○

I parked my car at the BP gas station around the corner from The Spot Pool Hall. Dusk was starting to set in and a fuchsia-colored sky hung over Baltimore, embellished by a luminous, full moon. That night, my intent was to escalate the murder rate. I had boldly come back to kill old man Humphrey. He had killed my nigga and had the nerve to sell death, talkin' 'bout a bounty on me or my family. One of us had to leave the earth.

○ ○ ○ ○

As I walked up on the crime scene, tape was strewn on the ground. I saw old man Humphrey through the window. He and two other men were sitting around drinking. The streets were full of people as usual.

The bell chimed on the door when I walked in. "Pool hall closed, can't you see the—" Humphrey was saying when he

Leo Sullivan

looked up and realized it was me. B.B. King crooned from the ancient juke box, "The thrill is gone baby …"

I could still smell the blood and death in the air.

"Somebody said you was lookin' for me." My voice carried in the dank pool hall. His two companions got up and walked away.

"I … I ain't lookin' for you. Lookin' for you for what?" Humphrey said, his voice trembling with fear. His eyes were wide as he gestured with his hands, palms facing me. I noticed a band-aid on his index finger.

"Nigga, you got a fifty thousand dollar reward out on me and my family?"

Humphrey jerked his neck back like he had been slapped and stared at the window. I held my burner at my side.

"Son, I swear to God! Swear to God, I ain't got no reward on you. I'm a old man, just wanted to protect mines."

"Fuck that!" I spat with my hand on the trigger, about to squeeze on his old ass and keep it true to my nigga, Rock. I saw a nervous twitch in his face, like he was about to cry.

"Please, let me go home to my family. Please!"

Someone called my name. "Jackie Boy, go home. Stop the killin'." I glanced over at the window and saw a thousand faces. Witnesses. I sighed, stepped off that long voyage of insanity and returned to my humanity. I decided not to kill him.

I backed out the door with the pistol in my hand. Outside, the crisp night air felt cool on my damp skin as I realized I was sweating profusely. Nocturnal noises enveloped me as I walked back to my car with my mind in a daze, people staring, me not caring. I racked my brain trying to figure out just who the fuck had a bounty on me. If it wasn't Humphrey, then who? The voice in my head warned me, *You should have killed him.*

It was 9:14 p.m. I decided to stop by Ashley's crib, so I

picked up a bottle of Patrón to have something to sip on. I smoked half a blunt of some purple. By the time I arrived at Ashley's place, I was fucked up, mellow with a nice buzz, bumpin' Jeezy's joint, *"I Luv It."* I couldn't help reminiscing about her kiss and that phat ass when she walked off. I wondered if it was true that Ashley was still a virgin. Better yet, would I ever find out?

I rolled up in the spot with my pistol tucked in my drawers and knocked on the door. I saw a big-ass rat scurry across the walkway. Music was coming from the house next door. I heard someone laughing in a high-pitched cackle. The front door opened and the most adorable little girl I had ever seen in my life was standing there with pink barrettes in her hair. She snickered with two front teeth missing.

"Hi, I'm Jamal," I said, squatting down to her height. "Is Ashley here?"

She placed her finger in her mouth and giggled. "You her boyfriend?"

I smiled. "Nawll, I'm—"

"Hold on, wait." The little girl slammed the door in my face. I looked up and saw a late model car with its lights off doing a slow creep up the street. My instincts kicked in. I had touched too many niggas on the strength they got caught slippin' at some bitch crib, tryna get their dick wet. Not me. Just as I was about to pull out my strap, the door opened.

Leo Sullivan

Seven

Ashley

I swung around with the hot skillet, about to throw it in Frank's face. Jasmine screamed my name. The hot grease spilled over, damn near burning Frank. He moved out the way just in time.

"Gurl, wha-da-fuck wrong wit'cha!"

"Ashley got a boyfriend ..."

The grease splashed on the floor.

"What?" I asked, carefully setting the skillet back on the stove. I gulped air, pulse racing, heart revving a mile a minute as I exchanged looks with Frank. It felt like he read my mind as he looked down at the grease on the floor, then back at me.

"Your boyfriend Jamal at the door!" Jasmine exclaimed.

"Jamal?" I retorted. I wiped my hands on my skirt, picked up Jasmine and ran out of the room.

I opened the door. Jamal had his back turned, hands in his pants. His eyes were opened wide, trained at a car moving up the street.

"Haaay, Jamal!" I caroled with glee. I was so elated to see him. I gave him a big hug and a kiss on the cheek. As I set Jasmine down, Frank's large shadow loomed in the doorway. Nervously, I grabbed Jamal's hand. For some reason, he kept peering over his shoulder behind him. I saw his flabbergasted expression when I said, "This is my boyfriend." His handsome face lit up as he looked back and forth between me and the

B–More Love

streets with a smile, then a sneer, his top lip curled slightly.

"Jackie Boy!" Frank called out. From the shocked expression on his face, it was easy to tell he wasn't happy to see Jamal.

"Wuz up, Cuz?" Jamal drawled. His eyes were slanted, red and heavy-lidded. I guessed he'd been smokin'.

"Uh, it's kinda late for Ashley to be having company. She gotta get up early for sc—"

"No, I don't!" I interrupted with steel in my voice. "Tomorrow, we gonna see Mama in the hospital," I added. I could sense Frank's disdain for Jamal as the two stood, considering each other. Frank was almost twice Jamal's size.

"Yo, Frank, lemme holla at shawty for a second, namean?"

Frank made a face, took a swig of his beer and flexed his muscles. He wiped his mouth with the back of his hand and belched loudly. The moment lingered too long, finally Frank said, "Okay." Then out of spite, his perverted ass looked down at my baby sister. "Come on, Jazz, let daddy give the baby a bath. Say goodnight."

Jasmine ran over to me and grabbed my waist.

Irate, I looked at Frank and spoke in clipped tones, barely able to contain my anger. "You are not her daddy and you will never bathe her."

Jamal watched our exchange of words. He was about to say something then glanced over at Frank and changed his mind. "Let's go sit in your car," I said to Jamal, feeling emboldened by his presence.

Jamal hesitated at first like it wasn't a good idea, then reluctantly changed his mind. He grabbed Jasmine's hand and took her outside with us.

As soon as we walked to his car, he turned around and faced me. His eyes searched mine. "Wuz up wit' dude in there?" He gestured with his forehead.

Leo Sullivan

I turned my head and bit down on my bottom lip, undecided if I should risk telling him. Could I trust him? I was so afraid.

He reached inside his car and turned the stereo on. Akon was singing, "Nobody wanna see us together." Jasmine tugged on Jamal's pant leg.

"Gimme some money, boy!"

"How much?" he replied, amused.

"I'on't know." Jasmine then placed a finger in her mouth.

Sometimes my little sister embarrassed the hell out of me. "Don't be askin' him for money," I scolded her.

Jasmine shrugged her shoulders, thought for a second, then asked, "You got some candy then?"

Jamal cracked up in jovial laughter. I could tell he was high, tripping off my little sister.

"Jasmine! If you ask him for one more thing, I'ma send you in the house!" I screeched.

With a child's petulance, she pouted. Jamal bent down and whispered something in her ear. Together, they laughed. I had a feeling the joke was on me. Again, Jamal's eyes scanned the streets. I began to wonder if perpetual paranoia was part of a gangsta's mentality. He opened the car door and Jasmine climbed in with mischief in her eyes.

Jamal walked back over to me as I leaned against his car, a beautiful blue automobile with nice rims and a slick paint job. He stood close and glanced down at the wide spread of my hips. He then made a face when I caught him looking.

"You gon' tell me what's up with dude or what?" he asked. Behind him, a full moon hung in the sky, illuminating the waves in his hair as the ambient streetlight sparkled in his eyes. I inhaled his cologne with a sigh.

"Ain't nothing wrong," I finally replied. He seemed to sense

B–More Love

I was lying.

"Dat nigga used to smoke crack. I personally served dude one day," Jamal said vehemently.

"Mama said he don't smoke no more."

I just happened to glance inside the car and saw Jasmine munching down on a Snickers. The glove compartment was open.

"Gimme that," I said and moved to reach for her.

Jamal grabbed me in a bear hug. Jasmine squealed in laughter as Jamal held me in his embrace, his laughter euphony to my ears, like his embrace—enrapturing, intimate. It was the first time I'd let a guy hold me like that, so close. It felt good. I wanted to be enshrined in his arms. I squeezed him, needed him … if he only knew. He whispered in my ear, "You're trembling. Why?"

"It's cold."

"Um humpf, yea, right," he muttered incredulously. It was one of those beautiful summer nights in B-More, and we were young and not so innocent.

"I used to not be able to stand you," I said.

"Why not?"

"Because all the other girls like you and you a thug. You rob and shoot people. You a gangsta."

"I've changed."

"Uh huh," I murmured.

"You still don't like me?"

I couldn't help but smile. "I like you. I like you a lot," I said in a breathy voice. I kissed his cheek. Mary J. Blige's *"Take Me As I Am"* came on the radio.

He palmed my ass with both hands and squeezed. "Be my lady," he intoned, like a Jodeci song.

Silence.

Leo Sullivan

Finally, I answered in a sultry voice, "Let me think about it." I could feel his manhood pressing against my thigh, and a gun on his waist. I was caught up in the rapture of the moment. He kissed me. His tongue searched out mine.

"Ooh ... I'm telling Mama!" my little sister exclaimed, interrupting the enchanted spell.

My first kiss.

I pulled away. "You little snitch. Gimme back my candy," Jamal said playfully.

Just as he was about to reach for Jasmine, a car drove by. He watched it closely then walked to the front of his car to make eye contact. He pulled out his pistol to let them see he was strapped.

The car passed.

I exhaled.

He walked back over after he put his pistol back in his pants, eyes narrow slits, watching the car while talking to me.

"Lemme go inside and holla at dude—"

"No!" I said.

Jamal ignored me. "Where yo' other sister at?"

"She cried herself to sleep. She took Mama's illness really hard, plus she probably tired from skippin' school all the time."

Jamal picked up Jasmine and began to walk back toward our house. I had a bad feeling there was going to be some drama.

"Go to your room, lil mama," he said to Jasmine as soon as he stepped inside.

To my surprise, she waved.

"Bye bye." She walked to her room.

Frank was standing in front of the window when Jamal spoke slowly and deliberately.

"Dig, my nigga. I'm gettin' bad vibes from you, namean, and I peeped the shit you spit about bathing Jasmine. I ain't feelin'

B–More Love

dat, yo." Jamal frowned.

I watched Frank's Adam's apple bob as he swallowed hard.

"Uh, nawll, dawg, it ain't like dat. We all family here. Ain't that right, baby girl?" He turned and looked at me to cosign his lie. I turned my lips up and gave him a cool stare.

"Humpf," I groaned.

"Well, nigga, you know how I roll. I rep West Port to the fullest, so I'ma keep it one hundred wit'cha. If something happen to one of these girls, I'ma come back."

Frank screwed up his face. "You threatening me?"

Jamal walked over to him and got up in his grill. "Nigga, I don't make threats. I dress niggas up in caskets, send 'em home to they mama in a box. You got a problem wit' dat?" Jamal reached into his pocket and Frank flinched like a bitch.

"No! No! No!" he cried out. I started to dive behind the couch as I watched Jamal come out his pocket with a cell phone. I couldn't help it—I holla'd laughing at the sour expression on Frank's face. Dude had been reduced to a shivering coward.

"Put your number in here," Jamal demanded, never taking his eyes off Frank. "If dis nigga try any funny shit, call me. I might come back later on tonight. Okay?"

I smirked as I punched in my number. Afterward, he kissed me and palmed my ass in front of Frank, the way dudes do to stake claim and show off. I watched him turn and mean mug Frank before he walked out the door. I couldn't help thinking, *Thank God for creating thugs!*

I strode over to the window and watched Jamal drive off in his car. As soon as he drove off, the dark Crown Victoria followed suit. I was almost certain it was the car Jamal pulled out his pistol on.

"You know what dat nigga hustle is?" Frank asked acrimoniously.

Leo Sullivan

I turned around and fixed him with a contemptuous stare.

"Nawll, tell me. What does he do for a hustle, Frank?" I asked sarcastically, then added, "is it any different than what you wanted to do to me?"

"I was just playin', but he's not. He a muthafuckin' gangsta, robbin' folks for a livin'. I don't think it would be a good idea to let him back in this house."

I tilted my neck and crossed my arms over my chest. "Why didn't you tell him that while he was here, Frank?" I sassed. "To be truthful, I don't think it would be a good idea for you to be in this house. Tomorrow, I'm telling Mama what you tried to do to me."

Frank furrowed his brow. "She ain't gonna believe shit you say!" he shouted in anger.

"Jamal will," I shot back. He flinched then looked at me. I read the smoldering resentment in his beady eyes, saw his hate and treachery. He clinched his jaw tight.

"That nigga got a fifty thousand dollar hit out on his ass. His days are numbered."

"Whaat?!"

Frank staggered off to the bedroom drunk and slammed the door.

That night, there was no way in hell I was going to sleep in my room alone. I still didn't trust him. I slept in the bed with Jasmine. She and Vanessa shared a room. Jamal called me three times that night to check up on us.

Eight

Ashley

Bam! Bam! Bam!

I awakened, startled, with Jasmine's leg wrapped around my neck. I glanced at my watch. It read 8:10 a.m. Damn, I had overslept.

Bam! Bam! Bam!

Someone was banging on the front door. I staggered down the hall and peeped out the curtain. It was Mr. Johnson, our landlord.

"Shit!" I cursed. Backing up from the door, I bumped into someone. I spun around, startled. It was Vanessa. "Landlord," I whispered, then placed my finger over my lips. "Shhh."

Barefooted, we padded down the hall over wooden, barren floors and knocked on Mama's door. Frank always slept late. I needed to get the rent money Mama had stashed in the closet. Vanessa pulled out her razor. I frowned and made a face at her. "Put that away!"

She frowned back. "Nope!"

I knocked at the door.

No answer.

Vanessa banged on it with her fist.

No answer.

Vanessa and I exchanged glances. She pushed in front of me, opening the door.

"Ughhh!" The stench of crack smoke and malodorous funk

Leo Sullivan

permeated the room. Beer cans, ashtrays and cigarette butts littered the floor as we stepped over clothes. A crack pipe made from an antenna sat on top of the nightstand next to the bed. I rushed over to the closet with my heart racing. As soon as I looked inside, I knew the money was gone, but still I fumbled around on the top shelf with my hands.

The money was gone. So was Frank. "Shit!"

"I swear to God, I'ma kill that nigga!" Vanessa said.

What am I going to do now? I wondered.

There was another knock at the door just as Jasmine walked into the room. I walked past her to look outside the window. To my surprise, it was Jamal. Behind him, I saw the landlord walk off, get into his truck and drive off. I hesitated before I opened the door. I looked like shit. My hair wasn't combed, I hadn't even washed my face and had on the same clothes from yesterday.

Reluctantly, I smoothed my hair back, pulled my panties out my ass and opened the door. I had to do a double take. There was a big-ass sign taped to the door. It read: Eviction Notice.

Jamal snatched it down, balled it up and threw it. I had never been so embarrassed in my entire life.

"I hit dude off with a coupla bills, namean? Y'all good." He blushed boyishly.

I didn't know whether to hug him or thank him, so I did both. "Thank you, Jamal." I squeezed his neck. Say what you want about a thug, but Jamal showed a sista love.

"You still want to go see yo' Mama?"

"Yeees!" voices intoned in chorus. I looked behind me, and Jasmine and Vanessa were standing there all smiles. That day, I told Jamal about Frank stealing the rent money and about him trying me for sex. Jamal was pissed to say the least.

○ ○ ○ ○

B-More Love

As usual, Bond Secure Hospital was a madhouse. That day, people were everywhere. The sick, the dying, folks bleeding. The night before, there had been a shooting at a club called B-More Live. The lobby was so congested I decided to bypass the nurses' station and head straight for the elevator.

Finally, we reached Mama's room. Number 511. Jamal stalled outside the door. It wasn't hard to read the pensive expression on his face.

"Want me to wait out here?" he asked with Vanessa standing next to him. For the first time in a long time, all dressed up to see Mama, Vanessa looked like a fifteen-year-old instead of a thugstress.

"Come on," I mouthed and pushed the door open. We walked in. My knees almost buckled when I saw Mama.

Her face was severely swollen and disfigured. She had thick gauze wrapped around her head. It was ringed, encrusted with dried blood. She was unconscious. There were many tubes and other apparatuses running from her body. She was connected to several machines. Episodic beeps chimed from a machine monitoring all of her vitals. In the next bed, the old woman was still there. She looked dead. It took a moment for Jasmine to recognize Mama, lying in the bed with her face disfigured and head swollen.

Jasmine completely lost it.

"Mama! Mama! Mommy, wake up!" She ran to the bed crying hysterically. Jamal scooped her up in his arms. Next to me I heard sobs. It was Vanessa crying softly. Together we held each other. I didn't realize it but my cheeks were wet with my own tears. Tentatively, we walked over to her.

"Mama?" My voice quivered. Vanessa cried louder and placed her head on Mama's chest. "Mama!" I yelled. She had to wake up. She had to.

Leo Sullivan

I glanced over at Jamal. He cradled Jasmine in his arms, rocking her back and forth. Finally he mouthed, "I ... I'm sorry." He blinked and pinched his eyes closed. He then turned and walked out the door. Mama just lay there in bed in a comatose state. I tried my damndest not to look at the old woman in the next bed. I wiped at my tears and decided since I was the oldest, I needed to be strong. I also needed to see the doctor. Someone was going to tell me what the hell was wrong with my Mama.

Vanessa and I exited the room. Out in the hall, people hurried by. I looked up and saw Jamal standing by a big picture window that overlooked Baltimore. He was still cradling Jasmine in his arms as she cried. He whispered in her ear, a dulcet lullaby. For some reason, I found myself staring. He turned and saw me coming. Vanessa walked to the nurses' station in search of the doctor. I came and stood next to Jamal and just stared out the window into the vastness of the ghetto, our home. He paused and then punctuated the stillness with a sigh that turned into a groan.

"Ahh fuck! I got a little sister, love her to death ... my Mama work two jobs and all the overtime them white folks give her. Can't neaah nigga tell me a nigga ain't got no heart. I felt that shit back there, seeing all y'all girls crying and yo' Mama in that damn bed!"

He stopped talking, pulled in his lips. I saw a large vein on the side of his forehead then realized he was ashamed at me seeing him all emotional. Somberly, I nodded my head and watched our reflection in the glass as a tear slid down my cheek.

Vanessa appeared and spoke in a broken voice, "The nurse said Mama's doctor is making his rounds. She wouldn't tell me what's wrong with her." She began to cry again.

I reached out and held her in my arms. Jamal shuffled his

feet uncomfortably and turned to look at all of us.

"We can't do it like this … not like this." He shook his head dismissively and then looked down at Jasmine. "You love your Mommy?"

"Yes," Jasmine sniffled.

He turned to us. "We gotta give your Mama life, positive energy, yo. Not all this cryin' and shit! Be strong. She can feel us … hear us. I once had an uncle who was in a coma for three months. He was shot nine times. They said he wasn't gonna make it but he woke up from his coma and said the only thing that made him want to stay alive was the love he felt. We was all there, laughin', crackin' jokes, sangin' and everything. We acted the way we would if we was home. I swear to God, y'all, she can hear y'all," Jamal said poignantly with his face twisted in a passionate plea.

We all nodded our heads and took that long trek back into Mama's hospital room. "Y'all gotta believe," were the last words Jamal spoke to us. Words that ruminated in my mind.

Back in the drab room, Mama lay motionless. Jasmine began talking with her finger in her mouth. "Mommy, guess what? Ashley got a boyfriend."

Jamal smiled like cracked glass.

I fidgeted. There was a clock radio on the nightstand. I reached, turning it on 92.0 FM. A melodious Mary J. crooned soulfully, "We been too strong for too long and I can't be without you, baby …" Vanessa closed her eyes and sang off key. We all knew that was one of Mama's favorite songs. Jasmine continued talking to Mama. I reached out and squeezed Jamal's hand and held onto it like I never wanted to let it go.

The doctor walked in the room and looked around at us in shock. The radio was loud, Vanessa was singing and Jasmine was talking to Mama about school. Dr. Turner looked haggard

Leo Sullivan

and weary; his clothes were wrinkled like he had slept in them. He took his glasses off and massaged the bridge of his nose.

"You're the young lady I spoke with yesterday, the daughter, right?"

"Yes," I replied, taking a step toward him. "These are my two younger sisters and uh ..." I momentarily stopped talking, searching for an appropriate title for Jamal.

"I'm her husband," he lied with a straight face.

The doctor didn't question it. "May I speak to you two in the hall?" His voice hinted that he wanted to talk to us in private.

"Hell nawll, I want to know what's wrong with her, too!" Vanessa screeched, walking up to the doctor. I shot her a warning glare, like "chill out."

She caught my glare and decided not to disagree with me. She stayed inside the room with Jasmine while Jamal and I left the room to talk to him.

Once outside in the hallway, the intercom system sounded as people rushed by. The doctor threw his hand back and wiped at a tuft of blond hair on his forehead.

"Does your mother have health insurance?"

"No."

"Any kind of hospital insurance?"

"No," I said again and looked at him like "what part of *no* don't you understand?"

"What happened with the surgery? She looks bad."

As I spoke, a nurse passed by, pushing a pregnant girl in a wheelchair.

The doctor cleared his throat. "The surgery was difficult. It took longer than expected and the prognosis isn't good. Your mother has Glioblastoma."

"A what?" Jamal asked with a sour expression on his face.

B-More Love

The doctor explained. "Glioblastoma. It's the deadliest form of brain cancer. Only three percent of Glioblastoma patients survive. Most die within a year."

My hands went to my mouth.

"So you mean ta tell me ain't a damn thing you can do to save dat lady in there?" Jamal raised his voice.

The doctor shrugged uncomfortably and reverted his eyes back to me. Just then, two policemen walked by with an inmate in county oranges, shackles on his wrists and ankles.

"It's just that, hmmm, er, if you had insurance or some type of financial resources, I could have moved her to a better hospital, like Mercy or Maryland General. This type of tumor doesn't respond to chemotherapy or radiation, but there is another type of treatment," he said with enthusiasm, and continued, "it's a vaccine and it works by training the immune system to attack the cancer cells."

"How much to get her moved outta this butcher shop into a better hospital?" Jamal interrupted. The doctor expelled a deep breath, rubbed his red, irritated eyes under his glasses.

"About two hundred thousand," he finally said.

"Two hundred thousand," I grumbled.

"But if you could come up with ten percent, that should be enough to have your mother moved and begin treatment. I mostly volunteer here, but I'm on staff at Maryland General. There, I feel she would have a much better chance."

"I'll bring the ten percent," Jamal confirmed, "but what happens if we have trouble getting the rest of the money?"

The doctor gave him a blank stare and then responded, "We'll be forced to return her here." The doctor arched his brow. I couldn't help feeling terrible and full of pain.

Once the doctor left, I looked at Jamal. "Where you gonna get all that money from?"

Leo Sullivan

"I'ma do me, shawty. Don't sweat it," he said and placed his arm around my neck.

That day, we all left the hospital sad and confused. Vanessa continued to blame Frank for Mama's illness, plus she swore she was going to kill him for stealing the rent money.

Nine

Ashley

Jamal managed to come up with the ten percent for Mama's hospital bill and that same day she was moved to Maryland General. From that point forward, all we could do was wait with faithful anticipation as we continued to visit her, talking to her as if we expected her to answer back. As she lay in a coma, all Jamal would say was, "You gotta believe!"

The days quickly turned to weeks and the weeks into months. Even though no one would admit it, Mama's body started to show signs of deterioration and our lives were starting to show the strain of Mama's absence. Vanessa got kicked out of school. I was having trouble with my boss at McDonald's and it wasn't long before heads in the hood started to pick up on the fact that Jamal and I had become inseparable. Some days he would pick me up from school in his new, pearl-white Cadillac Escalade with the big 26s.

Pretty soon, hoes started hating and speculating that I had given up the goodies. Truth was, it wasn't like I didn't want to, and thugs are hardly gentlemen. That nigga used to beg me to death. I can remember many a night when he stayed over my house in my bed, dick hard, him horny.

"Ash, just let me put the head in," he would beg, fingers in my wet panties. I knew he was having sex with other chicks and that upset me, but officially, he was not my man, at least that's what I kept telling myself.

Leo Sullivan

Finally on August 7th, my eighteenth birthday, Jamal bought me a fly-ass, tight-fitting Donna Karan dress with a matching Marc Jacobs bag. After we dropped my sisters off at a friend's house, Jamal took me to a tattoo parlor in West Baltimore. I had a tattoo of a pink and purple butterfly placed on my right ankle. Jamal got tatted up on his arm.

"R.I.P. My nigga Rock. See you when I get there," I read on his right forearm.

That night, Jamal took me to a club called Hammerjack's. I was surprised to see all of his homies there. We had a good time taking pictures. Jamal played the wall with me and most of the night I sipped Hpnotiq and danced solo for him, pressing up on him against the wall. As we were leaving the club, twenty deep, it dawned on me that Jamal's homies were actually acting as security. *For what?* I wondered.

As we prepared to drive off, Jamal placed his pistol in his lap, and his eyes roamed the parking lot. It was like his mind stayed on automatic alert. As I looked at him thinking how handsome he was, I reached over and caressed the waves in his hair.

"Don't you ever relax, chill?" I asked, feeling mellowed by his presence. The Hpnotiq was stirring my young hormones into a riot of horny emotions.

He checked his rearview mirror for the second time. "It's yo' birthday. I can take you home or I can take you to the telly. Relax, chill, like you askin' me to do," he said casually.

"Humpf," I muttered, tongue tied. I liked how slyly he campaigned for the thang. Even though I wasn't ready to drop it like it was hot, he had my mind open, so I turned all the way around in the seat facing him. "If I let you take me to a hotel, what would you do to me?" I asked in a sultry, breathy voice.

He glanced down at my thighs and back up at me. "I'd make

love to you like I wanted you to be my lady, forever," he said and leaned across the seat and kissed me passionately. He squeezed my breast, causing me to purr like a kitten.

"You got a condom?" I asked him with his tongue in my mouth.

"Yep," he answered and then smiled at me sheepishly.

Ten

Ashley

Life is a trip. It was my eighteenth birthday and I was going to a Holiday Inn with Jamal. Jamal grabbed his large CD player and took it to the room with us along with a bottle of Patrón and a bag of weed. We had a nice room on the top floor. I sipped Patrón on ice and let Jamal talk me into taking a few tokes off his blunt. It was my first time in my life smoking weed. When I choked, he laughed at me. I don't even remember how he got me undressed down to my panties and bra. Still, I was nervous as hell, about to lose my virginity. Jamal was undressed down to his boxer shorts. He had somehow managed to get one of my breasts out of my bra and gently nibbled on it as I sat on the side of the bed.

Musiq Soulchild was crooning, "Teach me how to love, show me the way to surrender my heart, girl, I'm so lost. How I can get my emotions involved, girl, I'm so lost."

Jamal began to ease my panties down over my thighs.

"Stop … uh, let me go take a shower first," I said.

Jamal made a face at me and watched my ass bounce as I walked to the bathroom.

Once in the bathroom, I stared at my reflection in the mirror. I looked at my flat tummy, curvaceous hips and thighs, the plump symmetry of my hour glass figure. I gazed down at the nest of silky pubic hair between my thighs and decided I couldn't do it. I quickly took a hot shower. It fogged up the bathroom. As I stepped out with water cascading down my body, I looked up, startled. Jamal was standing there, nude. I gasped and tried my best to not look down at him, but I couldn't help it.

"I can't do this." My voice echoed, bouncing off the bathroom walls. He just stared at me. The misty fog looked like a halo around his body. His dick was so big, it looked like a baseball bat. I shuddered as he stepped close to me. It was then that I noticed the drink in his hand. He took a sip then smacked his lips. I tore my eyes away from him.

"If that's what you want," he finally said and stepped closer to me.

I nodded my head. "Yes." Chill bumps ran down my body.

"You got goose bumps," he whispered as his finger touched my neck.

"It's cold."

He snickered and for some reason, I felt a smile tug at my cheeks. We were both nude and close. He stepped forward, causing his manhood to touch my stomach. I backed up against the sink. He set his drink down as the steam started to dissipate. I could see his eyes full of lust and desire. They dared me as gently as he picked me up, light as a feather, and sat me on top of the sink, spreading my thighs wide. He stood between my legs.

"Stop," my voice squeaked, signaling my vulnerability. I pushed my palms against his muscular chest. His manhood, long, thick and throbbing, was pressed against my vagina. I could feel his heat, his unquenched lust for my body. He peered down between my legs at the dark delta of my inviting flesh.

"You want me to stop?"

"Y ... yes," I murmured.

"I'm not gong to do anything to make you feel uncomfort-

Leo Sullivan

able," he whispered.

I blinked in response, still staring down at his body. He had to be at least ten inches long, between my legs, aiming like a missile.

"If you let me touch you three times, and I ask you if it feels good, and you reply 'no,' all three times, I'll stop. But if you say yes, it feels good, I get to make love to you. Okay?"

I nodded my head, afraid to trust my voice as I scooted back away from what was between my legs.

"One more thing. You have to close your eyes," he said.

I hesitated for a moment, and then went ahead and closed my eyes. I saw an array of beautiful colors, placid blues, brilliant bright reds, explode under my eyelids. I was high off the weed. I felt his finger trace the top of my vagina, slowly, delicately. It honest to God felt so sensuous, so loving. While he slowly caressed my clitoris, involuntarily, my leg twitched.

"Does that feel good?" he asked, a breath on my cheek.

"No," I lied. I couldn't help blushing as I fought the urge to open my eyes. His hand lowered to my neck and lingered, then moved to my breast, tracing my nipple. Then I felt his lips replace his finger. He licked my nipple until it grew hard under his tongue. I began to squirm on the sink as he licked then kissed the savory water off my breasts like honeydew. I rewarded him with a sigh that somehow gave birth to a moan.

His head lowered, leaving a trail of hot saliva as his tongue slid down my body. He introduced his nose to my navel. He picked my legs up and placed my feet on the sink, opened my thighs wider. I felt something cold running down my body. He was pouring his drink on me, in between my legs. Slowly, he lapped at my stomach. With his forefinger and thumb, he spread the lips of my vagina and buried his tongue inside of me and popped an ice cube from his mouth inside of me.

B-More Love

"Oooh, oooh, oooh," I sucked and moaned. It was at that moment, I cheated and opened my eyes. I had to see what he was doing to me down there.

"Does that feel good?" he asked in between licks, looking up. He caught me cheating and smiled devilishly at me. There should be a law against smoking weed and getting your coochie sucked.

"N ... n ... nooo, it don't ... hummm .... feel good." I squirmed as he pushed my thighs wider and placed his fingers and tongue inside of my vagina, licking me like I was sweet molasses. He skillfully increased his pace, developing a rhythm, deep finger fucking me, one, then two fingers ... lick, lick, lick, suck, suck. He buried his face and tongue deeper and went faster and faster. He alternated between sucking my breasts then back down south ... that's when my toes curled, my back arched and my neck thrashed back, hitting the mirror. I would have called his name but I'd forgotten it. With a scowl on my face, like I was about to cry from sheer ecstasy with his tongue and fingers buried inside of me, my virgin world had become ultra sensitive. It felt like every nerve and every fiber had come alive as I was about to experience my very first orgasm, on a bathroom sink.

"Boy, w ... what yooo doin to meee!" I wanted to scream. Then his ass stopped, peered up over the mounds of my succulent flesh with his mouth ringed with my juices.

"You want me to stop?"

"Nooo, nooo, neva ..." I groaned. He smirked impishly and placed his tongue back inside of me and a finger in my ass. I came in convulsions, not once but twice. My feet started to slip off the sink and he placed his hands underneath my thighs, pushing me back, pussy forward, tongue diving in and out, flicking and lip boxing with my engorged clit, two against one.

Leo Sullivan

Finally, I was on the verge of tears.

I wanted to scream as I came again in his mouth. My body shivered. The sound of him lapping up my juices resonated in the bathroom. I watched him slowly rise from in between my legs. His entire body glistened with a light sheen of perspiration. I glanced down, and his dick looked twice as large as it dangled in between my legs.

I was so wet, I could feel cum oozing out of my hot vagina. In my heart and soul, I knew I was about to become his conquest. Maybe it was a primitive thing, but with a deft fingernail, I traced the head of his dick, causing it to throb. A sparkle of precum luster appeared.

"Grab it. Put it inside of you," Jamal commanded. I took hold of it and then the thought occurred to me—I was about to lose my virginity, high off weed, in a hotel bathroom, on a sink counter. I attempted to place it inside of me. It was too big, or I was too small. He pumped an inch of it inside of me. I screamed, raking my nails across his chest. He pushed again. I felt something tear as he began to stroke me lovingly. Still the pain was excruciating.

He squeezed my breasts and tried to kiss me and ease in another two inches. I cried out in pain and stared down at his manhood. I was too tight but somehow, he moved inside of me slowly, adroitly, loving me. My first time making love was sweet and innocent. Ghetto love, high off weed and Patrón. He carried me over to the bed and made love to me passionately with me panting and moaning, showing off my new sex faces.

Afterward, I padded to the bathroom nude and got a washcloth and bathed him like he was my king. He watched me through heavy lidded eyes. This brotha had been taking care of me, my mother and family, paying all the bills. After I bathed him, I asked him to show me how to love him with my hands and mouth. Tenderly, he taught me how to please him. It was the most beautiful thing—my newfound creativity, a woman's sexual virtuosity. For the first time in my life, I sucked a dick. Not only that, I let him cum in my mouth. Jamal Lawson, a thug, had turned me out.

Finally, satiated and depleted, we lay next to each other, coupled like spoons and pillow talked as lovers do. A splinter of sunlight shone through the curtain. I could feel the beat of his heart palpitating against mine.

"Jamal?"

"Yeah?" he croaked groggily.

"Hold me tighter."

"Okay."

"Jamal?"

"Yeah?"

"I love you."

No response.

"Ash?"

"Yes."

"Next time don't make me wait so long. I … I love you, too."

I smiled and drifted off into peaceful sleep wrapped in his arms.

Leo Sullivan

Eleven

Jamal

The day Ashley let me hit it was the day that made me realize I needed to slow down. I wasn't just rollin' solo no more, I had a chick on my side, someone who made me think more responsibly and I don't care what nobody say, a good woman can do that to a man, even a thug. Make him wanna change before it's too late in the game.

o   o   o   o

I was cruising down Annor Court listening to 50 Cent's new joint, *"Straight to the Bank."* I had my pistol under the armrest with my eyes alert for the kickers. I looked up and saw Ski Mask standing in the street, waving me down. It was one of those lazy Sunday mornings in B-More. The crack heads hadn't even awakened yet.

"Need ta holla at'cha. It's important. 'Bout yo' sista and that bitch you fuckin' wit'," Ski Mask said after I pulled over.

"Fuck you talkin' 'bout?!" I spat. He hopped his ass in the passenger seat.

"Word is niggas been tryin' to slump you but you stay on alert so now they plotting on someone you love. Nigga said he saw your pregnant sista at da mall and—"

I pulled my pistol from under the armrest.

"Nigga, who said it!"

"Ho, ho, hol' up man!" Ski Mask yelled, holding up both his hands. It suddenly dawned on me, Ski Mask was Frank's

B-More Love

nephew.

"It's Boo Man n'em," Ski Mask said. Boo Man was one of the cats I shot in the pool hall robbery at Humphrey's.

I had been driving for a minute. I bent a corner on Stripes Round Road. Boo Man had a "trip" he was working out of in a barbershop. I came to a screeching halt in front of the shop. Outside, a few ole wine heads stood, passing a brown paper bag around. I grabbed my nine, placed it in my drawers and hopped out my whip, leaving Ski Mask inside wondering what I was about to do.

I walked into the barbershop. The air conditioner was off, it was hot. On the walls were pictures of Malcolm and Martin. A small transistor radio played gospel music. I scanned faces as I walked to the back and saw a small boy getting his hair cut. His mother was a cinnamon-colored woman with freckles and red hair. She smiled at me as I passed. The barber, a young cat, followed me with his eyes.

I saw Boo Man perched in a chair with his back to me, counting money. One of his dudes gave him a heads up signal. He looked up and turned around. I was a few feet from him. Boo Man was a heavyset dude. He dressed nice. That day he had on a Southpole outfit and a black du-rag. I noticed the cast on his leg. He frowned at me and glowered.

"Nigga, you got a lotta balls walkin' up in this piece," he ranted. I watched his hands. Behind me I heard a door open. I resisted the urge to turn around. Boo Man was twice my age, and I'm sure, wiser, but I had to know.

"Hey, wuz poppin', my nigga? I come in peace. Heard niggas was plottin' on my lil' sista, namean?"

"Nigga come in here playing dumb. You know niggas been trying to get at you for months. Now you wanna come in peace? Soft-ass young nigga. When you robbed us, did you come in peace? Now niggas talkin' 'bout killin' yo' family and you want a plea bargain. Get the fuck outta here!" he said with finality.

I nodded my head. He had bitched me up as far as he was concerned.

"A'ight, Cuz," I said and slowly turned for the door. All eyes were on me. I pirouetted on the balls of my feet and spun around, catching Boo Man off-guard. He never saw it coming. I eased the pistol out of my drawers, all in one smooth motion.

The first shot caught him in the side of his jaw. I fired four more times to his chest. A woman screamed. Behind me, I heard tables and chairs being knocked over as people made a mad dash for the door.

"Punk-ass nigga! Leave my family and bitch outta this!" I ranted as Boo Man gasped for air, clutching his chest, eyes blazing with a dying man's fear.

I snatched up the money he was counting and dipped out the door. I stepped outside the barbershop with a quick pace.

Ski Mask was hunched down, hiding in the seat like he was trying not to be an accessory to murder. As I drove off, I hit Ashley on her celly.

Ring ... Ring ... Ring ...

No answer.

"Shit!" Just as I was about to hang up, Ashley picked up the phone. "Lock the door! Don't open it for nobody."

"What?" Ashley asked.

"Just do as I say. I got a burner stashed in the couch in the livin' room."

"What's wrong?" I heard fear in her voice.

"Nothing! I'll call you back."

"But—"

Click!

I called my Mama next. She picked up on the first ring.

"Ma, where Nikki at?"

"I don't know, but she ain't been home in two days. I'm about to go to the police and file a missing person's report," my Mama said, on the verge of tears.

Two days? I thought to myself, knowing something was wrong. Nikki never stayed out all night, let alone two days. I hung the phone up with my Mama and for the rest of the day, I drove around throughout Baltimore's boroughs, searching for my little sister.

The whole time, Ski Mask was chirping in my ear about a big lick. A million plus, four bricks of China White, heroin. He practically had my attention because lately, I had been splurging so hard, I was about to miss a payment on Ashley's mom's hospital bill. A bird of China White went for close to a hundred and eight g's. I needed that lick. Had to have it.

"Right there! Right there!" Ski Mask yelled and pointed as we passed through Carey and Lanve Street. In the opposite lane at the light was a gray Buick Park Avenue. I saw my sister, Nikki, in the back seat. Her face looked swollen and disfigured. They beat my little sister bad, plus, she was pregnant.

"Turn this bitch around," Ski Mask exhorted.

I made a wild u-turn in the middle of the street damn near causing a wreck as cars swerved to avoid hitting me. I caught up to the Buick at the light and saw two figures in the front seat laughing. Enraged like a man possessed with demons, I jumped out of my vehicle, leaving the door open in traffic. I acted without thinking, purely on hood instincts. I walked up to the side of the car with my nine in my hand. I'll never forget the terrified looks on their faces as I squeezed on their fuckin' asses.

Blacka! Blacka! Blacka!

The pistol sang, shattering glass and denting metal. I emptied the clip on both men, the whole time hearing my sister's

Leo Sullivan

bloodcurdling screams. The barrel smoldered as I opened the door to pull Nikki out. She was hysterical. She reached forward and grabbed the lifeless body in the driver's seat with his brains spewing out of his head.

"Oh God! Oh God! No! You kilt him!" I struggled to pull her off the dead man. She turned and began to fight me, kicking and scratching. "You killed my baby daddy! Oh God, nooo!" she cried with her face smeared in blood and tears. In the backdrop, I could hear police sirens blaring as I stood dumbfounded trying to wrestle her out the car.

"He just came back from Iraq. That's his daddy," she pointed to the other body slumped in the seat, bullet-ridden.

A wretching pain stabbed me in the gut as I somehow managed to wrestle her out of the ruined carnage of the bodies in the car. A father and his son. I felt like shit.

As soon as I pulled off with Nikki, next to me in the front seat, the police pulled up. In the wrath of her riveting hurt and dismay, Nikki lashed out at me, "You kilt him! You said you was going to kill him. I hate you!" she began to slap and punch me in the face as I drove. I didn't even try to block her blows. She busted my lip and bruised my eye.

"I hope you fuckin' die! All you do is steal and kill!" As she screamed at me, I realized the only reason her face looked swollen and disfigured was due to her pregnancy. If I had only figured that out earlier. I had just killed two innocent men.

Twelve

Jamal

After taking my sister home to my mother with her still crying and lashing out at me, I drove away from the West Port Projects. My heart was heavy like it was hemorrhaging in my soul. I knew it was time for me to hang up my tools and get out the game. As I drove, I picked tiny pieces of glass out of my clothes. I stopped at the light on 28th and Barkley Street, hit Ashley from my celly. She answered on the first ring.

"Baby, what's wrong? Tell me what's going on!" she said with her voice edgy and full of panic.

"Everything a'ight. I'll be there in an hour—"

"But I'm scared and what you doin' with a gun in the house?"

"Did you get it from out the couch?"

"Yes, Vanessa did. I'm scared of guns."

"Okay, I'm on my way."

"Alright … Jamal?"

"Yeah?"

"I love you."

I turned and looked over at Ski Mask. He was watching me like a hawk.

"Love you too, shawty."

I hung up the phone.

The night had grown dark with a constellation of stars dotting the sky. Friday nights in Baltimore are almost mystical, magical, alive. A festival teeming with folks, young and old. Ski Mask filled me in about the big lick on Park Heights in West Baltimore. It was at a house on a cul-de-sac. One way in, one way out. This would be my last caper—a million, plus bricks of heroin. I'd buy my sister Nikki a house and pay off Ashley's mom's hospital bills and take my ass back to school.

We had devised a simple plan to rob the house. Since the nigga who lived there had left to go out of town to take some "work," a female was left to watch the house until he returned. The dope and money were stashed in a bedroom closet on the first floor. All we had to do was a quick house invasion.

I parked down the street from the house. It was a nice Spanish-style brick home. Pink and fuchsia zinnias lined the flagstone walkway. There was an eerie quietness about the house as we approached. I had my nine in my drawers. Ski Mask had the .380. I could feel my palms searching, my pulse racing as I looked around prepared to knock.

It felt like I had been injected with high octane fuel in my veins. All the lights were off inside the house. I looked around suspiciously and knocked on the door. I looked at Ski Mask. He looked nervous as hell. Suddenly, there was a feminine voice on the other side of the door.

"Who is it?"

"Mike from across the street. There's a fire in your yard."

"A fire?" She opened the door and there stood one of the baddest bitches I had never seen. Fine like a model. Light skinned with hazel green eyes, long blond hair weave, big titties with nipples pointing right at me. I leveled my pistol to her head and rushed inside.

She looked like she wanted to scream.

"Bitch, if you make a sound, I'ma kill you!"

She nodded her head. "Take anything you want. Just don't

hurt me. I'll do anything you ask."

I turned around to shut the door and noticed Ski Mask was gone. *Scary-ass nigga,* I said to myself, and pushed the chick toward the hall where the bedroom was located. Second door on the right, Ski Mask had told me. I moved fast, according to the plan. The home was plush with expensive furniture and thick shag carpeting.

At the bedroom door, as I was about to open it, I thought I heard a floor board paneling creek above me on the second floor. This bitch was watching me closely as I turned the bedroom doorknob. Maybe it was my mind playin' tricks on me, but the chick didn't act as scared as broads normally do, all cryin' 'n shit. She was watching me, nibbling on her bottom lip. I noticed lipstick had smeared on her front teeth, so instead of going through the bedroom door first, I gestured for her to enter. She hesitated and walked in. I couldn't help noticing her fat ass jiggling in the short satin nightgown.

Inside the bedroom, it was handsomely decorated in a rich palatial splendor. There was a king-sized bed with lots of mirrors with fancy chairs and a matching mahogany dresser. Suddenly the strangest thing happened. It was surreal. The chick started to undress.

"Bitch, wha'cha doin'?!" I exclaimed. I thought I heard footsteps outside the bedroom door. This shit was bizarre. She slithered out the gown. The fur between her legs was trimmed like a heart.

"Lemme suck dat dick," she cooed. Stupefied, I frowned at her. It felt like I was having an out of body experience. I was moving slow and she was going fast. She sashayed over to the bed and lay on her back, spreading her legs. Pink pussy galore. She wiggled a finger at me, like "come here." Something about her startled my senses, tingling, alarming, signaling for me to

Leo Sullivan

go, run! But I couldn't if I wanted to. Not with a million dollars and enough dope to have a nigga straight for a lifetime. I walked over to the closet door with my eyes on the bitch. As soon as I opened the door, the bitch dove off the bed and onto the floor. I looked up and Box Stale was standing in the closet with a pistol aimed at my chest.

"Oh shit—"

Boom! He shot me at close range in the chest. I fell on my back. My burner slid across the carpet.

The chick screamed.

The bedroom door opened. It looked like an army of niggas stormed into the room. I looked up, dazed, and saw all familiar faces—cats I had robbed and shot in my lifetime. The world flashed around me as I realized I had been set up. Ski Mask set me up. Box Stale came and stood over me. The same old head I had given a vicious beat down to at the pool hall robbery. He chuckled derisively with a sneer on his face.

"Young nigga, we been tryna kill yo' ass for the last few months but couldn't creep you. Then I learned, by you being a greedy-ass nigga, you don't catch bees with vinegar, you gotta use honey, so when Frank and his nephew Ski Mask said they could deliver you to me for the fifty g's, I took them up on their offer." He snickered. I groaned in pain, clutching my chest as my blood soaked into the carpet. I saw Frank hover over me and next to him was Ski Mask. Then old man Humphrey and just about every nigga I had ever robbed. I saw my pistol a few feet from me on the carpet next to the bed.

"Here, Frank," Box Stale said and tossed him a wad of cash in a rubber band. I inched for the gun.

Closer.

Box Stale looked down and caught me. Frank walked over the kicked me in the face. So did Box Stale. They all began to pummel me, kicking and punching. Just as I started to black out, I saw Box Stale push everybody out of the way and lean over me with a menacing scowl on his face.

"You's a dead-ass nigga!" he yelled haughtily. He aimed his pistol and shot me five more times.

"Take his ass to the West Baltimore junk yard and dump 'im with the rest of the garbage," Box Stale commanded.

Ski Mask laughed.

Old man Humphrey grumbled, "You should have kilt me when you had a chance. I'm da one who put up half da money, dumb-ass nigga." He laughed.

I could feel Ski Mask going through my pockets taking my cash. They lifted my body and carried me to the trunk of a car that had already been installed with a plastic lining so that my blood would not leak inside of the trunk. After they slammed the trunk shut, Frank laughed. "I'ma fuck the shit out dat young bitch Ashley and I might let her suck yo' dick, nephew."

Ski Mask laughed.

Semi-conscious, I felt the car moving. I remembered the cell phone in my pocket and prayed Ski Mask hadn't taken it. I reached my hand inside my pants. It was there. I dialed Ashley's number.

"I'm … hurt … bad … junk yard."

Thirteen

Ashley

"Jamal ... Jamal ... Jamal!" I screamed into the phone, distraught with panic. Vanessa ran into the room.

"Gurl, what's wrong with you?"

"Jamal just called. He could barely talk. He's hurt."

"Where was he calling from?" Vanessa asked. She had her hair wrapped in a du-rag.

"He said something about a junk yard."

"West Baltimore junk yard?" Vanessa barked.

"I don't know," I replied, on the verge of tears.

"Let's go check. It's only a few miles from here anyway," Vanessa said and pulled the gun out of her pants like a dude.

By the time we rushed out the house, Jasmine was asleep. All I had on was my housecoat, slippers, bra and panties. My baby was in trouble and I was determined to get to him.

○ ○ ○ ○

Ten minutes later, we pulled into the West Baltimore junk yard, located just off Baltimore and Hilton Street.

A busy four lane street was next to the junk yard with cars constantly zooming by. I heard a dog barking. The night had a slight chill. I parked my car next to what looked like an abandoned old truck sitting on four flat tires. Something about the junk yard spooked me.

"Now what?" Vanessa asked.

I shrugged and wrapped my housecoat around me tighter.

B–More Love

Just then, a car pulled up with its lights out. It was directly in front of us. Instantly I recognized the dark Crown Victoria I had seen around the neighborhood. It looked just like the car Jamal had pulled his pistol out on a few months ago. I wasn't sure.

"Look! Look! Look! It's Frank with somebody else," Vanessa gestured, pointing.

"Get down!" I commanded. Together we slumped down in the seat. A Greyhound bus roared by. I felt my heart beating fast.

"Dat's Ski Mask punk ass with Frank," Vanessa said with her eyes squinted into narrow slants.

"Where the hell is Jamal at?" I asked out loud, talking to myself.

"I don't know where Jamal is, but I got Frank crack head ass!" Vanessa exclaimed and jumped out the car with the gun in her hand.

"Vanessa!"

Leo Sullivan

Fourteen

Ashley

Reluctantly, I followed behind my sister, scared to death, as I walked over rocks and broken glass in my thin slippers, clasping my housecoat around me.

Ski Mask and Frank were hunched over about to hoist something out of the truck.

"Nigga, where my Mama muthafuckin' money at?" Vanessa said in a threatening tone, almost sounding like a dude. A breeze tugged at my thin housecoat exposing my thighs and panties. Frank looked over his shoulder and grinned as his eyes roamed my thigh.

I trembled as cars passed, momentarily illuminating us. I saw nothing but fear in Ski Mask's eyes, but Frank was a different story.

"Gurl, put that gun away," he said with a wicked grin as he reached into his pocket and removed a wad of cash secured by a rubber band. "Here go yo' Mama money and more," Frank said.

Just as Vanessa stepped forward to retrieve it, he reached for the gun in his waistband. Vanessa never took her eyes off of him. In one smooth motion, she shot him in the head. His neck jerked back and then he crumpled over, dead.

Ski Mask took one look at his dead uncle and took off running across the street just as a mail truck came roaring past. It hit Ski Mask head on, dragging his body for nearly two blocks.

B–More Love

He was dead on impact.

Closed casket.

Vanessa picked up the bank roll with the rubber band wrapped around it. "Fifty thousand dollars in cash."

I peered over inside the trunk. Jamal lay in a puddle of blood with a cell phone in his hand. I pissed down my leg, screaming, "Jamal!" Together, Vanessa and I struggled to lift his body.

Fifteen

Two Months Later

It was a cold and bitter day. I stood staring out Mama's hospital room window and reflected back on my life, particularly the last few months. I graduated with honors and was accepted into Clark Atlanta University on an Academic scholarship. I didn't go to my high school prom even though a lot of guys had asked me.

We still didn't know if the treatment was working on Mama but we managed to pay her bill with some of the money Vanessa took from Frank. She gave me half. Ironically, Mama was on the sixth floor still in a coma and Jamal was on the second floor, hooked up to life support. I couldn't stand looking at him like that. The doctors butchered his beautiful body in an attempt to remove all the lead that had been pumped into him.

Jasmine was talking to Mama, all animated about a boy at school that she didn't like as Vanessa sang at the top of her lungs, a song by Akon and Bone Thugs-N-Harmony, "I tried so hard …"

"For God's sake, will you please stop hollering in my ear?" a voice croaked.

Silence hummed as the beep continued to chime from the machine. I turned around. Both Jasmine and Vanessa had their mouths agape in shock as they looked at Mama. Her eyes were closed, then suddenly they fluttered and opened.

"I'm thirsty," Mama managed to say. We all rushed to her

bedside. "I heard a man's voice talking to me. Where is he?" Mama asked.

I was too shocked for words.

"Mama, you woke up!" Vanessa said, caressing her hand. With jubilation, we began to talk to her all at once. She gave us all weak hugs with a slight smile. That day the doctor informed us the vaccine treatment for her brain cancer miraculously had worked.

"Mama, Ashley got a boyfriend! He's on the second floor—"

"No, I don't!" I lied. Mama didn't like me having boyfriends. She'd gotten pregnant at sixteen and was one of the reasons I stayed a virgin until I was eighteen. She'd forbidden me to date. Vanessa went on to tell how Jamal had been paying for the hospital bills. I avoided Mama's questions by tending to her every need. I even French braided her hair and wondered if it was too tight. She still had that awful scar on her scalp from the surgery.

With each new day Mama got stronger. She continued to ask who the male voice was she heard. Vanessa said it was the doctor, but Mama knew better.

"Come here, Ash," Mama said sternly when she saw me come into her room. I sat down at the foot of her bed. "Why you lying about your boyfriend? Why you ain't down there with him?" Mama asked with her eyes glistening. "Look, girl, you go down there and tell that boy I said thank you."

"But he can't hear me, Mama," I said on the verge of tears.

"Come closer, Ashley." Mama patted the side of her bed right next to her for me to sit down.

I sat down on the side of her and she continued talking. "I heard y'all. I heard him. Do you remember what he told you?"

I looked at her with questioning eyes.

Leo Sullivan

"You gotta believe." My eyes welled with tears. Jamal was right, she could hear us.

"Now go," she demanded.

Sixteen

Ashley

As I got off the elevator, I saw Jamal's mother standing in the hallway crying. She was accompanied by her daughter Nikki. She had recently given birth to a child. His mother and sister both greeted me teary-eyed. As I walked up, I noticed Jamal resembled his mother. She was a beautiful woman, even in her work uniform. I could tell she worked as a waitress.

"The priest is inside. The doctors have advised us to take him off life support."

"Oh my God!" I murmured and turned and rushed through the door to his room.

An older white man dressed in black wearing a white collar was standing over Jamal reading verses from the Bible.

"I need to talk to him in private," I said in a sharp, clipped tone.

The priest turned around. I noticed a crucifix ring on his index finger as he turned to me holding a black and gold Bible in his bony fingers.

He started to say something. I interrupted him.

"Please leave!" I raised my voice. He obeyed, mumbled something about two minutes, then the blood of Christ, and walked out the door.

I walked over to Jamal and looked at his battered and bruised body. He had lost so much weight. I looked at one of the tattoos on his arm. It read: R.I.P. My nigga Rock. See you

Leo Sullivan

when I get there.

I began to cry. I remembered he got that on my eighteenth birthday.

Sitting down on the side of Jamal's bed, I grabbed his hand. "You said we had to believe! You said you'd never leave me. You said you loved me. When Mama was in a coma, you said she could hear us. Jamal, you can hear me! Jamal, don't leave me like this!" I cried profusely. He just lay there on the respirator. I couldn't stand to look at him like this. I gathered myself and prepared to walk out of the door. Before I left, I bent down and kissed him tenderly on his lips. I wiped my tears off of his face. I felt something move inside of my hand. Was it my imagination?

"Do it again, baby, do it again. Please do it again!"

Jamal slightly wiggled his fingers.

I jumped for joy and screamed at the top of my lungs. His mother and sister rushed through the door.

"Ashley, what happened? Please don't tell me—"

"He can hear us! He can hear us," I cried, interrupting his mother's words.

"Baby, yo' Mama in the room. Show 'em you alive. Show 'em you can hear us!!"

As his mother and sister watched, Jamal moved his fingers twice.

That time everyone in the room erupted in tears. Jamal Lawson was going to survive.

B-More Love

Epilogue

Four Years Later

Jamal regained his health, other than the fact that he walks with a noticeable limp. It's hard to believe that we almost lost him, that his family was ready to give up hope. But Jamal was right, "You gotta believe."

I believed in Jamal, and after a long, grueling recovery, he moved to Atlanta with me. We got a small apartment together and I started college as planned. He got a regular job doing construction and works with troubled boys on the weekend. He knows their world, and he knows the consequences.

I am about to graduate from college, and joyfully, we're expecting our first child in May. Things are not easy but we're making it, thanks to the grace of God and a near tragedy that showed us what was really important—each other. My love for Jamal has gotten us through the hardest times. Who said a good woman can't change a thug?

Holla!

Leo Sullivan

315

Dedication for After the Storm
By Keisha Ervin

I dedicate this story to all the men and women out there who are crazy in love and don't know when or how to let go.

Acknowledgements

I wanna thank you god for blessing me with another opportunity to write and share my craft. You have blessed with me so much, thank you.

I wanna give a shout out to my momma, daddy and big brother.

What's up Kyrese?!! You know that I love you and thank you for finally calling me Momma and not Keisha after six years.

I wanna say what's up to my four closest friends, Tu-Shonda, Locia, Monique and Janea. You four chicks are the best.

Special big up to Locia!! Thank you for giving me so many fly and hip ideas. Without you, this story wouldn't be what it is. I appreciate ya, ma!!

Thank you to all the readers, book stores and vendors who support my work. Without you I wouldn't be where I am, so I thank you.

I wanna give a big thank you to the entire TCP staff.

And last but not least, special shout out and thank you to Vickie M. Stringer. You didn't have to ask me to be a part of this project but you did anyway and I appreciate it.

I hope you readers enjoy!!!

Hailing from St. Louis, Missouri, **Keisha Ervin** *is a prolific writer and devoted mother. Her success has drawn much deserved attention to herself and her hometown.*

Keisha Ervin is the Essence Magazine Best-Selling Author of Chyna Black, Me & My Boyfriend, Mina's Joint, Hold U Down *and the upcoming* Torn.

Acknowledgements for Allure of the Game
By Danielle Santiago

Thank you father God, from whom all blessings flow, for every single blessing that I have received.

Carlos, thank you for everything, you're the best husband for me! I'll always hold you down, baby. Love you forever. Kaden, Mommy loves you. You are my little man. You are the strength that gets me through the day.

Thanks to my Grandparents, Parents, Siblings, Cousins, Friends and Readers. I couldn't do any of this without your support.

~Danielle Santiago

Danielle Santiago draws her storytelling from her own life experiences of growing up between Charlotte, North Carolina and Harlem, New York. Along with writing books, Danielle devotes her time to aiding women who have been victims of domestic abuse. She currently resides in North Carolina with her husband and son.

Other titles by Danielle Santiago: Fair Exchange, No Robberies in Cream.

Acknowledgments for The Fink
By Quentin Carter

As always, God comes first. I thank Him for carrying me through the very hard times that I've faced during the past six years that I have been locked away from the outside world.

To my mother and father, Lois and Charles. I love you two people a whole lot. I owe y'all much more than I can ever give you.

My brothers and sisters, Fuzz, Black, Brad, Joey and Cheron. Y'all have really proven to me that my struggle is your struggle as well. I can't thank y'all enough.

To my cousins, Barbara, Nip, John and Ruby, for always keeping me in your prayers and for sending me all the wonderful cards and words of encouragement.

Until we can learn to get along, I will not list any women or children of mine in these credits. Not all of you deserved to be listed the first time, anyway. But still, y'all were tripping on whose name should've went first.

To Vickie Stringer, thank you for founding TCP, then hiring Mia and the rest of your hardworking staff. Your company has brought hope to all of the aspiring authors who thought they never had a chance.

To Cynthia Parker, even though you're picky as hell, thanks for doing such a great job cleaning up my work.

My new board of readers, who proofread my material in the raw and grade it before I am allowed to send it out. My cousin, Darryl Leggs, and partners, Gary Jones, Edward G. Mario Dodson, Rico, Gill, Joseph Ramsey, King, Jamario, Young Swerve, J-Wax and my celly, KK.

And to my fans who blessed me by picking up a copy of my first novel, *Hoodwinked*, to add to their collection of great urban novels.

A special thanks to those who took the time to write me and to those who posted their positive comments about my book on the Internet. Tiara Carmon, Nique C., Princeluva79, V. Darling, Rainbow Milon, Iris Rivera, L. Lattimore and Andrea Denise, who expects my next book to be as good as my first. I hope I don't let you down.

To all of y'all who don't know what a "fink" is ... look it up!

Quentin Carter is a 27-year-old native of Kansas City, Missouri. In the near future, Quentin hopes to grow as an author and become a writer of multiple genres.

Quentin Carter is the Essence Magazine Best-Selling Author of: Hoodwinked, In Cahootz *and* Contagious.

Acknowledgments for Cold as Ice
By T. Styles

I'd like to thank my fans. I'd like to thank my family.
And most of all, I'd like to thank God.

Born in Southeast Washington, D.C. and raised in Houston, Texas, **T. Styles** *now resides in Baltimore County, Maryland with her son. She has worked as a massage therapist and is an active participant in dialogues surrounding Health and Wellness.*

T. Styles is the Essence Magazine Best-Selling Author of: A Hustler's Son *and* Black and Ugly.

Acknowledgements for B-More Love
By Leo Sullivan

First, I want to thank God for giving me the strength and perseverance to not only survive, but thrive in a system that is designed to dehumanize and destroy black men and their families.

To my beautiful daughters: Jasmine, Lamaya, Desire and Christle Murphy. I love you all more than my own life.

To my cousins Alicia and Auriah – I can't wait, and thank you for hooking up my space.

To my soul mate and best friend in the world, Taya R. Baker – I know I drive you crazy. After all the difficult years, you're like my ebony angel. You've never abandoned me, not even one time.

To Leon (Booda) Baker, and a shout out to his mother Millicent Hester and brother, Antonio Harris (R.I.P.) Thank you for your patience with the millions of questions I inundated you with about the beautiful city of Baltimore.

To Kymberli G. with your fine, red, sexy, Amazon self. Bama! (smile).

All Rise! To my boss, the lovely Ms. Vickie M. Stringer. You have to respect her gangsta – fresh out of the joint with nothing but a handwritten manuscript and a dream. She built Triple Crown from the ground up and made it the most prominent African American book publisher in the country and abroad. Thank you for allowing me to be a part of your legacy, your history, and a part of the rising Triple Crown empire.

To Mia McPherson, the new Vice President of Triple Crown. Thank you for your kindness, but I could have swore I heard you chuckle at me when I complained about that deadline you gave me for this project. What's up with that? (smile).

To Cynthia Parker, my editor and dear friend. I apologize. I guess I was having a panic attack. The short notice killed me softly, but you once again came to my rescue. If they only knew how much of your feminine insight goes into my work. God bless you and your family.

To Sonya Gwynn. See, I didn't forget you and her sister Tajuana Hardison. You're my dawg, but damn! Are you ever gonna do some work?

Most importantly, to all my fans. It is because of you I am me. I promise to never let you all down. I don't write for the money. I write for the love of the craft and being able to touch people, and the joy it brings. If you like our short stories, please check with your local book store, or go online and purchase our books.

Oh, and I almost forgot my girl T. Styles. Thank you for your friendship. Also, Quincy Carter, thanks my brother. I'm looking forward to reading your new joint *Contagious*.

Leo Sullivan is a versatile writer, with Urban Fiction being one of the many genres that he enjoys. In the coming years, Leo hopes to be freed from prison, and looks forward to being a father to his children and a role model to others.

Other titles by Leo Sullivan: Life *and* Dangerous.

ORDER FORM

Triple Crown Publications
PO Box 6888
Columbus, Oh 43205

Name: _____

Address: _____

City/State: _____

Zip: _____

	TITLES	PRICES
	Dime Piece	$15.00
	Gangsta	$15.00
	Let That Be The Reason	$15.00
	A Hustler's Wife	$15.00
	The Game	$15.00
	Black	$15.00
	Dollar Bill	$15.00
	A Project Chick	$15.00
	Road Dawgz	$15.00
	Blinded	$15.00
	Diva	$15.00
	Sheisty	$15.00
	Grimey	$15.00
	Me & My Boyfriend	$15.00
	Larceny	$15.00
	Rage Times Fury	$15.00
	A Hood Legend	$15.00
	Flipside of The Game	$15.00
	Menage's Way	$15.00

SHIPPING/HANDLING (Via U.S. Media Mail) $3.95 1-2 Books, $5.95 3-4 Boo
add $1.95 for ea. additional bo

TOTAL $_____

FORMS OF ACCEPTED PAYMENTS:
Postage Stamps, Institutional Checks & Money Orders, all mail in orders take 5-7
Business days to be delivered.

ORDER FORM

Triple Crown Publications
PO Box 6888
Columbus, Oh 43205

Name: _____

Address: _____

City/State: _____

Zip: _____

	TITLES	PRICES
	Still Sheisty	$15.00
	Chyna Black	$15.00
	Game Over	$15.00
	Cash Money	$15.00
	Crack Head	$15.00
	For The Strength of You	$15.00
	Down Chick	$15.00
	Dirty South	$15.00
	Cream	$15.00
	Hoodwinked	$15.00
	Bitch	$15.00
	Stacy	$15.00
	Life	$15.00
	Keisha	$15.00
	Mina's Joint	$15.00
	How To Succeed in The Publishing Game	$20.00
	Love & Loyalty	$15.00
	Whore	$15.00
	A Hustler's Son	$15.00

SHIPPING/HANDLING (Via U.S. Media Mail) $3.95 1-2 Books, $5.95 3-4 Books add $1.95 for ea. additional book

TOTAL $_____

FORMS OF ACCEPTED PAYMENTS:
Postage Stamps, Institutional Checks & Money Orders, all mail in orders take 5-7 Business days to be delivered.

ORDER FORM

Triple Crown Publications
PO Box 6888
Columbus, Oh 43205

Name: _____

Address: _____

City/State: _____

Zip: _____

	TITLES	PRICES
	Chances	$15.00
	Contagious	$15.00
	Hold U Down	$15.00
	Black and Ugly	$15.00
	In Cahootz	$15.00
	Dirty Red *Hard Cover Only*	$20.00
	Dangerous	$15.00
	Street Love	$15.00
	Sunshine & Rain	$15.00
	Bitch Reloaded	$15.00

SHIPPING/HANDLING (Via U.S. Media Mail) $3.95 1-2 Books, $5.95 3-4 Bo
add $1.95 for ea. additional be

TOTAL $_____

FORMS OF ACCEPTED PAYMENTS:
Postage Stamps, Institutional Checks & Money Orders, all mail in orders take 5-7
Business days to be delivered.